THE GIRL FROM THE GOLDEN HORN

Also by Kurban Said
ALI AND NINO

THE GIRL FROM THE GOLDEN HORN

KURBAN SAID

Translated from the German by Jenia Graman

THE OVERLOOK PRESS
WOODSTOCK & NEW YORK

First published in the United States in 2001 by
The Overlook Press, Peter Mayer Publishers, Inc.
Woodstock & New York

WOODSTOCK:
One Overlook Drive
Woodstock, NY 12498
www.overlookpress.com
[for individual orders, bulk and special sales, contact our Woodstock office]

NEW YORK:
141 Wooster Street
New York, NY 10012

∞ The paper used in this book meets the requirements for paper
permanence as described in the ANSI Z39.48-1992 standard.

Library of Congress Cataloging-in-Publication Data

Said Kurban.
[Mädchen vom Goldenen Horn. English]
The girl from the golden horn / Kurban Said ;
translated from the German by Jenia Graman.
p. cm.
I. Graman, Jenia. II. Title.
PT2637.A433 M313 2001   833'.912—dc21   2001036472

Printed in the United States of America
ISBN 1-58567-173-8
1 3 5 7 9 8 6 4 2

THE GIRL FROM THE
GOLDEN HORN

ONE

"And this 'i,' Fraulein Anbari?"

Asiadeh looked up, her gray eyes thoughtful and earnest. "This 'i'?" she repeated in her soft, gentle voice. She thought for a little while and then said decidedly and desperately: "This 'i' is the Yakut gerund, similar to the Khirgiz 'barisi.' "

Professor Bang rubbed his long, hooked nose. Behind the steel-rimmed glasses his eyes looked like those of a wise owl. He wheezed softly and disapprovingly.

"Yes," he said. "But I still cannot really understand why the 'a' should be missing in the Yakut form." And he sadly leafed through the dictionary.

Goetz, another of his students, whose speciality was the Chinese language, proposed to explain the mysterious "a" form as being a petrified Mongol instrumental. "When I was young," said Professor Bang severely, "I too tried to explain everything as being a petrified Mongol instrumental. Courage is a young man's privilege."

Bang was sixty years old and the Chinese expert forty-five. Asiadeh suddenly felt a sharp scratching pain in her throat. The sweetish air of the yellowing old books, the tortuous flourishes of the Manchu and Mongol letters, the barbaric forms of the petrified languages—all these were unreal, hostile, numbing her senses. She sighed deeply when the bell rang. Bang lit his pipe, a sign that the seminar for Comparative Turkish Languages had finished. His long, bony finger tenderly caressed the yellowed pages of the *Uigur Grammar* as he said dryly: "Next time we will discuss the structure of the negative verb, using the machinaean hymns." His words seemed both promise and threat. Since the great Thomsen in Copenhagen had died, philology had lost its meaning for him. The young people of today did not understand anything and explained everything as being a petrified instrumental.

His four students bowed silently. Asiadeh went out to the wide staircase of the seminar for Oriental Languages. Other doors opened, bearded Egyptologists appeared, and idealistic youths who had dedicated their lives to the endeavor of deciphering Assyrian cuneiforms. Behind the closed door of the Arabic lecture room, the sobbing sounds of a ghazel by Lebid died away, and the lecturer's voice said, ending his discourse: "A classic example of the modus apokopatus."

Asiadeh went down the staircase. Her hand gripped her leather briefcase, and she pressed her bent elbow against the heavy outer door to open it. Outside, sad red and orange autumn leaves lay on the gray asphalt of the narrow Dorotheenstrasse. She crossed the street with short hasty steps and entered the forecourt of the university itself. Was it the wind that made the scrawny trees bow, or was it the weight of accumulated wisdom? Asiadeh looked up to the overcast sky of Berlin to the dark windows of the lecture rooms, the golden letters on the front of the university . . . People from another strange and unimaginable world rushed past her: students of medicine, law, economics—wearing thin gray overcoats, holding large briefcases under their arms.

The big clock in the dark crowded hall of the university showed eight minutes past ten. Asiadeh stopped in front of the notice board and read thoughtfully, if slightly bored, through the matter-of-fact announcements from the administration to the students, which had been there since the beginning of term, unaltered and already slightly fading, like the old prints from Cairo and Labore. "Prof. Dr. Hasting's lecture about English Gothic History has been canceled." "Chemistry textbook found, apply to Beadle." "Prof. Dr. Sachs has offered to treat fellow students free of charge. Daily 3–5 clinic for internal diseases." Asiadeh took a little notebook from her briefcase, put it flat on her arm, and wrote in tiny, downward sloping lines: "Laryngological clinic, Luisenstrasse 2, 9–1."

She put the notebook away and passed through the forecourt out into the avenue Unter den Linden. She looked at Frederick the Great's majestic monument, and the classical lines of the Kronprinzen Palais. Far away the Brandenburger Tor rose through the murky twilight of an autumn morning.

She turned right, went across the Louis-Ferdinand-Strasse, and ran up the marble staircase of the Staats Bibliothek. Before her was the entrance to the big reading room, to the left long corridors containing the catalogs, and on the right a small door led to the long, narrow Oriental Reading Room, the hiding place of Berlin's strangest scholars and eccentrics. Asiadeh walked in, went to a bookshelf, took out *Radloff's Comparative Dictionary*, sat down at one of the long tables, and wrote: "Etymology of the word 'Utsh—(end).' Utsh, according to phonetic law, becomes 'us' in the Abakan dialect. In Karagaian we find two forms: 'utu' and 'udu.' In Soyanic also 'udu' " . . . she stopped. "Soyanic"—she had not come across that word before, she did not know when and where this faraway language had been spoken, these letters that she was now deciphering. It seemed to her that in the sound of this word she could hear the rushing of a big river, and in her mind's eye she saw the picture of a wild, slit-eyed people who, armed with harpoons, dragged long, fat sturgeons onto moss-grown riverbanks. The men were clad in furs and had wide cheekbones and dark skins. And they killed the sturgeons, shouting "Utsh"—end, the Soyanic form of the basic Turkish word "Utsh"—end.

Asiadeh opened her briefcase and took out a small mirror. She put it between the backs of the dictionary's two volumes and looked timidly and furtively into the little glass. She saw a pale oval face, gray eyes with long, thick lashes, and narrow pink lips. Her first finger touched her brows and brushed over her clear skin, now a bit flushed. Nothing in this face reminded her of the slit-eyed, wide-cheeked nomads on the banks of the nameless river. Asiadeh sighed. She was living in Berlin, in the year 1928, and a thousand years separated her from her robust ancestors who had once come from the deserts of Turan to overrun the gray plains of Anatolia. During the thousand years the slit eyes, the dark skins, and the hard, wide cheekbones had disappeared. During these thousand years empires, towns, and vowel dislocations had arisen. One of her ancestors had conquered, founded, and lost cities and empires. What remained was a small oval face, light gray wistful eyes, and an aching memory of the lost empire, the sweet waters of Istanbul, and the house on the Bosphorus with its marble courtyards, slender columns, and white inscriptions over the entrances.

Asiadeh blushed like a little girl, put the mirror away, and looked around fearfully. At the next table sat a female philologist, dry and dusty-looking with sunken cheeks, laboriously translating the Tarik by Hak-Hamid. She saw the mirror lying between the two volumes, blinked disapprovingly, and wrote on a slip of paper: "*Horrible dictu! Cosmetica speculumque in collo-*

quium!" She pushed the slip toward Asiadeh, who wrote conciliatorily on the back: "*Non cosmetica sed influenca.* Am ill. Come outside, I'll translate the Tarik for you."

She rose, put the dictionaries away, and went into the big entrance hall. The phililogue with the sunken cheeks followed her. Then they sat on one of the cold marble benches, the Tarik on Asiadeh's knees. From the rolling verses the gray Spanish rock arose, and General Tarik crossed the Straits of Gibraltar by the fluttering light of torches in the night, to put his foot on Spanish ground, vowing to conquer the whole country for the khaliph.

The philologue sighed, entranced. It seemed terribly unfair to her that any Turkish child could speak the Turkish language while she, a diligent scholar, had to learn it so laboriously.

Asiadeh put the Tarik aside. "I am ill," she said, and looked thoughtfully at the black eagle inlaid on the marble floor. "I'm sorry, but I must go." She said goodbye and ran to the entrance, suddenly and without any reason in good spirits. She walked along the noisy Friedrichstrasse, the briefcase safely under her arm. Near Friedrichstrasse Station, the news vendors stood like soldiers on guard. A light autumn rain fell on Berlin. Asiadeh put up the collar of her thin raincoat. A car passed her and slushed wet dirt on her stockings. Her small foot stumbled in the mist near the Admirals Palast Theater. Asiadeh stopped on the bridge and looked down on the dull greenish-brown waters of the river Spree, and then up to the iron scaffolding of the station, into which a train was thundering. In front of her lay the broad Friedrichstrasse, glossy in the autumn rain. This town was beautiful in the classical straightness of its wet and naked streets. Asiadeh breathed in deeply the foreign air and looked at the pale faces of the passersby. Her romantic imagination sensed in the clean-shaven long faces ex-U-boat captains who made daring forays to Africa's coast, and in the hard blue eyes she saw melancholy memories of Flanders' battlefields, Russia's snow deserts, and Araby's glowing sands. She came to the long Luisenstrasse. The houses took on a reddish hue. A man at the corner wearing thick mittens was selling chestnuts. His eyes were deep blue, and Asiadeh thought that these eyes, full of otherworldly severity, had been fashioned by two people: King Frederick and the poet Kleist. Then the chestnut vendor spat noisily, and Asiadeh shrank away. She swallowed, and her throat hurt terribly. Men were incalculable, and the poet Kleist had been dead a long time.

Quickly she walked on, her head bowed and her thin shoulders drawn up. On her left the redbrick wall of the Charité Hospital rose up. She did not feel cold anymore. The wet mac smelled of rubber.

"Der Zug hält nicht an der Jannowitzbrucke," she thought sadly, for this was the first German sentence she had learned, and she always thought of it when she felt sad and lonely in Berlin's majestic stony splendor. For some reason it made her feel better to know that the train did not stop at Jannowitzbrücke Station.

She lifted her head and went up the three steps leading to the clinic's entrance. A robust nurse asked her name and handed her a card. Asiadeh stopped in front of a mirror, took off the little round hat, and her soft blond hair, wet at the ends, fell over her shoulders. She put a comb through it, looked at her fingernails, put the card into her pocket, and went into the dimly lit surgery.

"Concha bullosa," said Dr. Hassa and threw the instrument into a bowl. The patient looked timidly at his card and disappeared into the X-ray room. "Or it could be emphysema," murmured Hassa, and entered this idea into the case history.

Then he went to wash his hands. On the way he thought about life, and while the bright drops ran down his fingers and disappeared into the basin, he shook his head and felt very sorry for himself. "I'm carrying a pack of troubles," he thought, and two deep furrows appeared on his forehead. Three adenoidectomies in one morning were definitely too much. And two paracenteses—the second one was quite unnecessary. The tympanic membrane would have opened anyway. But the patient had become nervous.

Dr. Hassa dried his hands and thought of the rhinoscleroma. That was his problem child. The Old Man wanted to demonstrate it to his students. But the rhinoscleroma did not want to be demonstrated. It belonged to a stupid old woman who insisted that she was no guinea pig. It really was a shame that each illness had to have a patient attached to it. But the main cause of his anger was his assistant, who'd better go to Vienna and become a psychoanalyst. There he would be welcome to put the polypotome with the loop ends on the glass table. Bang in the middle of the Old Man's round head. The Old Man hadn't said anything, but his face had flushed crimson with fury. And Hassa was responsible for his assistant, including the silly ass's ideas of modern hygiene.

"Simply puts the loop ends on the table just before it's going to be used," grumbled Hassa. "And to think that it is strictly forbidden to inflict grievous bodily harm on an assistant." He took a handkerchief and, blinking angrily, wound it around the ebonite of the reflector. But he knew that neither the rhinoscleroma nor the assistant were the real causes of his bad humor. It was the weather, which made it impossible to drive out to the Stölpchensee. And that blonde who had been here yesterday, most probably would be today too . . . enough. It was the fault of the weather and the Stölpchensee, but certainly

7

not the news that Marion had spent all summer with Fritz in the Tyrolean Mountains. What did it matter to him what Marion did? "And the rhinoscleroma will be demonstrated, whether it wants to or not—what are we a university clinic for?" he thought.

Dr. Hassa put on a serious face and went into the big general surgery. Along the wall in a seemingly endless row stood the examination chairs. Next to each of them an electric bulb, an instrument table, and a few bowls. The patients were sitting on the chairs, vacant yet strained looks on their faces. On the left corner Dr. Mossitzki rattled a set of mirrors for the throat, and from the third chair on the right Dr. Mann shouted: "Nurse, an ear funnel, please!"

On Dr. Hassa's examination chair sat a blond girl with strange gray eyes. Their outer corners were slightly slanted, and their gaze seemed to be turned toward some fantastic dream. Dr. Hassa sat down on the low stool in front of the girl and looked at her attentively. The girl smiled, and suddenly a fountain of gaiety sprang from the sad, strangely formed eyes. She pointed her finger at Hassa's reflector, which was turned upward, and said in a foreign-sounding voice: "It looks like a halo."

Hassa laughed. Life was quite interesting after all, and what Marion was doing definitely had nothing to do with him whatsoever. He looked into the unfathomable eyes, and a quick thought hit him: "Hope it's vasomotor rhinitis, needs long treatment." He trapped this thought, rejected it as being unworthy of his professional ethics, and said, feeling a bit guilty: "What's your name?" "Asiadeh Anbari." "Occupation?" "Student." "Oh, a colleague," said Dr. Hassa, friendly. "Medicine too?" "No, philology," said the girl. Hassa fixed the reflector.

"And what brings you here? Oh, the throat hurts." His left hand searched automatically for the scalpel. "Germanistic?"

"No," said the girl severely, "Turkology."

"Oh—what's that?"

"Comparative Turkish philology."

"Good God, what'd you expect to get out of that?"

"Nothing," said the girl angrily, and opened her mouth.

While Hassa did his duty, slowly, softly, and minutely, his thoughts were running on two tracks, professional and private. Professionally he noted: "Rhinoscopic findings—anterior and posterior—nothing remarkable. Left eardrum slightly inflamed but not sensitive to pressure. No beginning otitis media. Purely local infection. Consider analgesia during treatment." Privately he thought: "Comparative Turkish languages. There really is such a thing, in spite of the gray eyes! Anbari—that's her name. I've heard that name before somewhere. She can't be more than twenty, and such soft hair."

Then he took the reflector off, pushed the stool back, and said very matter-of-factly: "Tonsilitis. Beginning of angina folicularis."

"Let's say quinsy." The girl laughed, and Dr. Hassa decided to drop Latin nomenclatures.

"Yes," he said. "Bed, of course. Here's a receipe for gargling. No poultices, but take a taxi home. Light meals—but really, why on earth Turkology?"

"It interests me," said the girl modestly, and the happiness in her eyes lit up her face. "You know, there are so many strange and wonderful words, and each of them sounds like the beat of a drum."

"You are feverish," said Hassa, "that's the drum beating. I've heard your name before. There was an Anbari who was the governor of Bosnia."

"Yes," said the girl, "that was my grandfather." She got up from the chair, and her fingers were for a moment lost in Dr. Hassa's broad hand.

"Come again when you're all right . . . I mean for after-treatment."

Asiadeh looked up. The doctor had brown skin, black hair combed back, and very broad shoulders. He was quite different from the enigmatic U-boat captains or the wild fishermen from the banks of nameless rivers. She nodded quickly and went to the exit.

Near Friedrichstrasse Station she stopped and thought. To take the train with its hard wooden benches would be the cheapest and quickest way—except walking, of course—but the doctor had said to take a taxi. She pursed her lips and decided to be extravagant. Head up, she passed the station and walked to Unter den Linden. There she got on a bus, and as she leaned back contentedly into the soft leather cushions, she mused that the German word "auto" meant both a private car and a taxi and was only a modest diminutive of the slickly rolling autobus.

"Uhlandstrasse," she told the conductor, and gave him a coin.

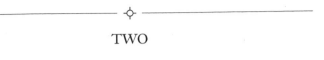

TWO

The room was dark, for it was on the ground floor, and both its windows looked out onto the narrow yard around which the block of flats was built. When the sun shone, its rays reached down only to the second floor. In the middle of the room stood a linoleum-covered table, and around it three chairs. A naked bulb was hanging from the ceiling on a long cord. Along the walls with the tattered wallpaper stood a bed and a divan, and at the other wall a wardrobe, its door kept closed by a wedge of folded newspaper. Next to that a few faded photographs had been pinned up. Achmed-Pasha Anbari sat at the table, straining his eyes to follow the familiar patterns of the faded wallpaper.

"I am ill," said Asiadeh, and sat down. Achmed-Pasha looked up, his small, dark eyes frightened. Asiadeh yawned and stretched out her slender arms. Achmed-Pasha got up and turned back the bedcovers. Asiadeh slipped out of her dress, sat on the edge of the bed, and told, shivering and a bit confused, of the Yakut ending on "a," and the strange man who had looked into her throat.

Achmed-Pasha's eyes filled with horror. "You've been to the doctor—alone?"

"Yes, Father."

"Did you have to undress?"

"No, Father, really not."

She sounded very indifferent. Asiadeh closed her eyes; her limbs felt like lead. She heard Achmed-Pasha's stumbling steps and the rattling of coins. "Lemons and tea," whispered Achmed-Pasha somewhere behind the door. Asiadeh's eyelashes trembled. Through half-closed lids she saw the faded photos on the wall: Achmed-Pasha wearing a gold-embroidered uniform, a decorous fez, and white kid gloves. Asiadeh breathed deeply and suddenly sensed the dust of Galata Bridge and the scent of dates that once had dried in a corner of her room near the Bosphorus.

From afar came a gentle murmur. Achmed-Pasha was kneeling on the dusty carpet of the room in Berlin and, his forehead touching the floor, was praying softly, lost to the world.

Asiadeh saw the big round ball of the sun and the old wall of Constantine at the gates of Istanbul. The Yanitshar Hassan climbed over the wall and, on top of the old citadel, hoisted up the flag of the House of Osman. Asiadeh bit her lips. Michael Paleologus was battling at St. Romanus Gate, and Fati Mohamed rode his horse over the dead bodies into the Hagia Sophia, where he pressed his bloodstained palm on the Byzantine column. Asiadeh raised her own hand and pressed it to her mouth. Her breath was hot and humid, and she said in a loud energetic voice: "Boksa."

"What is it, Asiadeh?" Achmed-Pasha bent over her bed.

"*Karagassian dativ* for the Djagatic Bogus—throat," replied the girl. Achmed-Pasha looked worried and spread his fur coat over her bed. Then he continued to pray, and Asiadeh saw in a confused waking dream the narrow shoulders of Sultan Wackheddin driving out for his morning prayer through an espalier of soldiers. Small boats went round and round on the Tatly-Su, and the newspapers reported victories in the Caucasian Mountains, German advances, and the great future awaiting the Osman Empire. Somebody was pulling her hair. She opened her eyes and saw Achmed-Pasha with a glass in his hand. She gargled a foul-tasting liquid and said very seriously: "Gargling is onomatopoeic, the whole issue must be researched according to the phonetic law." Then she sank back on her pillow. She was lying on her back, eyes closed, cheeks flushed. She saw steppes, deserts, wild riders, and the half-moon over the palace on the Bosphorus. Then she turned to the wall and cried long and bitterly. Her slim shoulders trembled, and with the back of her hand she wiped off the tears that were streaming over her face. Everything had come to an end on the day when a foreign general occupied Istanbul and expelled all members of the holy House of Osman. On that day Achmed-Pasha had, with a magnificant gesture, thrown his sword into a corner and wept in the small east pavilion of his konak. Everyone in the house had known that he was crying, and they had stood silently at the threshold of the pavilion. Then her father had called Asiadeh, and she had come to him.

The pasha had been sitting on the floor, his robe in rags.

"The sultan is exiled," he had said, looking away. "You know that he was my friend and ruler. This town has become an alien town to me—we will go away. Far away from here." Then both of them had stood at the window, looking for a long time at the lazy waves of the Bosphorus, at the cupolas of the big mosques and the faraway gray hills where, long ago, the first bands of the Osmans had risen against Europe.

"We'll go to Berlin," Achmed-Pasha had said, "the Germans are our friends." Asiadeh dried her tears. It had become quite dark in the room. From the divan came the soft breathing of

Achmed-Pasha. She sat up in bed, eyes wide open, and looked into the far distance. She was homesick for Istanbul, for the old house, for the sunlit mild air of the homeland. The minarets in the town of the Khaliphs seemed close, quite close, and a silent feat overwhelmed her. Everything had gone, everything was lost. All that remained were the soft sounds of the native language and the love for the wild tribes who had once founded the House of Osman.

"Grandfather was governor of Bosnia," she thought, and remembered suddenly how the doctor's knees had touched her thighs. She closed her eyes and saw before her his black, slightly slanting eyes. "Say 'A,' " said the doctor, and a halo shimmered behind his back.

" 'A' is the Yakut form. But I am an Osman. Our genetive is 'i,' " Asiadeh answered proudly and fell asleep. Her hand slid under the cover, and she caressed her thighs lovingly where the doctor's knee had touched them.

While she slept, Achmed-Pasha was lying in bed, eyes closed but sleepless. He thought of his two sons, who had ridden away to save the empire but had never returned. He thought of his blond daughter, who should have married a prince and was now suffocating in an ocean of barbaric hieroglyphs. He thought of his wallet, which contained one hundred marks—the whole fortune of the House of Anbari—and he thought of the sultan, far away in a foreign country, homesick, like him, for the soft air of Istanbul.

Then morning came, pale and gray. Achmed-Pasha made tea, and Asiadeh awoke, sat up in bed, and said proudly and sure of herself: "I am in perfect health again, Your Excellency."

The atmosphere in the café Watan in Knesebeckstrasse consisted of tobacco fumes and the smell of mutton fat. The proprietor was an Indian professor who wore glasses, was reputed to be of immense wisdom, and had therefore had to leave his homeland. His waiter was called Emerald and had a long nose and the rank of a minister in Buchara. At the little tables sat Egyptian students, politicians from Syria, and princes of the imperial House of the Kadjars. They were eating mutton fat and drinking fragrant coffee from tiny cups. The coffee brewer was a robber from the Kurdistan Mountains, with broad shoulders and thick eyebrows meeting above his nose. He knew eighteen ways of making coffee, but as a matter of principle he unfolded his art only before imperial princes, governors, and heads of tribes.

Achmed-Pasha Anbari sat at a corner table and looked into the dark round of his steaming coffee cup. At the next table the Tsherkess Orckham-Bey was throwing dice with a flat-nosed priest of the mysterious tribe of the Achmedians.

"Do you know, Your Excellency," said the proprietor, bowing before the pasha, "have you heard that Rensi-Pasha has arrived from Yemen. He is looking for generals and ministers to serve under the imam there."

"I'm not going to Yemen," said Achmed-Pasha.

"How right you are," said the proprietor indifferently, "the Yemenites are heretics." He disappeared behind the counter and rattled the cups. The Tsherkess won the dice game, lit a cigarette, and looked at the fat Syrian at the next table. "Shame," said the Syrian, "a man who believes in God should not play with dice." The Tsherkess drew disdainfully at the cigarette and turned away.

A bald man with dry, bony hands came in, paused at Achmed-Pasha's table, touching breast, lips, and forehead with his hand.

"Peace be with you, Your Excellency. We have not met for a long time."

The pasha nodded. "You come from Istanbul, Reuf Bey?"

"Yes, Excellency. I was wounded at Sacharia and am now working at Customs Administration. On our last meeting I was a deputy, and you the chief of the private cabinet. You wanted to arrest me that time."

"I am sorry you could flee justice, Reuf. How are things at home?"

"Flourishing, and the sun is shining on the Golden Horn. The harvest was good, and thick snow fell last winter in Ankara. You should come back, Your Excellency. Submit a plea for clemency to the government."

"Thank you. I am about to accept a partnership in a carpet store. I don't need anyone's clemency."

The stranger went, and Achmed-Pasha's eyes became sad. He thought of his unpaid rent; of the landlord, who thought him a Levantine racketeer; of his cousin Kyasim, who had fled to Afghanistan and promised to send money; of Mustapha, his other cousin, who had gone over to the enemy and did not answer any letters; and of his blond Asiadeh, who walked about in Berlin unaccompanied, wearing a thin raincoat in this autumn weather, and had fallen ill. Then he smoked, and Emerald took his money and sat down at his table. "Very bad, Excellency, cold and poor," he said in his near-unintelligible dialect. "In Buchara war. I minister again." He laughed, but his eyes were as sad as before.

In a corner a Persian put his hand behind his left ear, in the age-old gesture of Oriental singers, and softly sang an old bayat. The Indian sat behind the counter quarreling violently with the Achmedian priest about God's true nature.

Achmed-Pasha hung his head and thought that perhaps he really could join a carpet shop as an expert and adviser for the ignorant European customers. He sighed and felt a little pain in his left side. He loved that pain, for it was the last souvenir of a wound he had received many years ago, during the Arabic campaign.

The Tsherkess at the next table hummed a melody and smiled as if he did not mean it.

"I would like to be a pianist in the restaurant Orient, Excellency," he said half questioningly, for robbery and warfare, the ideal occupations of his ancestors, were now closed to him. Once his forebears had come in martial hordes to the Osman court, and he was born to rule and give orders. But the past was dark and seemed to disappear behind a whirling wall of desert sand, and the present was here on the hard asphalt of Berlin. The Tsherkess could do only two things: give orders and make music. And giving orders was obviously out of fashion.

From the table of the exiled Kadjar princes came soft whispering: "Bitter is the bread of the strange land," said one. "No," answered the other, "in the strange land no bread at all is baked for the homeless ones." Achmed-Pasha rose. He left the café and, his head bowed, walked slowly about on the streets of the foreign town, where the houses looked like odd, unconquerable fortresses. Silently Achmed-Pasha walked about in the noisy town and did not hear any of its noises.

"I will buy potatoes," he thought, "and tomatoes. I will mix them. That makes a good meal."

He stopped at Wittenberg Platz. The sun sent slanting rays to flood the front of the big department store. Foreign women were walking past with wide empty eyes, silk stockings on their legs. Asiadeh did not have any silk stockings. Suddenly the pasha walked on quickly and turned in to a side street, for along Tauentzien Strasse came a fat, brown-skinned man. Achmed-Pasha looked away with despairing, tired eyes. It was bitter that an imperial minister had to turn into a side street because he owed a rich countryman fifty marks. He was overwhelmed by an excruciating wish to fight, to hit, to strike. He longed for a dark alley where an unknown man would push him and have his ears boxed in return. But the streets were sunlit, people moved out of his way politely and indifferently, and he bought potatoes, tomatoes, and radishes. Then he went home to the respectable house with the greenish-gray front and the door between the marble pillars with the inscription *"Nur für Herrschaften."* Not for him . . . He was not *Herrschaft* anymore, not gentlefolk, for whom this noble entrance was reserved. For him it was the little door with the inscription *"Gartenhaus"*—Garden-House (it seemed an ironic description)—the little door that yawned like a gullet next to the marble glory of the main entrance. He crossed the narrow yard with its tuberculous trees and stopped before the broken handle of his flat, opened the door, and walked along the corridor that led into their room. Asiadeh was sitting on the divan, holding a thread of cotton between her teeth, mending a stocking. On the chair before her an open book was lying, and she mumbled unintelligible barbaric sentences.

Achmed-Pasha poured his tomatoes, potatoes, and radishes on the table, and when she saw the red round balls and the brown clumps smelling of earth, Asiadeh clapped her hands gaily. For some reason she was suddenly very happy.

THREE

The Mensa Academica was about as cheerful as the waiting room of a railway station in the outer provinces. Students were sitting at long wooden tables, closely packed, eating quickly and unselectively the food that a huge man was serving with acrobatic ability. Left of the counter a blackboard was hanging with the menu written in chalk. The low prices made the imaginative denomination of the simple dishes rather bewildering.

Asiadeh concentrated hard on the menu and for a long time could not make up her mind between peach melba and königsberger klops. At last her hunger won the battle with her sweet tooth; she gave the waiter twenty-five pfennig and received a plate with an immense meat dumpling, hot and savory. Carefully balancing her plate, she traced her way to a table, sat down, and sniffed contentedly at the dumpling.

"All right again, Fräulein Anbari?"

She raised her head.

Dr. Hassa stood before her, looking down at her plate.

"Since when do doctors come to the students' Mensa?" asked Asiadeh, and was happy that at last she could talk to someone who was neither a Turk nor a Turkologue.

"Doctors without their own practice are always counted

as students," said Dr. Hassa, and sat down at her table. "You are a Turk, aren't you? I did not know there were blond Turks."

Asiadeh looked at him, astonished. So there were people who did not know that the light-colored eyes of the Istanbul princesses were famous from Tibet to the Balkans.

"It does occur," she said modestly, and pierced the steaming meat with her fork. "You aren't German either, are you?"

"How do you know?"

Asiadeh laughed contentedly. "Even if I'm just a Turkologue, I do know about German dialects. Apart from that, Hassa is not a German name."

The doctor sipped his glass of beer and, with his black slanting eyes, looked at Asiadeh, at the childlike forms of her body, the soft lips and the slightly veiled gray eyes, and in his imagination, harems arose with marble fountains, mysterious veiled women, and evil eunuchs who, as a result of a successful surgical intervention, played an important if rather hazy role among Asiatics. Suddenly he wished he could grab this child of the Arabian Nights, and under the table his knees touched cautiously her slender thighs. The Asiatic child looked daggers at him and said: "If you get familiar, I'll open my mouth and say 'A.' Then I'm your patient, and your professional ethics will put a stop to you."

Obviously this child was no child anymore, or at least a very clever child. He emptied his glass quickly.

"I am an Austrian," he told her graciously. "Do you know Vienna?"

The name of the Imperial City did not bring any noticeable reaction. Asiadeh brought the last morsel of meat to her mouth and looked rather sadly at her empty plate. "Do you know Kara Mustapha? The one who besieged Vienna under Suleiman the

Magnificent? Well—he was my ancestor. If he had won, I might perhaps appoint you to be my physician inordinary."

This, actually, was not quite correct. Grim Kara Mustapha was not really related to the House of Anbari. But the Viennese was duly impressed. "My most grateful thanks, Princess," he said. "I may call you Princess?"

"No," said the girl, "don't call me Princess." She became sad and thought of Prince Abdul-Kerim, whom she had never seen, and who had been destined to become her husband. He had gone to America, and no one had ever heard of him again. He probably had become a waiter.

Dr. Hassa sensed the sadness in the girl's eyes. He rushed to the buffet and brought her a chocolate cake with whipped cream. Asiadeh looked at him indulgently and ate the cake. The white sticky mess covered her lips, and she licked it off with a pointed tongue.

"I am a Viennese," repeated Hassa emphatically, for he was hurt that his announcement had made no impression on the strange girl. "I got my title in Vienna, and for further experience, I went to Paris and London for one term each. Till the end of this term I'll be here in Berlin, and then I'll settle down in Vienna."

This also was not literally true, but the truth was so deeply hidden in Hassa's heart that it would have been senseless to drag it out suddenly. For of course it was quite absurd for a qualified doctor to gad about all over Europe, giving guest appearances at diverse hospitals.

But if Asiadeh should happen to ask about that, she would be told of Dr. Hassa's scientific interests and zeal. Perhaps he might even have informed her that the main cause of his coming to Berlin had been to study the latest discoveries about oto- and rhinoplastic. But she certainly would not have been told about the scandal of Marion and Fritz, who had been together all summer in the Tyrolean Mountains . . . but enough of that. That was nobody's business, and anyway, it was all a long time ago. He bowed his head and smilingly looked down at Asiadeh. "Yes," said Asiadeh, taking no notice of what he had said, "I have now been in Berlin for four years. We left Istanbul after the revolution. Everything is rather strange. I was fifteen years old then and already wearing the veil. At first I could not get accustomed to walking along the streets alone and unveiled. Now I quite like it. But really it is a shame. At home I had learned music and languages, and now I'm learning the language of my wild ancestors. It's a link with home—can you understand that?"

"Yes," said Hassa. "After the next term I'll settle down in Vienna. I'll live on the Opernring. I'll have all the singers as patients." So they talked across each other for a while, and both left something unsaid. Hassa did not mention the existence of a Viennese girl called Marion, and Asiadeh did not mention that this morning a strange man, wearing the uniform of a postman, had knocked at the door of their room and said, "Post." The strange man had given Achmed-Pasha a gray sealed letter, and when Achmed-Pasha opened the envelope, there were, in many-colored splendor, one thousand Afghan rupies and greetings from cousin Kyasim. An hour later a kind bank clerk had looked at the notes, shaken his head, telephoned the head office, and paid Achmed-Pasha seven hundred and forty marks, after which Achmed-Pasha had paid Asiadeh's college fees and she had eaten königsberger klops. But these details had nothing to do with Dr. Hassa.

"What are you doing this afternoon?" asked Hassa suddenly.

"Osman history. Paleography. The sects of Anatolia."

"Is it something very important? I mean—perhaps it's the last warm day of autumn today, and you need some fresh air. Come with me to the Stölpchensee. That's doctor's orders."

Asiadeh looked at his square forehead and narrow smiling lips. She thought of the sect of the Kisilbash and the holy Sary-Saltyk-dede who were waiting for her. She blushed. "Let's go to Stölpchensee," she said calmly, and Hassa did not know that, for the first time, in her life, Asiadeh had accepted a strange man's invitation.

They rose and went out. Asiadeh headed straight for the bus stop. "Where are you going?" cried Hassa, and grabbed her arm. He took her to a side street and opened the door of a car, which showed a big white "A" next to the number plate. "Austria," said Hassa proudly, and Asiadeh's mouth opened in silent astonishment. Never would she have believed that a man of such lowly standing could afford a car. Europe was indeed a land of miracles.

They were lying in the sand on the slope of the low hill by the lake. Asiadeh's body trembled imperceptibly. She looked at the green bathing suit that Hassa had bought for her on the way, and she felt that the whole situation was quite confusing and fantastic. Her rosy fingers groped about in the sand, and she was ashamed that soon she would have to put on this costume of a bayadere. During all the four years she had been in Berlin she had come to know the university, the streets, and cafés. But she had never seen a beach and had only a very hazy idea of these places where European men and women, half naked and closely entwined together, offered their faces to the mild rays of the northern sun. Her eyes opened wide with terror when the attendant took her into the small cabin, gave her the key, and closed the door.

The narrow dark room smelled of water and wood. Asiadeh felt wretched and unhappy—it was like the beginning of a difficult exam. She sat down and stared at the tiny bit of wool that was to cover her body; she pursed her lips and longed for the familiar world of Uigur suffixes and Middle Eastern sects. Then she took off her shoes and stockings and turned them slowly this way and that way until she had calmed down a bit. Then she closed her eyes, hastily took off her clothes, and slipped into the bathing suit. She looked into the little fly-blown mirror and froze. From the wide neck of the tricot her little bosom looked out, naked and naive. She sat down on the bench in despair and cried helplessly. No, she really could not go out like that, even if all the women in Berlin did. Outside she heard strong naked feet trampling about, and she raised her shoulders anxiously. In the twilight of the cabin she looked like a frightened bird in a trap. At last she opened the door just wide enough to put her head through and beckoned to the attendant. In the cabin she looked at the woman with eyes full of smiling shame and said: "Do you think I can go out like that? I mean—I can't see very well in this mirror."

"No," said the attendant in a deep voice, "of course you can't go out like that. You've got the bathing suit the wrong way around." She helped to turn it the right way around and went away, shaking her head.

Asiadeh came to the beach like a sinner to the gates of hell. Her hands were tensely folded over her stomach and her eyes were closed. She felt dizzy—she had seen women's naked backs and men with mops of hair on their breasts. "Bismillah, in the name of God," she whispered and, death-defying, opened her eyes again. A man, a complete stranger, stood smiling before her. She saw spreading toes and two sun-burned legs. Slowly her eyes traveled upward, and the legs became thighs, covered by a woollen tricot. She gave herself a little shake and forced her eyes to open wider. There was a well-formed, tricot-covered stomach, a broad brown breast with curly black hair, and arms with no hair but strong muscles moving under the skin. For the very first time in her life, she saw a strange, nearly naked man, and it was very exciting.

"I am a depraved woman," she thought sadly, and forced herself to look into Dr. Hassa's face. Hassa smiled, uncomprehending but enchanted, and took her to their place. Asiadeh threw herself down and did not know which part of her body she first wanted to bury in the sand.

"Would you like to swim?" asked Hassa.

"No, much too cold," answered Asiadeh, and did not tell him that neither could she swim, nor had she ever even seen anyone swimming.

Dr. Hassa went slowly to the diving board, and Asiadeh saw, greatly astonished, a grown-up throwing himself into the water without any reason, but with a loud splash. She saw men and women romping about with unnecessary energy, or lying about lazy and immobile in the sun, like tired snails. The beach was covered with bits of paper and food, and a fat woman was smearing some yellow stuff on her nose. Asiadeh sat up, drew up her knees, put her arms around them, and felt her shame disappear. But slowly she felt a strange nausea coming up. These people seemed to be animals in a weird zoo; they were all hairy, like apes, there was hair on their feet, their breasts, their arms. Even women had hair in their armpits. Asiadeh thought of her own body, from which she carefully removed each little hair, and of the glossy hairless skin of her father and brothers. Silent disdain filled her. She looked up to the sky, away from the half-naked bodies. The soft white clouds had strange shapes—sometimes they looked like Professor Bang's nose and sometimes like the geographical map of the Roman Empire at the time of its greatest expansion.

A drop of cold water fell on her back, and she flinched. Dr Hassa stood beside her, dripping and wild like a wet poodle.

He sat down next to her and looked, silently enchanted, at this strange girl, whose upper lip was a bit too short, which made her look awkward and childlike.

"How do you like it here?" said Dr. Hassa.

"Nice, thank you. This is my first time at Stölpchensee."

"Where do you usually swim?"

"At the Rupenhorn," lied Asiadeh, looking down innocently.

A little later they were both lying on their stomachs, facing each other, groping in the sand with their fingers.

"Did you grow up in the harem, Asiadeh?" asked Hassa, still overwhelmed by the fact that he was allowed to take a beauty of the harem to Stölpchensee.

Asiadeh nodded. She told him that the harem was a very nice place where men were not allowed and women were among themselves. Dr. Hassa did not quite understand. He thought he knew all about harems.

"Did you have many eunuchs?"

"Eight. They were very faithful people. One of them was my teacher."

Hassa, flabbergasted, lit a cigarette.

"Pfui," he said. "It really is barbaric. And your father had three hundred women, didn't he?"

"Only one," said Asiadeh, proud and offended. No man she had known so far had dared to talk about the harem with her. But Hassa was a doctor—perhaps that made a difference.

She frowned and pouted childishly. "For you the harem is barbaric," she said angrily, "and for me even your name is barbaric." The effect of this sentence was stupendous—much more remarkable than Asiadeh had expected. Dr. Hassa rose up and stared at her, aghast.

"Why my name?" he stuttered, obviously embarrassed.

"Because it's no name at all," said Asiadeh, ruffled. "There is a county Hessen, and a name Hass. Hassa is barbaric and not German at all. The ending 'a' simply does not make sense."

Dr. Hassa lay down on his stomach again, looked at her, and chuckled, relieved. Thank God the girl had no Viennese friends, so did not know about the scandal with Marion and the shame that had come over Hassa's name. Philologues were harmless creatures. "Hassa' is an abbreviation, quite legitimate," he said. "Our name used to be Hassanovic, long ago, because our family originally came from Sarajevo in Bosnia, even before the annexation. I was born in Vienna myself."

Now Asiadeh rose up. Completely dumbfounded, she looked at the doctor. "From Sarajevo?" she said. "Hassanovic—excuse me—the ending surely stands for 'son.' The root must be 'Hassan.'"

"That's right," said Hassa innocently. "Our first ancestor must have been some Hassan or other."

"But Hassan is . . ." began Asiadeh, then stopped, astonished at her own perceptiveness.

"What is?" said the astonished Hassa.

"I mean," stuttered Asiadeh, "I mean . . . surely Bosnia was part of Turkey until 1911, and Hassan is a Muslim name. One of the prophet's grandsons was called Hassan."

At last Hassa understood what the strange girl was driving at.

"Oh yes," he said, "of course. We really are Bosniacs, that is, Serbians who converted to Islam after the Turkish invasion.

I believe I have some wild cousins knocking about somewhere in Sarajevo. I even remember that during the Turkish regime, we used to have some estates somewhere in Bosnia, but that's a long time ago."

Asiadeh took up a handful of sand and let it slowly trickle through her fingers. Her short upper lip was trembling.

"Well—then surely—you must be a Muslim too?"

And then Hassa laughed. He was lying flat on his stomach, his whole body trembled and his eyes became very small. Then he sat up on the sand, his legs crossed.

"Little Turkish lady," he said, laughing, "if Kara Mustapha had conquered Vienna, or the Peace of San Sebastian had turned out differently, my name would be Ibrahim-Bey-Hassanovic, and I would wear a Turban. But Kare Mustapha did not conquered Vienna, so I have become a good Austrian, and my name is Dr. Alexander Hassa. Do you know Vienna? When the sun is setting behind the vineyards and you hear the singing in the gardens . . . there is nothing more beautiful than Vienna in the whole world."

He stopped and looked at Asiadeh patronizingly. She looked up and felt the blood slowly mounting up into her cheeks, her ears, her lips, and her forehead. She wanted to jump up and hit this person in the face—this man sitting there in the sand, making fun of her world—she wanted to run away and forget this town, where the power of the old empire had been broken. Then she saw the stranger's happy smile, his dark eyes, alluring yet childishly unaware of any discord between them, regarding her harmlessly.

Overwhelmed by sadness, she closed her eyes and thought of the broken empire and of the downfall that had begun before the gates of Vienna.

"Is it too hot for you, Asiadeh?" asked Hassa, worried.

"No, not hot—rather cold. Perhaps I am still not quite well. After all, it's autumn."

She looked down, embarrassed, and her eyes were quite dark.

Hassa became suddenly very busy. He threw his bathrobe over her shoulders and fetched hot coffee. He rubbed her hands, cold and lifeless, in his, and enumerated the names of countless bacilli that attacked people in autumn while bathing. When he came to the streptococci, he noticed that Asiadeh's face had become distorted with fright, and he began to enumerate the antitoxins in the same order. That calmed him down considerably, and he caressed Asiadeh's cheek, not sure whether this was prophylactic or erotic. At last he proposed going home.

Asiadeh rose, her cheeks aflame. Dr. Hassa was the first man allowed to caress her, but that was nobody's business. She ran to the cabin, threw her bathing suit, hating it, into a corner, and dressed quickly. Then she came out and stood, proud and unapproachable, by the car, while Hassa twiddled with the motor.

They drove along the dirty asphalt road. Cars sounded their horns, whizzed past them, and Hassa meandered on, past buses, cyclists, and taxis. While driving, he told her about his work at the hospital, and of a temporal septum resection he had done this morning that had only taken eight minutes. The great Hajek himself in Vienna could not have done it quicker. And on top of it, he had had to dab himself, which, judging from the tone of his voice, was obviously an aggravating circumstance. Asiadeh was leaning back against the seat. Her face was all attention and sympathy, but she did not listen to the doctor's words. She was looking at the streets, straining to try and take notice of all the posters, which urged her to take

Bullrich Salt in any ups and downs of life, or which showed a fat man holding his hands up in despair to tell the whole world about his disaster: "The Ullstein Book stayed in the train—I might as well go home again!"

"I'm on the road to ruin," she thought, and her upper lip trembled. "I'm definitely on the road to ruin."

She imagined a long slide and herself slowly gliding down into a boiling lake. On the far side of the lake her father was standing, shouting unintelligible threats to her, with endings that were very interesting from a philological point of view. The she looked sideways at Dr. Hassa and was angry with herself for liking this strange, godless man more and more.

At last her eyes discovered the mirror. In the polished glass she saw his narrow severe lips, a longish nose, and two slanting eyes looking attentively into the distance. She stared into the mirror until the man's features became quite distinctively Mongolian. That made her feel much better.

Meanwhile the car turned into the Kurfürstendamm. Hassa finished his report about the temporal septum resection and thought of Asiadeh's soft lips. The lips moved, and a foreign voice said: "To Uhlandstrasse." For a moment Hassa saw two dreaming, frightened eyes looking at him. He sounded his horn long, excitedly, and quite unnecessarily, and turned in to Uhlandstrasse. At the four-story house with the respectable greenish-gray front, he stopped and looked over his shoulder. Asiadeh looked at him, and the blond windswept hair fell over her forehead. Then he bent toward her, and his lips enclosed her little trembling mouth. He heard a quiet stifled moan and felt Asiadeh's knees contracting. Her soft lips opened, her head leaned back, and he did not have to hold it any longer.

Then Asiadeh slid into a corner, inclined her head, and

looked up at Hassa, breathing heavily. Slowly she opened the door, stepped out, and stood smiling on the pavement. Then she brought her right hand to her mouth, took off her glove with her teeth, and boxed Hassa's ears with a resounding slam. Her eyes glittered, half furiously and half astonished. She smiled softly and disappeared behind the door with the inscription *Gartenhaus*.

◇

FOUR

Half-moons and sentences from the Koran hung in black frames on the wall. The lion of Iran with his mane shone next to the gray wolf of the Turkish coat of arms. The three small stars of the Egyptian half-moon hung peacefully next to the kingdom of Hedsha's green flag. In the big hall, carpets and rugs had been laid out, pointing toward Mecca. On the carpets and rugs, and on the chairs standing against the wall, men were sitting, wearing their best clothes, fezes, and turbans, with their feet bare, among them the faded glitter of a court uniform or that of a high-ranking officer. Persian greetings mingled with Arab blessings and Turkish congratulations. The Orient Club of Berlin was celebrating Prophet Mohamed's birthday. The imam, the same Indian professor whose sideline was the café Watan, conducted the prayer. Persians, Turks, Arabs, generals, waiters, students, and ministers stood barefoot close together and recited the sentence of the Koran. Then they prostrated themselves in the dust before the Almighty, and the Indian professor sang the prayer in his high, sad voice. After that they all embraced, kissed each other's shoulders, and took their seats again in the great hall, on the chairs, sofas, carpets, and rugs. Servants

32

brought coffee, Turkish delight, small Arab cakes, and Persian sherbet. The club's president, a small dehydrated Moroccan, made a short speech, thanked the Almighty for his mercy, the German state for its hospitality, and those present for coming. Then he dipped an Arab biscuit into Turkish coffee and recited a Persian blessing, for he was a learned man and knew how to behave in exactly the right way.

Asiadeh sat on a little divan, eagerly breathing in the scent of deserts, lonely camps, and camel rides, which she sensed in the guests' robes. Men came near her and looked at her shyly, somehow frightened, for she was a woman, and the men in this room were not used to having women among them. Their hands took Asiadeh's, and Achmed-Pasha solemnly pronounced long names that belonged to the hands. Asiadeh looked into the dark brown and black faces of her neighbors. There they were—people of all countries, unified by the word of the Koran. None of these young and old, brown and black people would dare—as that long-legged one from the hospital had dared—to grab her and tear at her lips. She looked down into her small palms and smiled silently and thoughtfully.

A Negro with flashing teeth and sad eyes stood before her.

"*Anto min misri?*" You are from Egypt? she asked in Arabic.

"From Timbuktu" said the Negro.

"Timbuktu," repeated Asiadeh. The name sounded like a magic spell. "That's in the Sudan, isn't it? Once King Dialliaman reigned there, and the House of Aksu. You had a sage whose name was Achmed-Baba. That is all I know about you."

The Negro smiled happily. "We have a saying: The salt comes from the north, the gold from the south, the silver from the west, but God's wisdom and songs in God's praise come only from Timbuktu." He grinned proudly and thoughtfully.

"What are you doing here?" asked Asiadeh.

"I am caretaker in the house of the Egyptian ambassador," said the Negro with great dignity. "You are right, our sage's name was Achmed-Baba. He wrote the book *el-Ihtihadshi*, but he has been dead a long time. Since the Moroccans destroyed Timbuktu, it is a desert, and no one sings there anymore." He fell silent and looked disapprovingly at the little Moroccan, the club's president.

A young olive-skinned man bowed before Asiadeh. "Why do you come to us so seldom, Hanum?" he said in broken German, and Asiadeh answered in Persian: *"Zeman ne darem,"* I have no time, for the young man was a Persian prince.

Achmed-Pasha flushed proudly. Anyone could see how well he had brought up his daughter. She spoke Turkish—the language of his ancestors; she spoke Arabic—the language of God; and she spoke Persian—the language of love. It had not been God's will that she should come into the prince's harem. God was great. He alone knew why this had happened and why the empire had crumbled.

All those present made a big circle. A lean Egyptian sat down on the floor and began to sing in a high, melancholy voice. Two young Syrians with big black eyes appeared, their supple limbs swathed in white bedouin robes. In their hands they held long, crooked swords and round shields with martial sayings on them. They moved to the rythm of the wild song. *"Yah sahib,"* they cried, and the crooked swords glittered. Their movements became short and hasty. The steel blades touched with a melodious sound. The shields crashed against each other. The young men's eyes grew wild. They were well-mannered sons of Beirut merchants, but through their veins coursed the savage blood of their ancestors, who had came from the desert and conquered Beirut. *"Ya—h—i—i—i—,"* they cried, long, drawn-out, and hoarse, and the steel blades glittered. Behind their shields they crouched on the parquet floor and watched each other, like bedouins behind a desert hill. Then they jumped up and charged at each other, carried away by the heat of the sudden fight. Their burnooses waved in the tobacco-filled air. Higher and higher, quicker and quicker, trilled the Egyptian's song, and suddenly the fighters were circling one another—round and round, as if in the whirl of the desert wind. Their glances became rigid, their movement cramped. The bedouins' fight had become the wild convulsions of the dancing dervishes. Abruptly the Egyptian stopped his song, and the wild dervishes changed again into the civilized sons of Beirut merchants. They bowed, and the steel swords touched in friendly greeting.

Asiadeh clapped, carried away by the enchantment of the whirling dance. The air in the hall had become pungent and thick with smoke. Faces suddenly appeared only to vanish as suddenly, like bodiless masks. A beard swam toward Asiadeh in a cloud of smoke. When it stopped in front of her, a face emerged: bushy eyebrows and long teeth behind red lips under a mustache.

"Peace," said the beard, and Asiadeh bowed her head, tired and uneasy.

The old man sat down next to her. He had the small, darting eyes of a lizard a thousand years old. "I am Reza," said the old man, "from the brotherhood of the Bektashi."

"Bektashi," repeated Asiadeh, and thought of the holy band of warriors, ascetics, and monks.

The old man's eyes were spiky and restless. "We have all gone," he said, "Istanbul has spat us out. The master now lives in Bosnia. There we chastise the body. Ali-Kuli is his name."

His lower lip hung down, and his mouth stayed half open.

"You are a wise man," said Asiadeh faintly.

"We keep the faith," said the old man fervently. "Everything falls to pieces in the world of the unbelievers. Light and shadows unite, and God punishes the erring ones. Sin has many faces and stalks those not firm in their belief."

"I do not sin very much," said Asiadeh, and the old man laughed with indulgent melancholy.

"You do not wear the veil, Hanum," he said. "That is not a sin, but it invites sin in others."

He rose and for a second hid his eyes behind his right hand. Then he went away, bowed and lonely, and people looked shyly at him as he passed. Achmed-Pasha came to her, his eyes laughing.

"The whole hall wants to marry you, Hanum," he said softly, and Asiadeh looked at him mockingly.

"They are all good people, Father. Whom will you give me to—the Negro from Timbuktu, or the prince from the House of the Kadjars?"

"To nobody," said the Pasha. "I will travel to Afghanistan and dip my sword into the blood of my enemies. I will build a castle, and you shall marry the king."

Asiadeh looked up at her father. Behind him hung the black banner of Afghanistan and the picture of a man with a nose like the beak of an eagle, a long white feather on his hat.

"The king," she said softly, and caressed her father's arm. "Father—what would you do if a strange man kissed me?"

Achmed-Pasha was puzzled. "Kiss you—a strange man? But no one would dare!"

"But if—"

"My God, Hanum, what makes you think of such things? I would take my knife, I would cut off the lips that have kissed you and gouge out the eyes that have seen you. He would be very sorry that he had kissed you."

Gratefully, Asiadeh pressed her father's hand. She felt she was the guardian angel of Hassa's eyes and lips. "So I will marry a king?"

"No," Achmed-Pasha said, laughing, "on second thought, you'll marry the president of the United States and convert him to Islam. Then the president will send his whole fleet to Istanbul and we can go home. That will be his bride price."

"So be it, my father," said Asiadeh ceremoniously. "I will now go home and ponder your words. It's too smoky here, and the Day of the Prophet has come to an end."

She rose and walked across the hall. Shy glances followed her, but she did not return them. There were slit eyes and narrow lips emerging from the smoke, and they looked like those of Dr. Hassa. Asiadeh turned away and went to the door. A servant helped her into her coat, and the Negro from Timbuktu smiled at her. She left the club and felt, even on the staircase, forsaken in a foreign hostile world. Behind her was home: eager servants, Negroes, princes, blood relations who would protect her honor, and pious dervishes who would remind her of sin. That was the world she knew, the world where she could feel safe. Before her was the dusty staircase of a badly lit house, and the faraway gleam of the street lanterns. She went down and opened the door. The wind swept along the wide empty street, dim light fell on the asphalt from the windows, and drops of a passing rain spattered from the panes of the lanterns. Asiadeh stepped out into the street.

Greedily she breathed in the cool evening air. The stones of the pavement were mathematically correct squares. Asiadeh looked at them, wrinkled her brow, and felt a slight trembling in her knees. Suddenly she wanted to run back, to go on talking to the Negro from Timbuktu about the wise Achmed-Baba, who had written the famous book *el-Ihtihadshi* and had been dead a long time.

She did not. She looked up, dark and serious, into Dr. Hassa's eyes. He took off his hat and bowed. "Good evening, Fräulein Anbari," he said softly.

◇

FIVE

While he was puncturing a paranasal sinus, Dr. Hassa thought of his boxed ears. The suspicion of suppuration was unfounded, but the thought of the boxed ears persisted. He catheterized the eustachian tube of a fat grocer who was behaving like a baby, asking idiotic questions. Later he went to the operating theater and supervised the clearing of a labyrinth, and that made him think that boxing people's ears was not only an impertinence but could actually produce a disturbance of the labyrinth.

Later again he watched the Old Man carrying out a tracheotomy and once again admired the surprising agility of his hands. Then he went to the second floor and thought of the general futility of life, and of the siege of Vienna under Kara Mustapha. He made the rounds of the wards and spoke soothing words to the grumbling hag with the wonderful scleroma. The patients were dutifully lying in their beds, on the blackboards above their heads were the names of their complaints according to regulations, and the nurse on duty reported that the "otitis media" in bed eight on the right had received a morphine injection. Dr. Hassa nodded, went into the basement, and shouted at the assistant, who had used the same bandage

39

over the eyes of three separate patients while they were having their aereted baths.

"Hygiene!" he said, and raised his finger.

Then he returned to his place, gloomily convinced that the only thing which could jolt him out of his general indifference would be a phlegmon with the origin in the paranasal sinus.

Instead of this, a thin woman with a chinorrhoe appeared, which Dr. Hassa, bitterly disappointed, treated with chlorine, and then a student who had nothing wrong with him at all but came only because he was curious, and also because it did not cost anything to be examined by all kinds of specialists. Then nobody came for quite some time, and Dr. Hassa stared at the wall, lost in thought about the routing of the Turks from Europe. His right hand moved toward the instrument table and fiercely rattled with catheters, speculi, funnels, and myringotomes until his neighbor on the left squinted at him and said, "Er, excuse me . . ." Brought back to reality by this remark, Dr. Hassa leafed through several reports and noted with strange satisfaction that the Anbari case was filed between a retromaxial tumor and a chorditis tubrosa. Then he got up, washed his hands, took off his white coat, and felt a private person again.

He drove along the Linden exceeding the speed limit, and on the Charlottenburger Chausee had a difference of opinion with a taxi driver, whom he promised some boxing of ears, and who informed him that he was a flabby Austrian with no idea of driving.

When he reached the Knie, he parked the car, went to his flat, and concentrated very hard on leafing through the *Archives of Oto-Rhino-Laryngology*. He learned that in the Baptist Hospital of New York, ray treatment had lately been used for persistent and relapsing peloidscars hypertrophies, and that Negroes practically never had any pathological septum anomalies. For no reason at all this made him absolutely furious, and he closed the archive.

His glance fell on Marion's photo in its silver frame. He frowned and was suddenly convinced that having one's ears boxed was not the worst thing that could happen. It depended on whose hand did the boxing.

He stretched out on the divan and closed his eyes. As usual, Marion appeared in his mind beside the divan, and he began to reproach her severely because of Fritz, of the way she had behaved, and the shame she had brought on the name of Hassa. Marion's image inclined her head to the side and said, as always, that it was not her fault—which, if one looked at it from the psychoanalytical point of view, was perhaps not so far from the truth but nevertheless infuriated Dr. Hassa beyond measure.

Suddenly he jumped up, went to his writing desk, and put Marion's photo into the drawer. "And that's that," he said, and snorted contentedly. He paced up and down, trying to think of all those Negroes who practically never had any pathological septum anomalies, but it was no good—his thoughts turned the usual way.

The fact that he had married Marion at all had now been demonstrated as completely and utterly wrong. But even more difficult to understand was that he had chosen as his best friend a psychoanalytical colleague—a colleague who had treated a female patient complaining of sleeplessness for acute melancholy, while all that was wrong with the little girl was that she had an adenoymoma. Yes, just a common—or garden adenoymoma! And only he, Hassa, had established that!

But Marion had a soft spot for psychoanalysis and did not understand the first thing about exact science. And on top of it all, the scandal! Just to run away! And up to the last minute her eyes had been so innocent, as if she had not for months and months with Fritz . . . oh well.

And afterward Fritz had said in the café that laryngologists were just failed dentists, and had no understanding at all of a woman's soul. Hassa should have taken Fritz before the Disciplinary Board. When they had stood before the judge who, according to law, proposed a reconciliation, Marion had worn a yellow hat and inclined her head to one side—as if she had a brain tumor.

At this point Hassa used to drink a glass of cognac and immerse himself in an incomprehensible work about the *nervus sympathicus*. But this time, strangely enough, he felt no need for cognac or heavy reading. Astonished, he found himself standing in the middle of the room and knew with absolute certainty the secret reason for this: it was the gray-eyed Turkish girl who had, without any idea of the consequences, stumbled into his clinic.

"A savage child, or rather an Angora kitten," Hassa thought, and suddenly felt the irrepressible urge to cuddle this Angora kitten. He sat down and shook his head sadly. Everything had been going wrong since Marion had left him. Strangely enough, it had always seemed to rain ever since. "I would call her Asi," he thought—quite by the way—"in the Medical Assembly, they would say on every Thursday that I have married, an Angora kitten. My closer friends will call me a sodomite and die of jealousy. I wonder whether Turkish girls are inclined towards psychoanalysis?" He took hat and coat and drove very slowly—which was just as annoying for other motorists—to Uhlandstrasse, where he went through the front door marked "For Gentlefolk Only." But not one of the plates at the doors to the flats bore the name Anbari. A bit out of breath, he arrived back on the ground floor and learned from the caretaker that the "savages" lived in the right wing, through the yard. He rang the bell on the scruffy door until a sleepy landlady appeared and told him that tonight the savages were celebrating their Turkish Christmas or something. He found out where these celebrations took place and drove there quickly.

But on the way he was overcome by doubts and did not dare to invade the club's premises, for to have his ears boxed in front of all these savages was too great a risk. Still—there was always the possibility that the savage girl might go home alone. Too nervous to sit quietly in his car, Dr. Hassa paced back and forth, stood under a balcony while rain was pouring down, and was very surprised that Turks were celebrating Christmas.

At last he saw a dainty figure looking up to the sky and down to the pavement, trying to make up her mind.

Quickly he stepped forward and took off his hat.

"Ohu," said the girl, obviously nauseated. But she did look at Hassa and stopped, her chin slightly thrust forward.

"I am crushed, my child," said Hassa.

Asiadeh pursed her lips. "I am not your child, I am Asiadeh," she said. Then she moved her weight from one foot to the other and added thoughtfully: "It's raining. If we stand here much longer, my father will come and cut off your lips. What will you do then?"

"I will never be able to kiss anyone again," said Hassa sadly, and tried to touch Asiadeh's arm.

"No! No!" she said severely. "My father is very strong." Then she fell silent, and finally added with sudden resolution: "Oh well, let's go, or my father will really come."

She set off and Hassa followed, pointing with despair at the waiting car. But Asiadeh shook her head energetically.

"No," she said, "just follow me." Hassa followed.

When they came to Wittenberg Platz it began to rain again, and Asiadeh stopped, undecided, under a protruding roof.

"Mercy," said Hassa humbly, "please—may I follow you into the café? It looks crowded and well lit."

Asiadeh turned to him.

"Terrible climate," she said. "I can understand why we never conquered this country." Then she looked up to the sky and added charitably: "You may accompany me into the café."

It did not sound like capitulation. She walked across the street and Hassa opened the glass door. They went in and Asiadeh bent silently solemnly over a cup of mocha. She breathed in the flavor and felt her heart beating—a pleasant feeling. "Don't be mad at me, Asiadeh," pleaded Hassa, on his part feeling slightly confused. "I promise never to do it again."

Asiadeh put her cup down, aghast. "Really?" she said, sounding quite frightened, and bit her lip. A load off his mind, Hassa put out his hand, and Asiadeh took it graciously. Softly and reverently Hassa kissed the back of her hand, and peace was declared.

They sat close together in the crowded café, and Asiadeh told him about the Negro from Timbuktu, the eunuch who had taught her Arabic prayers at home, of the Grand Rue de Péra, so much more beautiful than all the streets of Berlin put together, and of Prince Abdul-Kerim, whom she was supposed to have married.

"But you won't?" asked Hassa anxiously.

"I've never seen him. All I know is that he is thirty years old. He disappeared after the revolution. Strictly speaking, he has deserted me. But I suppose it could not be helped."

Hassa looked at her understandingly and felt that sometimes there was a lot to be said for a revolution. "What are you going to do when you have finished your studies?"

Asiadeh looked dreamily at the display of pastries on the table and chose a chocolate cake.

"I'll marry the president of the United States or the king of Afghanistan." Her lips were white with sugar. Happily she spread her fingers and accepted a cigarette from Hassa's case.

"But have you ever loved?" asked Hassa.

Asiadeh put the cigarette away. She blushed hotly, her gray eyes flashed.

"Nobody in Europe knows how to behave," she said furiously. "One doesn't talk of love with strange ladies. And one doesn't stare at them either with eyes popping out of one's head. We know just as much about love as you do, but we are more reserved and quiet about it. That's why they call us savages here."

She was wonderful in her rage. Her pupils dilated, she inhaled the cigarette smoke and blew it upward, and knew with absolute certainty that she had fallen hopelessly in love with Hassa.

Hassa looked at her. "I did not want to hurt your feelings, Asiadeh," he said sadly. "I did not ask out of curiosity but—well—because—you understand? How can I put it? Er—" He became silent and looked around, embarrassed. Perhaps one ought to read an introduction to psychoanalysis after all.

Asiadeh looked at him with silent amusement. These Europeans were terribly naive in matters of feeling. They just didn't have the Istanbul polish. She put the cigarette away and looked at him with pity in her eyes. "Tell me," she said simply.

"A strange thing has happened in my life. That's why I'm

trying to find out about love by asking others. I have been married, and now I am divorced."

Asiadeh looked at him quietly and innocently. Her mouth was slightly open, her upper lip curving upward.

Suddenly she bent forward and coughed vehemently. Europeans were strange people.

"I understand," she said pityingly. "The woman could not have children, and you have disowned her."

"Children?" Hassa was astonished. "What have children got to do with it? Marion did not even want any children."

Now it was Asiadeh's turn to be astonished. "She did not want children? But that's what she was for."

"Oh my God," groaned Hassa, "the problem was quite different. I had a good friend. He was always coming to see us. And one day Marion ran away with him." He shrugged, and Asiadeh's eyes became round with astonishment.

After awhile the situation seemed to become clear to her.

"Ah," she said, "I understand now. You followed them and killed them. And now you're hiding in a foreign country from the courts of justice and from blood feuds. There are many cases like yours."

Hassa felt a bit hurt that Asiadeh thought him capable of murder. "I needn't hide from anybody," he said proudly, "and the courts are on my side."

Asiadeh shook her head. "In my country," she said, "the woman would be put in a sack with a wildcat and thrown into the Bosphorus. The man would be stabbed to death. Everyone would think justice had been done. Are your enemies then hiding so well that you can't do anything?"

"No," said Hassa. "This summer they were in the Tyrolean Mountains. But by the way, why enemies?"

Asiadeh did not reply. It was no good trying to explain love to this person. He was sitting there, awkward and bowed, as if behind a glass wall. She looked at her empty cup and felt a slight satisfaction. It was rather nice to know that he was so alone.

"What do you think of psychoanalysis?" he asked suddenly.

"I beg your pardon?" Asiadeh was extremely surprised. These people had trains of thought so utterly different from those of the pashas at the Bosphorus.

"Psychoanalysis," repeated Hassa.

"What is that?"

"Psychoanalysts are people who look into other peoples' souls, the way I look into your throat."

"How horrible." Asiadeh shuddered. "How can one show one's soul to a stranger? Surely that is worse than rape. Only a prophet may do that, or an emperor. I would kill anyone who tried to look into my soul. You might just as well go naked on the street." She paused and brushed her hand across her forehead. Suddenly she looked at Hassa with a happy smile. "I much prefer people who look into other people's throats," she said submissively.

Hassa had to take a strong grip not to throw himself there and then at this gray-eyed girl. "Let's go!" he cried suddenly, and Asiadeh, nodding, felt she had no will of her own.

Holding hands, they went back to the car. Night had fallen. The straight line of the street lanterns met in the far distance. Asiadeh stared into the lights without thought of either the house on the Bosphorus or the Pasha, who was by now sitting at home, waiting for her. Hassa was big and impossible to understand, like an exotic animal, and his car, in the nocturnal lights and shades, looked like a big armored elephant. They sat down in the car, and the asphalt disappeared mistlike under the wheels. They drove along the Kurfürstendamm and turned on to the Autobahn. The square houses with flat roofs abruptly flashed by in the lights of the car. The scaffoldlike Radio Tower pointed up to the sky, a steel lance. They drove along the wide Autobahn, close together and quiet. Hassa pressed the accelerator, and the needle rose. A moist breeze beat against Asiadeh's face. Hassa looked at her flying hair and gray unmoving eyes. Again he sped up and, at a turn, felt Asiadeh's hand on his shoulder.

The car was tearing through the night as if driven by magic. The forms of the outer world disappeared and merged into one magnificent uniform gray. Blood was pounding in Hassa's temples. In the hectic speed he felt the first reelings of a love he had never experienced before. The asphalt under his lights was an endlessly rolling ribbon. The woman at his side had suddenly come close, to be his forever in the mad whirl of speed. Asiadeh sat unmoving, eyes half closed, overwhelmed by the unexpected sense of yielding. She gripped the handle, and everything seemed to disappear in the intoxication of the world racing past. She looked at the speedometer. The hand showed a number, but she did not know anymore whether it was high or low. She had become one with the wind, the speed, the spooky beams of light from the faraway Radio Tower. "Enough," she whispered, overcome by exhaustion. Slowly and silently he drove back to town.

When he stopped at the house in Uhlandstrasse, he looked white and tired. Asiadeh's hand came around his neck, and he bent toward her. "Thank you," said Asiadeh's soft voice, which seemed to come from far away. Then Hassa felt the warmth of her face and the agitated breath of her childish lips. His hand touched her cheek and he closed his eyes. Asiadeh's lips were very close. He bent forward and opened his eyes. Her face did not move; she seemed to be looking anxiously and longingly at something only she could see—something far away.

"Thank you," she said again and stepped out of the car. Without another word she disappeared into the house, and Hassa stared after her, baffled and enchanted.

SIX

"And thus spoke the people of China: 'Let us annihilate the Turks. There shall be no Turkish people anymore.' But thus spoke the heavens of the Turks and the holy earth and the holy waters of the Turks: 'There shall be no destruction of the Turks. Let them be kept safe for us.' Speaking thus, heaven gripped my father, Ilteres Khan, by his hair and raised him high above all people. And my father, the khan, spoke . . ." Following the runic letters of the inscription with her finger, Asiadeh was concentrating hard. " 'Made known' rather than 'spoke,' " she thought tiredly, and the enigmatic square strokes of the ancient script began to swim before her eyes. Many thousands of years ago a wild people in the steppes of faraway Mongolia had erected barbaric monuments of their greatness. The people wandered away, but the rough script remained. Weatherbeaten and secret, it looked over the emptiness of the Mongolian steppes into the dark mirror of cold, nameless rivers. Stones fell apart, nomads passed by and looked shyly and fearfully at the half-buried monuments of long-forgotten glory. Wanderers from faraway countries lost their way in the wild wastelands. They brought back to the West stories of mysterious inscriptions. Expeditions set out, skillful hands copied the unknown signs. Then the copies were printed on clean white paper and lay in the quiet rooms of learned men. Dry veined hands caressed lovingly the age-old script, furrowed brows bent over the paper. Slowly the veil of secrecy was lifted, and from the square weatherbeaten symbols sounded the howling of steppe wolves, arose the faraway nomad people, rose up a wild leader on a small long-haired horse, came the story of ancient adventures, wars, and heroics. Asiadeh looked tenderly at the rough script. It seemed to her that she was reading the story of her own dreams, desires, and hopes. She sensed something immense, something calling behind the chaos of these primitive forms and structures of words. She sensed the mystic of the beginning hidden in the oldest sounds of her race. She saw the first people of an emerging tribe as they wandered long ago over the snowy ice-bound steppes, creating the first sounds of a language from the enigma of their souls. Her small fingers followed the lines of the script, and she read slowly: "Sixteen years old was my brother Kül-Tegin, and behold what he did! He went to war against the people of the pigtails and beat them. He threw himself into the fight, and his hand, the hand of a warrior, reached the enemy Ong Tutak, who commanded fifty thousand men."

A shrill bell rang. Asiadeh looked up and rubbed her tired eyes. She was sitting in the small reading room of the seminary, and around sounded the guttural whispering of the Sinologues, the compressed throaty cadences of the Arabists, and the faint lip intonations of the Egyptologists, swallowing the consonants. It was said they had solved all the mysteries of the Nile except for the correct pronunciation of the word "Osiris."

Asiadeh rose and looked at the curriculum. "The first Osmans," she read. "Lecture room 8, Lecturer: Dr. Meyer." When she went up to the lecture room, the Hungarian Dr. Szurmai met her in the corridor and told her charmingly—

himself obviously quite enchanted—about a newly discovered Turkish element in the Finno-Ugonist agglutination. Asiadeh listened distractedly. Only once in her life had she seen a real live Ugro-Finn. He had been a fat blond steward from Helsinki who smelled of rum and used senseless swear words. It was perplexing to think that the cradle of his kind had stood in the same faraway steppes from which the first Osmans had arisen and flooded westward.

"It is an aorist," said the Hungarian, "you understand, an aorist." Asiadeh understood. They went into the lecture room, where the Chinese expert Goetz was bending his bald pate over a piece of paper, explaining the cypher "Tü-Ke" to the Tartar Rachmanullah. He drew the beautiful curved lines and said in his hollow voice: "You understand, colleague. In this case the meaning does not matter. It is the sound that matters. The Chinese do not have the sound 'R.' 'Tü-Ke' is therefore the sign for 'Türke,' or 'Turk.' "

Rachmanullah sat there, his mouth open, his brow furrowed. His small eyes looked angrily at the cipher, the meaning of which did not matter. Meyer came in with his youthful face, gray hair, and ability to speak all languages of the Orient with a Swabian accent. He talked about the Golden Mountains of the Altai, from which the people originated; about the great hero Oglus-Khan, the son of Kara-Khan, who gave the army to the people; and of Ertogrul, the ancestor of the Osmans, who, with four hundred and fourty-four riders, threw himself against the Greeks and founded the holy Empire of the Osmans. "Ertogrul had three sons," said Meyer in his Swabian dialect: "Osman, Gedusalp, and Surajaty Savedshi. The first of these three was the real founder of the movement, and this movement is the task we have set ourselves to examine." Then he finished, for the bell rang, and he was a worried man, and a long way from becoming an established academic.

Asiadeh ran down the stairs. She hid in the library like a snail in its shell. Without choosing, she took the first thick volume from the shelf and read with surprise the front cover: *Kudaku Bilik, The Blessed Knowledge, Uigur Ethics of the Second Century.*

Opening the book, she gave herself an order: "Page fifteen, verse fifteen." Trembling with excitement, she began to decipher the mysterious Uigur sentences. The script was irregular and the forms unusual. The bell had rung a long time ago, but she disregarded it, completely immersed in the secrets of the past. At last she deciphered: "Everything which is offered to you comes and goes. Only the Blessed Knowledge remains. Everything which this world holds must end and vanish. Only the written word remains, everything else flows away."

It sounded very grand but had no bearing at all on Asiadeh's thoughts. She bowed her head and looked thoughtfully at her translation, feeling that she had, at vast expense of energy, drawn the cork from an empty bottle. She pocketed the slip of paper and looked around. Satisfied she was alone in the room, she stealthily scratched her head. One thing was certain: Things could not go on as they did. Every day Hassa would wait for her in front of the house and take her to the university. Or to the Grunewald, the fir forest in the west of Berlin. He would give her flowers and make remarks about the joy of family life. Sometimes he would caress her hand or brush her forehead with his lips.

Asiadeh looked grimly at the long rows of bookcases. Everything would have been different if she, still following the laws of decent behavior, had hidden her face under the veil. Dr. Hassa never would have seen her, her life would have remained uncomplicated, and she herself would not have to wrack her brain about the mystery of love instead of examining Turanic prefixes.

Thoughtfully she scratched at the dark wood of the table with her fingernail. It really seemed a mistake to leave one's own country. But her father had decided, and now disaster was approaching her—the love of a foreign man whose feelings, thoughts, and actions were so completely different from all she had ever known. Asiadeh sighed, deeply despising herself. She felt powerless and ashamed. Hassa was pursuing her, and there was no escape from the alluring circle of his words, looks, and gestures. Asiadeh rose and went to the bookcases. The bald administrator who sat at the door, leafing through the catalogs, looked at her questioningly, but she pretended to look for a special book, and her harrassed glance passed over the *Swahili Grammar* and the *Introduction to Persian Poetry from the 11th to the 12th Century.*

"Marriage," she thought perplexedly, and went back to her seat. She took a piece of paper and began to draw demons' heads, geometrical figures, and nonexistent endings of words she had never heard. Then she put the pencil away and was surprised to see on the paper, in beautiful Arabic letters: "Prince Abdul-Kerim." She shook her head and wrote the same name in Latin letters. Then she crossed it out, wrote the full title in Turkish: "Shah-Sade-Abdul-Kerim Effendi Hasreklari," and knew suddenly that all the time she had not thought of anything but the lost prince.

She had never seen him but had felt his presence when she was in a boat, passing by his palace, and saw lonely servants on the terraces. Surely he would have the pale skin and the long, hooked nose of the Osmans. Perhaps his eyes were sad and his mouth closed-lipped. Perhaps he inclined toward gloom and melancholy, like Sultan Abdul-Asis. Perhaps he was sly, weak, and brutal, like Abdul-Hamid. Perhaps, like Memed-Rashi, the quiet dreamer, he lived in idle boredom and had hooded eyes behind which a hidden world of beyond could be sensed.

She did not know; she knew only that this prince, who had lived in the palace on the Bosphorus, had been meant for her, that she was forbidden to love anyone else and yet had fallen in love with a barbarian who had long legs and smiling eyes. The prince had gone, and he had never seen her either, perhaps hardly knew that she existed. Perhaps he had soft, well-cared-for hands and felt a tired longing for death, for quiet and forgetfulness, like the late Yussuf Izzeddin.

There was not much of life in the tired House of the last Osmans. Hassa was stronger, healthier, nearer. Asiadeh shrugged. She did not know what to think. Here she was mourning for a prince who was not a prince anymore and whom she had never even seen. She took her pencil and drew a beautifully curved ornament around the prince's name. Then she wrote underneath, "Asiadeh is a silly goose," and felt suddenly that during her whole life she had been submerged in a confused half-dream. Slowly she brushed her hair from her forehead, then searched in her briefcase, found a sheet, took her fountain pen, and wrote slowly and deliberately:

"To His Imperial Highness, Prince Abdul-Kerim Effendi Hasretlari." She looked at these words for a long time, convinced that she was just as mad as the last Osmans. Then she took up her pen again and wrote: "Your Imperial Majesty! You have never seen me, and perhaps you will hardly remember my name. His Majesty, our August Emperor and Protector of all Believers, had once ordained that—if it be God's will—I should enter the palace of Your Highness to become your most obedient slave and most faithful spouse. I am very unfortunate, Your

Highness, for God has not willed it thus. I now live in Berlin and frequent the House of Wisdom, where I study the history of Your Majesty's ancient ancestors. I am filled with grief, for I am utterly lonely, I do not wear the veil, and many strange men can see me. Punish me, oh mighty Lord! But for a woman who does not wear the veil, it is very difficult not to fall prey to sin. I throw myself at your august feet and entreat you: Take me to you wherever you are, so I can serve you and breathe the same air as you do. If you have deigned to become a waiter, I will, in the evening, after your work is done, massage your feet. If you should drive a taxi through the narrow streets of a strange town, I will give you thermoses with hot coffee and wave good-bye to you when you depart. But should Your Highness's mercy forever be denied to me, I implore you to disown me so I can feel free to rush to the abyss called love, which is the fate of the unveiled ones. For I am young, Your Majesty, and my education in my father's house was not finished when this house was taken from us. Therefore I am weak and have not yet achieved the patience and self-control that is the duty Allah has put upon women. I often think of you, of your palace on the Bosphorus and the trees growing in your garden, which I saw when I was rowed past, at the time when I still believed that in the future I might repose in their shade. Do not frown on me, Your Highness, for I am your slave, chained to the duty of having to obey you, which our Emperor and Master has laid upon me."

Asiadeh signed this letter and put it into the envelope. Then she took it out again and, blushing, put in the postscript:

"And should Your Highness's answer be denied to me, I fear that this will be a sign of your displeasure and final disfavor, which will drive me into the arms of a foreign love."

She closed the envelope and looked at it, undecided. Nobody

knew where the prince was. The tip of her tongue came out and moved slowly from the right corner of her mouth to the left. Then she wrote:

"To the exiled Prince Abdul-Kerim, c/o the Government of the Turkish Republic. Very important! Please forward!"

There was no hope at all that this letter would ever arrive at its destination. She rose and left the library. The bald librarian looked at her retreating back with approval and respect. "What a hardworking student," he thought. "I wonder whether she will establish herself? A pity if she doesn't."

Meanwhile Asiadeh was walking along Dorotheenstrasse. Hassa waved to her. She stepped into the car, and Hassa said it would be very nice to have a honeymoon driving through Italy. "Stop," said Asiadeh, and Hassa stopped. She got out, went to the mailbox, and posted the letter. When she returned, she leaned back and said a bit listlessly: "Italy? You think so? Yes, I suppose it could be very nice." Then she fell silent and looked out of the window. She really did love Hassa.

SEVEN

Achmed-Pasha sat in the café Watan and realized that his life was becoming chaotic. The Indian behind the counter fingered his rosary; Emerald, the waiter from Buchara, served coffee; and the Tsherkess Orchan Bey gave his opinion that Allah's ways were unfathomable. "The religion does not forbid it," said Emerald, for there were no secrets in the café Watan.

"No," said the Pasha sadly, "our religion does not forbid it."

Caressing his beard, the priest of the Achmedian Sect sat down next to him. "All is one, and one is all," he said enigmatically. "By the unity of the flesh, man achieves the unity of the blood." He drank a sherbet and gave the pasha a cigarette.

The Indian professor put his rosary away and said darkly: "God has spoken through the mouth of the prophet: 'Better to be a believing slave than an unbelieving dog.' "

"That only applies to the heathen," Emerald interrupted. "The imam of Buchara has written a commentary on it."

All fell silent, and the Tsherkess disappeared into the next room.

"Strictly speaking, he is not really an unbeliever," said the pasha. "He is a freethinker."

He nodded sadly, and the Indian said indifferently: "How very right you are, Your Excellency, and apart from that, he is rich."

The fat Syrian came into the café and immediately fell into the stance of a prophet.

"What is money?" he said. "Dust before the throne of the Almighty. Where are Abdul-Hamid's millions? Did they save his throne? A holy man from the desert of Netsh said . . ."

He did not finish his sentence, for Emerald put a cup of coffee in front of him, and the professor said indifferently in his melancholy voice: "How very right you are."

Minutes passed, then the pasha raised his dry brown finger and ordered another coffee. His eyes looked at nothing in particular, and he thought that if the Kabul cousin did not send money again very soon, he really would have to become an expert in the carpet trade.

Whisperings disturbed the silence of the coffeehouse. A Moroccan was talking to Emerald: ". . . and he gripped his saber and massacred a thousand unbelievers. The whole Rif is on his side. All Kabyls. He is marching toward Fez. He will become khaliph, and then the bell has tolled for the unbelievers."

"How very right you are," said Emerald enthusiastically, and poured coffee.

From the next room came the voice of the Tsherkess: "Do come in, brother, the pasha will be pleased." He came in, holding a well-built man with a beard and dark naive eyes by the hand.

"Excellency," said the Tsherkess, "may I introduce Ali Sokolovic, merchant from Sarajevo."

The Bosnian bowed and was obviously very flattered that he was being introduced to a real pasha.

"From Sarajevo," said the pasha, raising his eyebrows. "It is a famous town."

"Yes, Excellency." The merchant's voice sounded pleased.

"I hope your people are devout and follow the commandments of our faith?"

"Indeed they do, Your Excellency. What is a people without God?" He spoke of the schools and mosques of Sarajevo, about the time of the Turkish rule, and of the Pasha's father, who had resided in Bosnia and commanded armies. "The world knows little about us," he said, "but we are a quiet, pious people. We have wise men, imams and mosques, and several of us have made pilgrimages to Mecca. Is Your Excellency considering travelling to Sarajevo?"

"Perhaps." Achmed-Pasha tugged at his mustache and looked rather vaguely into the distance. "Do you know a family called Hassanovic in Sarajevo?"

"There are several, sir."

"I mean the one that is split in two parts. One part lives in Vienna."

The merchant nodded, pleased but also a bit embarrassed.

"It is not our fault, Excellency, there is no flock without a black sheep. There was a man called Memed-Bei-Hassanovic. He traveled from Sarajevo to Mostar. That was in those days when your father gladdened our country with his wisdom. A man called Husseinovic attacked him in the mountains—or he attacked Husseinovic—God alone knows the truth. But one of them was left dead there, and it was Husseinovic. At that we were simple people, and much blood was flowing in the mountains. For three years the family carried out a blood feud. The Hassanovic, with all his earthly belongings, his wife and son, took the walking staff into his hand and traveled to Vienna. There he fell into the trap of unbelief. His son became a rich man and his grandson a wise man. But God punishes the apostate. They all have bad wives who bring shame on them."

The merchant had finished. Quietly he sat at the table, drinking and munching, his mustache moving steadily. Then he went, broad and round, like a clump of earth. The pasha kept on sitting there. He was silent, smoking thoughtfully. "That's what has happened," he said suddenly to the professor. "That's what has happened because my father did not have a well-organized police force. If there had been law and order, Husseinovic would not have attacked Hassanovic, and everything would be all right. Thus the parents' sins are visited on the grandchildren. And yet I'm going to say no."

The professor bent forward. "If I were you, Excellency, I too would want to say no, but I would not do it."

"Why not?"

"Because one does not say no unless one has got something better. You haven't got anything better, Pasha."

"Everything changes."

"It is good, Pasha, if two people love each other."

"In our days, Professor, one did not love before marriage."

"In our days, Pasha, women wore the veil."

"You are right, Professor. I will see whether he is a good man."

He rose and left the café. The professor's eyes followed him, and Emerald noted with melancholy: "Five new coffees and eighteen old ones—twenty-five."

"Twenty-three, Emerald," said the professor, for he was a learned man.

"Twenty-three," wrote Emerald, and said wistfully: "A very beautiful hanum. Can she be happy with an unbeliever?"

"One does not talk about these things, Emerald. A hanum from Istanbul can do anything, even be happy."

He fell silent and rattled the coffee cups. He was glad that he did not have a daughter who went about unveiled and fell in love with strange men . . .

EMPIRE STATE BUILDING, FIFTH AVENUE, NEW YORK.

One hundred and two stories, a penthouse with a revolving parquet floor, a jazz band and an all-girl band, glass walls, and behind them the long shape of Manhattan.

John Rolland sat at a table next to the window. The parquet floor revolved, girls were swinging their legs wildly. "A martini," said John Rolland, looking at the girls' legs. "Extra dry," he added, and drank the bitter, ice-cold fluid in one gulp. He rose and walked across the revolving parquet. Beneath him one hundred and one stories lived, loved, worked, and slept—a whole vertical town. He went out on the glass veranda. Square towers loomed from the darkness, a multitude of windows glowed through the night. Whole lighted stories seemed suspended in the air, as if held there by some unearthly force. The abysses of the avenues were like dried-up riverbeds, and far away lay the one dark and fragrant spot in this light-flooded city: Central Park.

John Rolland bent forward. A cutting wind came from Riverside Drive, from the wide, opaque Hudson. John Rolland looked down, far down, into the street, and for a second he felt dizzy. "No," he thought, and stepped back. "No." Then: "A martini," he told the waiter, and looked at his wrist with the pulsating blue vein. "No," he thought again. "Sometime, but not yet." He tugged at his white waistcoat and looked into the mirror. The jazz band howled its wild, yearning rhythm. John Rolland moved his hand lovingly over his breast pocket. There, wrapped in soft silk, was his bulwark against the world. The bulwark consisted of two thin booklets: the passport of a United States citizen named John Rolland, quite legitimate and correct, and a checkbook of the Chase National Bank of New York in the same name.

John felt very safe and protected by these two booklets. He had a whiskey and thought that on the next morning he would have a headache. He had had morning headaches for years, but he still was not going to jump down into the abyss of the avenues. It was his ambition to have a different ending from that of his brother, father, and grandfather.

"Another whiskey," he shouted, as his thoughts became clearer. He was now absolutely sure that it was wrong to let the young scientist make his entrance after only one thousand meters. The young man would have to come on in the first two hundred meters, and furthermore in a close-up. Perhaps like this: "The young scientist in his jungle laboratory, fighting tropical malaria."

"Very good," thought John Rolland, and hoped he would not have forgotten it in the morning. He rose and threw a few dollars on the table, went to the elevator, and saw in its mirror his own lean form, wearing white tie and tails. His ears were singing in the racing mahogany box of the elevator. On the street he opened the door of his car and drove slowly along the empty Fifth Avenue to Central Park, where he turned and stopped at the Barbizon Plaza Hotel. At the front desk the clerk handed him his key and a packet of letters. John Rolland looked at the clerk, and suddenly his eyes were sad and tired. In his own room he put on his dressing gown, poured—after some hesitation—a whiskey, and sat down at the writing desk. He opened the big envelope and thought of the sender, the film agent Sam Dooth, whose real name was Perikles Heptomanides, but that was an old story.

"Dear John," wrote his agent, "enclosed a few letters that have arrived for you. The one from the producer seems to be important. I think that for his $10,000 he really can expect that the abduction scene should be transferred to Hawaii."

John Rolland sighed and read the producer's letter, thinking that really he should write lyrical poems instead of film scripts in which the abduction scene had to be transplanted to Hawaii. Then he thought of the producer, who had many thousands of unused Hawaii shots, and decided to alter the script, for $10,000 really was a lot of money.

Now for the other letters: offers, bills, inquiries, all in oblong envelopes, with the firms' names printed on the front. But one letter was in a rectangular envelope, with no sender's name on it. John Rolland took out the letter, unaware of holding a miracle in his hand. Suddenly he blushed furiously and a blue vein swelled on his forehead. His heart beat loudly as he read: "To His Imperial Highness . . ."

He threw the letter into a corner and jumped up. "Idiot," he thought, meaning the agent, then went to the phone, dialed, and waited until he heard the agent's voice.

"Perikles Heptomanides," he shouted furiously, "how often have I told you: Letters of this kind go straight into the wastepaper basket."

The agent was drunk. He lisped something in a foreign but only too understandable language that sounded like "Imperial Highness." "Idiot!" shouted John Rolland and slammed down the receiver. Then he walked up and down in the room and squinted at the letter. Suddenly he took it up, tore the envelope, and read the beautifully curved Turkish lines. He shook his head, at a loss to understand.

"Anbari," he said aloud. "Some minister or other, wasn't he? So he's got a daughter. Well well. Yes, I think there was some such idea." He closed his eyes and for a minute felt transported into another, unreal world. Then he shook his head again and went to his writing desk. Feeling like a sick monkey, he wrote in Turkish, from right to left.

"Dear Asiadeh, I am not I anymore, and wish for your sake that you will not remain you forever. Our emperor and master has dreamt of both of us; that was in another incarnation. Your conscience can remain clear, for I do not exist anymore. Therefore you are completely free. Not everything that is called sin is really a sin. But perhaps I am wrong, seeing that I am not I anymore. You study the life of my ancestors and long for me. That surprises me. Please forget me. Should I ever come to life again, I will call you, but it is better for you not to wait. Be happy. I will not sign this, as I do not exist."

John Rolland stamped and sealed the envelope and threw it into the dark mailbox in the corridor. "Very nice," he said, and did not know himself whether he meant the mailbox or the strange girl whose name was Asiadeh and who studied the life of his ancestors. He undressed and lay down on his bed. A creeping pain began mounting up. Quickly he drank another whiskey. "Hawaii," he thought. "Two thousand meters. Yes."

"Yes," Achmed-Pasha said too, and embraced Dr. Hassa. "You seem to be a good man. I give you my daughter, even though she was meant for someone else. May God help her to serve you. I believe it is not easy. Give her many children, she will like that. I have brought her up well, and she knows how to behave. If she does not behave well, disown her."

Again he embraced Hassa, sobbing with a few short gasps. Hassa looked at him, embarrassed and happy.

◇

EIGHT

Asiadeh was lying on her back on the divan, looking at Hassa, who seemed a big awkward child. He bent over her, and she was conscious of the scent of his skin and the warmth of his open lips. Her hands were buried in the cushions, and in her eyes were both longing and fear. Hassa's lips came closer and closer, bigger and bigger. They enclosed Asiadeh's mouth, they covered her face, and Asiadeh's whole body seemed to dissolve in the narrow slit of those open lips. Hassa's hand touched her neck. She felt his fingers gliding over her hand, and her body stretched toward this hard, alien touch. She turned her face aside, and Hassa's hand pressed against her bosom.

"Asiadeh," said Hassa, and she gripped his head to lay her burning cheek against his forehead. Hassa's body was very near. From under her half-closed lids, Asiadeh saw his dark jacket and the white triangle of his shirt. His lips again enclosed her mouth; she heard his breath and abruptly felt transported into another strange world, a world of dreams, where feelings were more tangible, more sharply defined than in the world of normal, everyday life. Hassa seemed a mighty scorcerer with a mysterious power that ruled her senses and from which she could not escape. She felt his hands on her slim body, and her

66

whole being seemed lulled to rest in these strange, hard palms. "Enough," she said very seriously, and sighed, relieved and perplexed.

Embarrassed, Hassa rose and glanced sideways at Asiadeh, for he did not know how he had suddenly found himself on the divan, so indecorously close to the gray eyes, which were looking at him with laughing disapproval. Asiadeh seemed to know this perfectly well. She motioned him to sit down, then she put her head on his knees, humming a strange, monotonous song. She looked up at Hassa and was glad she was born on the sweet waters of Istanbul, where one learns love's forms, enigmas, expressions, and mysteries.

The room became quite dark, and Hassa lit a small table lamp. The light fell on his face and he began to talk about the honeymoon in Italy. "I won't go to Italy," said Asiadeh, and raised her head. "After the wedding we'll go to Sarajevo."

"To Sarajevo? But why?" Hassa was genuinely astonished.

"Oh, we'll just go," said Asiadeh, and that was that, for she had gray eyes, and Hassa was only a man. Then Asiadeh rubbed her chin against her knees and looked longingly into the darkness. Suddenly her pupils were very big.

"My wet nurse," she said, "my wet nurse told me that when Timur the Lame had conquered Sivas, he assembled his bravest warriors and the sickest of lepers and condemned them all to death—the ones so they could not infect others with their bravery, the others with their weakness. He ordered them all to be buried alive. Their heads were bound down between their knees, they were bundled together—always ten together—into round balls, and then they were thrown into holes, where they suffocated. My nurse told me that so I would remember never to be too brave or too weak. But I'm afraid it was not much good."

"Will you be faithful to me?" asked Hassa, because he did not know what to say, and because he had a past.

"Adultery—that is something in novels, but not for real people. Of course I'll be faithful to you." Asiadeh raised her head proudly. "Take the hundred most beautiful men in the world and put me on a desert island with them. Come back in ten years' time. Not one of them will have possessed me. Man and wife are like a double nut kernel in its shell, thus spoke the wise Saadi."

Her legs crossed, she sat up on the divan, obviously disgusted.

"Do you love me so much?" Hassa was honestly surprised.

Asiadeh bowed her head, smiling. "One does not talk about love. Hands, eyes, and the veil that slides down on the wedding night—they are the ones to speak of love. A kiss is not an inscription on a gravestone—thus said the great Hafiz."

Hassa grumbled: "Saadi says one thing, Hafiz another. What does Asiadeh say?"

Asiadeh got up and hopped about the room. "Asiadeh says nothing. Asiadeh does not talk about her love—she shows it." She went into a corner, raised her hands, and turned cartwheels all across the room. Then she got on her feet again, quite out of breath. "That's how much I love you," she said, very satisfied with herself.

"You'll have to do that in Vienna, on the Ring, when my friends ask if you love me."

Asiadeh's lids fluttered. "Do you mean to say your friends will ask me whether I love you?"

"Of course they will."

"I'll bite off their noses if they do. It's got nothing to do with them."

She stood before Hassa, her hand touching his arm, and said half in jest, half really entreating: "Oh Hassa, let me wear the veil. It will be better."

Hassa laughed, and Asiadeh shook his shoulders.

"Don't laugh like a fool," she cried furiously, "you're getting a very good wife."

She ran into the entrance hall and put on her coat. Hassa said he would take her to the café where Achmed-Pasha was waiting for her, and she gripped her handbag closely. In this handbag was the letter of the nonexistent prince.

She came into the café and sat down at the little marble table. Achmed-Pasha's hands were folded on the tabletop, his small black eyes looked at Asiadeh, he talked, and Asiadeh thought of the exiled prince, of Hassa, and of the Imperial City of Vienna, where the power of the Osmans had broken.

"Yes," she said, "I love him." She looked straight ahead and pressed her lips together.

"Nobody knows what is written," said the pasha, "if tomorrow he loses his leg, or his mind, or the fire of his love, what will you do then?"

"I will still love him and be a good wife to him."

"Men are sometimes moody or cross. It is not easy for women when God puts their men to the test."

Asiadeh thought for a few moments, then said decidedly: "If he gets nasty, I'll lock him in for a while and play with his children. He'll have many children, and it will never be dull."

The pasha looked approvingly at his daughter. "She is a clever woman," he thought. "She knows what to do."

"Men are fickle," he said, "and people of today often have not the genuine understanding of morals anymore. Unthinkable horrors happen in marriages today. There are men who waste their semen on women other than those God has given them."

"I know," said Asiadeh, and pushed her lower lip out. "That is called adultery. But people do not behave like that. Only animals do, and surely Hassa is an educated man."

She shrugged awkwardly and looked at the marble tabletop, at a loss to understand. Achmed-Pasha cleared his throat. He had a good daughter, but there were so many animals among people, and a young woman was such a helpless and unexperienced thing.

Asiadeh seemed to guess his thoughts. "I was fifteen years old when we left Istanbul," she said, blushing. "I was to marry a prince and was being prepared for it. Sexless servants have instructed me in those things that bind one sex to another. I can hold my own against the women of the unbelievers."

She looked proudly ahead, and her face became pale again. The pasha was embarrassed. By God—he had underestimated his daughter. Hassa would not deceive her.

"We are a warrior people," he said. "We were four hundred and forty-four men when Ertogrul led us toward Anatolia. But we were brave and adventurous, so God gave us the rule over one half of the world. Our women have to be brave, beautiful, and clever, and they must never cry. Don't forget that. A woman has only one duty—to serve the man and educate the children. But the man has more duties—he must fight and defend his house, today as ever. Therefore he can never wholly belong to the woman. It is important to know that if one wants to be happy. But a clever woman both serves and is served, and whoever is born to reign will reign, even behind the veil."

The pasha was silent for a while, lost in thoughts and memories. Then he said in a hard voice: "The greatest treasure on earth is a virtuous wife. Thus spoke our prophet. You will not bring shame on me. But if a shadow should fall on you, come to me—I will kill you myself. I do not want an unbeliever to do that. Can you remember your mother?"

"Yes, Father. Mother stood by the fountain and wore a long, full robe. Her skin was pale and on her first finger she wore a ring. More than that I do not remember."

The pasha nodded. "Your mother was a good woman. I had disowned three wives until I found her. I gave eight big diamonds for her, and the revenue of four villages, for good women are rarer than even good diamonds. She died honorably, before sin came to our country. Be like her, or your husband will disown you."

Asiadeh bowed her head. She thought of Hassa's slanting eyes and the awkward figure in the twilight.

"My husband will not disown me," she said decidedly, "only if I myself would want him to."

She laughed, and the pasha did not understand what she meant, for he too was only a man, and had given eight big diamonds for a wife whom God later took away from him again. He looked at Asiadeh and thought that she too would leave him in a week's time—in a different way from his wife, but a departure nonetheless. He blinked his small black eyes and felt he was being destroyed. Once there was a house with a marble court and a fountain. Once there were regiments in colourful uniforms and flags with the half-moon. There were quiet women, palaces, and worthy men with whom one took council. There was an empire that ruled over three continents and millions of people. Everything had gone, and what remained was breaking up or going away, like his blond Asiadeh, who was marrying a barbarian, and like his sons, who set forth to defend the House of Osman and did not come back, and like himself with his old body and halting steps, with the memory of

71

Istanbul's radiant sun and the red-clad Negro battallions on Fridays, on the Ak-Maidan Square, in front of the big mosque.

"In a week's time you will be a wife," he said softly, and got up.

Asiadeh looked at his perturbed wrinkled face and suddenly felt a deserter from the battlefield of exile.

"Be a good wife," said the pasha tiredly, and she nodded and said bravely: "At your service, Excellency."

NINE

The hotel was called Srbski Kralj, the café was called Russki Tsar, and the town was called Belgrade. Hassa strolled along Prince Michael Street, and Asiadeh stopped in front of the shops in Terapia Square and had profound conversations with the owners.

In the evening they wandered though the quiet park between the hotel and the river Save, on the glass-covered veranda they ate immense Serbian oysters, strange dishes, and spices that Asiadeh ordered, the names of which Hassa could not even pronounce. After the meal Asiadeh dropped eyes and nose into a steaming coffee cup, emptied it in small sips, and looked at Hassa gratefully and submissively. Then they passed the smiling hall porter, walked across the big hall, Hassa locked the door behind them, and Asiadeh's body was small and fragile. She stretched her hands out to him, and in the faint light of the covered table lamp her eyes were yielding and her lips childlike and open.

Hassa put the light out, and she was humble in her shy, touching curiosity. During the night she half-woke, spoke long, twittering Turkish sentences that Hassa did not understand but which seemed to hold a secret tenderness. Early in the morning she jumped over Hassa's body and disappeared into the bathroom. Hassa followed, won the battle for entry, and grabbed the shower. Asiadeh's face became distorted with fright, but with baited breath, she too went bravely under the cold stream of water.

Then she rubbed herself dry and, shaking her head, looked at Hassa, who was paddling around in the water, baring his teeth.

"Barbarian," she said grandly and happily.

She dressed, and sitting at the breakfast table, she looked a real princess.

"The ideas you have!" said Hassa. "Nobody ever goes to Belgrade on their honeymoon." But he did not sound at all dissatisfied, and Asiadeh hardly heard his words. She was looking at the green avenues of the park and the waters of the wide river Danube shining in the bright morning sun. She thought of Suleiman Pasha, who had once, with two hundred men, defended this town against the bands of Black George, and how they had fallen before the walls of this town, every man. But that was long ago, long before Asiadeh was born, and it was certain that Hassa would not understand anything about it.

"It is the gate to the Orient," she said, and pointed at a man wearing a fez and glasses, carrying a walking stick. "I am just visiting the provinces my ancestors once conquered and then wasted."

"The Orient," said Hassa contemptuously, "unhygienic housing and reactionary customs. It is losing more and more ground. In a hundred years' time, the Orient will be just a geographical term."

"Mm," muttered Asiadeh and played with her knife. "But still love . . ." and Hassa thought her soft words meant the Orient.

Afterward they walked the streets, and Hassa was proud when his wife's eyes filled with joy and laughter. She dragged him along the darkest alleys, went into the lowest cellar taverns, and spoke Turkish to everyone in the strange belief that the people could not have forgotten Suleiman Pasha and the official language of his times. In a wide street behind the National Bank she suddenly stopped and, overwhelmed with astonishment, looked at a low, square building with a round cupola and a little tower.

"A mosque," she said, and forgot to close her mouth in her delight. She went into the yard. An old man was sitting at the well, thoughtfully washing his feet. Asiadeh spoke Turkish to him, and he answered brokenly but disdainfully.

Asiadeh fell silent and looked away.

"What did he say?" asked Hassa.

"He says the Turks have forgotten God and women go about unveiled. Come away."

She turned and walked quickly to the exit, Hassa following.

They went to the café Russki Tsar, Asiadeh still frowning, her eyes pensive. She drank coffee, and Hassa admired her soft, girlish profile. "Enough of sightseeing," she said severely. "Tomorrow we'll go to Sarajevo." Hassa took her hand and played with her little rosy fingers. He looked into laughing, half-closed eyes, at the short, slightly upturned upper lip, and it did not matter to him at all where he was doing that, in Belgrade or in Sarajevo. Asiadeh was a fairy tale, impossible to grasp with the laws of exact logic. He gave up trying to find his way in the labyrinth of her thoughts, to find any reason for her sudden laughter or misery.

"All right," he said, "let's go to Sarajevo."

They went to the hotel, and Asiadeh packed with the skill of a nomad woman moving to a new camp.

"You'll see," she said, "we're now going to a pious Muslim town where people will honor me despite of you, for I am living a righteous life while you are a heretic, worse than an unbeliever. But do not be afraid. I will defend you, for you are my husband, and I am responsible for your well-being."

"All right," said Hassa, a bit afraid of his robust cousins in Sarajevo whose name was Hassanovic, and who would surely despise him. In the sleeping compartment, the little room with red walls and curtains, he stood at the window for a long time and looked at the Serbian plain, at the fields, the little white-washed station houses, and the lean farmers who jumped hastily from the train to drink water. Asiadeh touched his shoulder. He turned, and she embraced him. He looked at her head bending backward and at the strangely formed eyes. She drew her feet up and hung on his neck, small, dainty, and impossible to understand. Carefully he gathered her in his arms and put her on the bed, and obediently she let him cover her up and seemed to fall asleep at once. He climbed the small steps to the upper berth. The car trembled in rhythmic elasticity. Hassa looked out of the window. There were trees, suddenly, unexpectedly coming out of the darkness, for a few seconds hiding the narrow crescent of the moon.

A slight sound from below. "Hassa," cried Asiadeh, "shall I wear a veil tomorrow? We are going to a very pious town."

Hassa chuckled at the thought that he should be married to a wife in hiding. "I don't think that will be necessary," he said softly. "Sarajevo is a civilized town."

Asiadeh did not reply. The little blue bulb over the door was the one point of light in their compartment. Asiadeh looked at the leather-covered wall and made little scratching noises on it.

"Listen, Hassa," she cried, "can you tell me why I love you so much?"

Hassa was touched. "I don't know," he said humbly. "Perhaps it's got something to do with the way I am."

Asiadeh sat up in bed. "I loved you when I did not know anything about the way you are," she cried in an injured tone. "Are you asleep, Hassa?"

"No," said Hassa, and put his hand down. Asiadeh gripped one of his fingers and held on to it as if it were a talisman. She put her mouth close to his palm and spoke into it as if it were a telephone. Hassa did not understand the words, but her lips touched his palms and were soft and warm.

"Asiadeh," cried Hassa, "it is wonderful to be married."

"Yes," answered Asiadeh, "but I am still a beginner. What will it be like in Vienna?"

"Wonderful. We'll live on the Opernring. I've got a beautiful flat, and all the singers of the opera will come to me for treatment."

"Female singers?" growled Asiadeh. "I'll help you when you are operating."

"Good Lord, no! You're far too young, and you'll think the whole thing disgusting. No, you'll just be my representative."

"What's that?"

Hassa did not really know himself.

"Well—" he said, "you'll go about in the car, receive our guests, and so on . . . it will be wonderful."

Asiadeh was silent. The window had turned quite black. The car swayed on the curves of the rails. She closed her eyes and thought of Vienna and of the children who would have Hassa's eyes.

"In my country," she said, "a man becomes either an officer

or a civil servant. What made you choose such an extraordinary career?"

"Today it's much more extraordinary to be a civil servant. To be a doctor is a good thing. I'm helping humanity."

Hassa said this rather pompously and thought, as always in similar situations, that the average life span had risen from fifty to fifty-five lately. Hassa felt he was taking part in this success.

Asiadeh did not know anything about the average life span. Hassa was incomprehensible yet familiar, like a machine one owns without having any idea of what goes on inside.

He was lying in the bed above her, and she heard his soft breathing.

"Don't sleep!" she cried. "Your wife is all alone. Are we in Bosnia yet?"

"I suppose so," said Hassa sleepily.

Asiadeh jumped up and was suddenly very excited. She took hold of the steps, and Hassa saw her fingers straining to catch the edge of his bed. Then her head with the tousled hair came into view, and at last the blue pajamas, black in the darkness. Hassa supported her, drew her up to him, and her naked feet crept under his covers. She pressed her body against his and said with solemn enthusiasm: "Here reigned my grandfather."

Then she put her head on his pillow and said haughtily: "I'm staying with you. It's dark down there."

She fell asleep immediately, and Hassa clasped her body tightly, lest she fall at a turning. He lay for an hour or two, he did not really know how long.

Suddenly Asiadeh woke up and said sleepily, in a reproachful tone: "Go down, Hassa. What an idea, to get into strange beds at night."

Feeling quite ashamed of himself, Hassa climbed down into

the empty lower bed, where Asiadeh's scent still lingered on the pillow, and fell asleep.

When he awoke in the morning, Asiadeh was standing at the open window, leaning far out into the cool morning air.

"Come here!" she called. "Come here!"

Hassa came to the window. The sun was rising, flooding the jagged rocks with rosy light. The train was going across a ridge, the rocks fell into steep precipices on either side, and down in the valley the square white houses looked like scattered toy cubes. The domed cupolas of mosques rose on little hills, minarets towered up against the sky and seemed, in the rays of the morning sun, to be made from pink alabaster. Figures in many-colored robes stood on the minarets' balconies and brought their hands to their mouths like funnels. Asiadeh thought she could hear the mullahs' voices, though the train's noise seemed to drown them: "Arise for prayer!" sounded from the minarets. "Arise for prayer! Prayer is better than sleep!" Veiled women wearing heelless slippers stopped at the roadside to watch the train go by; barefoot children lay down in the grass, praying playfully yet earnestly.

Asiadeh's hand was on Hassa's shoulder. "Look!" she cried triumphantly. "Look!" She pointed at the mosques, the priests' flowing robes, and the rising sun.

"Do you understand now?" she asked, and waved to the valley.

"Understand what?" asked Hassa, for he saw children in rags, small, poor houses, and lean goats on the mountain slopes.

"How beautiful it all is," said Asiadeh. "There is nothing more beautiful in the world. And the people of the prophet have built all this."

She turned away, biting her lips. But Hassa had not seen her tears. He was taking photos of the fairy-tale valley and worrying whether the light was right.

"Hassa." Asiadeh's voice was deep. Her cheek touched his face and rubbed against the unshaven upper lip. "Hassa," she repeated, "for five years I have longed for a country that looks like my homeland."

Hassa put the camera away. "Yes," he said, "it is nice to see the world from the window of a sleeper. Then it's so different from the way it really is. But you are a romantic, and that is good. For you have come straight out of the Arabian Nights."

Asiadeh was packing. The train began to slow down.

"I am just a girl from Istanbul, nothing more," she said, and covered her face with a thin veil.

The train stopped at the station of Sarajevo.

TEN

Three days after the train, rattling astmathically, had
driven into the Sarajevo Station, Achmed-Pasha was
entering the carpet shop of Bagdadian & Co. in Kantstrasse. The smell of old carpets and rugs was comforting.
There was no doubt about it: It had been the best thing to do,
accepting a paid job, even though it was a definite comedown.
The carpets' soft lines were memories of a vanished world, the
delicate curves of ancient patterns were revealed as gardens,
hunting and fighting scenes, old warriors, lingering gestures,
expressed by slender virgins with elongated eyes and delicate
faces.

Achmed-Pasha sat down before a pile of old carpets in the
back room. His hands caressed the many-colored softness.

"A Kerman," he whispered, and noted the price. Carpets
were gliding through his fingers: carpets from Smyrna, Kash-
mir, Koshant, carpets of many colors, mirroring the rich
splendor of the Orient. His face earnest, wrinkled with concentration, he noted the prices and wrote short explanations
meant to teach the rich barbarians to see behind the perplexing
glory of the colors in a Buchara carpet, a classical war scene
from the epos by Firdousi.

At twelve o'clock he slipped off his shoes, took a prayer rug from Tekin, and prayed long and fervently, looking toward Mecca. Then he sat behind a little shelf, armed with a magnifying lens, in front of a stack of Persian miniatures, and explained them to the merchant.

"This drawing, sir, looks as if it came from the school of Achmed-Fabrisi in the sixteenth century. But you must not mislead the customers. It is not by the great Bahsade. Bahsade loved to lay out the background of his pictures in well-ordered designs. He would, for instance, draw gardens, behind them lakes, and behind the lakes, a deer. This here is by a lesser artist of the same school."

"Oh yes," said Bagdadian, and wrote into the catalog: "Drawing by Bahsade. Very rare."

Achmed-Pasha saw it and worriedly pressed his lips together. Obviously this was the way in which other nations became rich and powerful while the Osman Empire fell into ruin.

He worked in the carpet-filled room until dusk. Then he went home, and on the table lay a letter with the stamp Sarajevo. He read it, his hands trembling slightly, and learned that Sarajevo was a God-fearing town, and the Zarska-Djamij resembled the Blue Mosque in Istanbul. He learned that Hassa was the best husband in the world and that his relatives were good people who knew exactly what was due to a princess from Istanbul. He learned further that there was no better state for mankind than the married state, and no better honeymoon than in Sarajevo. The letter was short, the lines running upward.

"Very good," said the pasha, and folded the letter.

"Very good," said John Rolland, sitting at midnight in the gutter of a narrow lane in Greenwich Village. He was trying to make a beautiful bow on his cane from his agent's white tie.

"Very good," he said again, and tried to make the cane stand up without support. The cane trembled slightly and fell. Sam Dooth laughed loudly and clapped John Rolland on the shoulder. Then they both looked sadly and silently at the fallen cane. From behind the doors of the little bars in New York's artist quarter came shrill shouting. Dimly lit lanterns were hanging over the entrances, and a policeman crossed the street, looking tolerantly at the two gentlemen sitting in the gutter, playing with the cane.

The gentlemen pushed their top hats back, and one of them put his left palm behind his ear. He opened his mouth, and a wild howling cut through the night.

"*Amanamana-a-a-a,*" sang the gentleman, full of fervor and enthusiasm. The other one blinked happily and joined in.

"*Gjashiskjamana-a-a-a,*" he sang, raising his face to the moon. Then they both embraced and roared, long, drawn out, up to the stars:

"*Ai-diribe-e-e-eh, Wai-diribe-e-eh.*"

The door of an all-night-bar opened, and a frightened commissionaire, bedecked with gold braid, looked out. The policeman walked up to the two gentlemen and touched their shoulders with his truncheon.

"What's going on here? Why are you shouting?"

"Sir, we are singing, we are musically inclined."

The policeman looked sternly at them. His watery light eyes seemed to have taken their color from the ocean and the green coast of Ireland.

"That's not singing," declared the authority, "that's shouting. Better go home."

"My friend," said one of the gentlemen, "this is the Indo-Chinese scale. It is, as you remarked so correctly, rather different from the Irish one. Yet you cannot deny that millions of people feel the whole range of emotions, from the erotic to the divine, at the sound of this scale."

"Is that so," said the policeman threateningly, and took out his notebook. "Ten dollars," he added matter-of-factly, and gave them the receipt.

The gentlemen paid. One of them struggled into a vertical position and dragged the other one up. Stumbling rhythmically, they disappeared, heading toward Washington Square.

On the way they embraced, and one of them whispered into the other one's ear: "This is a wild country. They don't know anything about music here."

At Washington Square they stopped. From Greenwich Village, behind them, came the sound of cheap jazz. Youths with high ideals and curly, greasy locks appeared in the fluttering light of the streetlamps. From time to time a big dark colored car would drive along the narrow cobbled streets, and from its windows, curious eyes would look out disdainfully. From afar came the sound of broken glass, and a high female voice cried, "Joe, a drink!"

"Galata," said John Rolland, "definitely Galata. Or Tatwala. They wouldn't let me go there, but it can't have been very different. You ought to know, Perikles."

Sam Dooth pressed his lips together haughtily. "Haven't even visited the sewers of your capital," he said with immense dignity. "For I was born on the Phanar, at the patriarch's seat. Even at the time of Michael Perfirogenetos, a Heptomanides was a patrician."

"You're lying," said John Rolland reproachfully. "You were born in the criminal quarter of Tatwala. How else would you be able to take ten percent of my earnings?"

"What is money," wheezed Dooth, spreading out his palms.

"The peace of one's soul—that's the only thing that matters. Incidentally, I take fifteen percent from all the others."

He took a flat metal bottle from his hip pocket and gave it to his partner as a proof of reconciliation. John drank, and as his head bent backward his eyes followed amazedly the endless rows of windows in the skyscrapers. The shabby triumphal arch looked poor and lost in their middle. It had been built when the pious Puritans had a cemetery on Wall Street and the streets of the city had names instead of numbers.

"The Dutch are a loose and extravagant people," said John Rolland, and returned the bottle to his friend. "Twenty-five dollars they paid the Indians for Manhattan. Much too much."

Sam Dooth looked at the majestic abysses formed by the rows of buildings. "They should ask for their money back, or take the Indians to court for willfully unfavorable dealings." He put his hand on his friend's shoulder. "But I suppose the time limit for that has expired long ago," he sighed, and did not know himself whether he had been born in the criminal quarter of Tatwala or the aristocratic hill of Phanar. Dawn broke. The dark giants of the square shimmered in rosy silver.

"Hiun-Hu," said Rolland suddenly, and his eyes had a glazed look. "Hiun-Hu," he repeated. "They called them Huns in Europe. They were a people, and the Chinese called one of their tribes 'Tü-Ke'—Turks."

He fell silent as the first unsightly bus drove across the square. "Tü-Ke," he went on, "they were a robust tribe and went to war against the Chinese. At that time there ruled a wise emperor, Shi-Huan-Di. He built the Great Chinese Wall to protect his people against the outer barbarians. But it wasn't much good. The barbarians put a ladder against the wall, scaled up into China, and there learned the Indo-Chinese scales."

John Rolland adjusted his tie and felt ready to face life again. The first rays of the fallow sun fell on Washington Square.

"These wild sounds," he continued, "brought the wild people to the shores of the Mediterranean. Only much later the holy House of Osman arose, and the Palace of Stars on the Bosphorus."

Sam Dooth looked at his friend with the pride of an owner and inventor. "You're a lyrical poet, John," he said admiringly, "we should use the Indo-Chinese scales in a film. Something from the Far East—you know. Perhaps with the title 'The Building of the Great Wall.' Wonderful costume film. Think about it."

"I'll think about it," said John Rolland obediently. "The sun rises over the sandy hills, and the people are building the Great Wall. But I will have a headache. I will swallow pills and sit at the typewriter in my underpants, and in the evening I will drink whiskey, and life will be good again."

Sam Dooth looked at Rolland's narrow, pale face. They were all like that—these last Osmans. Shy and commanding, lonely, tender and brutal at the same time, with delicate bodies and strange fantasies that could, with the help of a good agent, be turned into lots of dollars. Sam Dooth understood very well why the empire had crumbled and Rolland's films sold so easily. They had not been statesmen, these rulers who had sat on the throne of Osman and reigned over three continents. They had been fantasists and idealists.

"Let's go," said Rolland, and leaned on his friend. "You know—I was a prisoner in the palace on the Bosphorus, and now I am imprisoned in the stony sepulchres of this city."

"Well—that's life," sighed Sam. "But you've got money. Perhaps you should go away somewhere, have a look at the world. All you know is the Bosphorus and the Barbizon Plaza

Hotel. I'll come with you. I'll talk to the clerks and do the telephoning. You're not up to that anyway."

They walked across the square. On the terrace of the café on Fifth Avenue, the waiters were standing around, still half asleep. The green tables gave the illusion of dewy lawns, but nobody was sitting at them. They went in and sat down, heavy and tired.

"Two coffees, very strong," said Rolland, and was suddenly quite sober.

Then he bent forward toward his friend and began: "The location is China. The present is caught visually by the past. The Wall is the symbol of the self-satisfied, limited and conceited peace . . ."

The agent looked at him gratefully.

ELEVEN

"Hosrev Pasha was a rich and powerful man." Asiadeh stood in the court of the great mosque. A thin veil covered her face. Her head was thrown back, her enchanted eyes followed the slender line of the minarets. "A very powerful man indeed," she repeated. "When he came here, there were three villages on this spot. He had them pulled down and built a *serai*—a palace—in their place, and that is why the town is called Sarajevo."

She sat down on the marble steps at the mosque's entrance and stared at the fountain with the Arabic inscription. Children played at the fountain, and a white-turbaned priest walked across the courtyard. Hassa stood in the shade of the colonnade, looking at Asiadeh's legs and the pigeons tripping across the marble tiles—they reminded him of Venice. Everything was quite different from those days when he had walked across St. Mark's Square with Marion and she had fed the pigeons and sworn eternal faith to him. Asiadeh did not feed the pigeons; she was sitting there, quietly thoughtful, the sun shining on her hair.

"It is beautiful here," she said, and Hassa did not reply, just kept looking at her legs. Life was wonderful indeed. He leaned back against a pillar and thought the right thing to do was to be married, and that his whole life had been just an interlude between school and the final exam. He was thirty years old and knew the University of Vienna, the hospitals of Europe, and Marion. And now he knew Asiadeh. He wanted to bend down to tell her that there are phlegmons caused by a disease of the paranasal sinus, and that he would like to submit a report about this to the Medical Association. But he did not tell her, for Asiadeh would not understand him and would only ask for the etymology of the word "phlegmon."

An old man, bowed and weatherbeaten, came into the mosque. He took off his shoes and prayed, his face serious and thoughtful. It was a strange world into which Hassa could not enter. He thought of his wild cousins, who came to his hotel, drank tea with him, and stared at him as if he were an exotic animal. And they venerated Asiadeh—imagine, a real pasha's daughter! The cousins clicked their tongues, and Asiadeh accepted this veneration with quiet dignity. She visited the wives of the wild cousins and talked to them long and profoundly about the soul of the Orient. The wild women poured coffee and stared at her, for she was a pasha's daughter and spoke wise and incomprehensible words.

"All Muslims are brothers," she said conceitedly. "Our homeland begins in the Balkans and ends in India. We all have the same customs and tastes, that's why I feel so much at home with you." The women were gratefully and anxiously silent and poured coffee for the pasha's daughter.

"Come," said Asiadeh to Hassa, and rose. They walked along the narrow alleys of Sarajevo, looking at the blue doors of the bazaar shops and the little donkeys who, ears wobbling, stumbled thoughtfully across the small squares.

"I do like it here," said Asiadeh, looking at the donkeys, "people here seem to be happy."

They went into a small coffeehouse. On the counter stood a plate of olives and tiny slivers of cheese on toothpicks. Hassa learned, to his astonishment, that the toothpicks were used in place of forks—a sensible and hygienic idea, he thought. Then he ordered, as counseled by Asiadeh, a raki, which was served in little carafes and was to be drunk from them. It tasted like a mixture of water, toothpaste, and absynth. Asiadeh speared olives on toothpicks and chewed happily. It was wonderful to travel the world with Hassa, carefree and gay, to look at mosques and eat olives.

The town was suddenly familiar and dear to her, and Hassa was, without any doubt, the best husband in the world, even though he was neither an officer nor a civil servant.

"You've got such nice relations," she said, and spit out a stone.

Hassa was astonished. The wild Hassanovic tribe seemed very foreign to him. "They are practically Turks," he said, "and the Turks have subjugated the country and enforced an Asiatic way of life on it."

Asiadeh's eyes became round with amazement. She laughed angrily, and her white teeth glittered.

"Poor Hassa," she said and shook her head. "The Turks are better than their reputation. We have never subjugated this country. The country called us. Even three times, under Mohamed I, Murad II, and Mohamed II. The country was torn by civil wars, and King Twrtko entreated the sultan to come and give them law and order. Later it became the most God-fearing and faithful province of the empire. And we did all we could to bring civilization to the country. But the country refused to become civilized."

Now Hassa laughed. "Everybody knows the Turks were against any kind of progress. We were taught that at school."

Asiadeh bit her lips. "Listen," she said, "on the eleventh Silkadeh 1241—you would say on the sixth June 1826—Sultan Murad II decided to reform his country. He therefore decreed a liberal constitution, the Tansimati Hairieh. This constitution was far more liberal than any other constitution of that time. But the people of Bosnia did not want to become liberated. Hussein-Aga Berberli instigated an uprising against the padishah, the unbeliever. He conquered Travnik, the seat of Marshal Ali-Pasha, Bosnia's governor. The marshal was taken prisoner while he was wearing the uniform of a field marshal, cut to the latest European pattern. The pious rebels tore the sinful uniform from him and bathed him three days and three nights to expurgate the smell of Europe from him. Then they gave him old Turkish robes and made him sing psalms day and night to repent his sins. Now say for yourself, Hassa—who was the retrograde there?"

Hassa emptied his carafe. His wife was a learned woman, and it was no use quarreling with her. "Let's go home," he said humbly. "We're just barbarians who know about medicine."

Asiadeh rose slowly. They walked to the hotel, and Hassa thought how very nice it would be if she would just once ask him something he could tell her. For instance: What exactly do you do when you take tonsils out? But she did not ask anything, and that made Hassa sad. She walked at his side like an earnest and thoughtful schoolgirl, her short upper lip slightly pushed out. It was obvious that to her all matters of medicine were just as alien as the barbaric endings of exotic words was to him.

In the hotel, in the dazzling light of the chandeliers, sat several men with black beards, hooked noses, and glowing black eyes. The family Hassanovic greeted the foreign cousin. Hassa ordered coffee and Asiadeh translated the relatives' simple questions.

"Yes," said Hassa, "I like it here very much," and "No, there are no mosques in Vienna."

The cousins twittered something unintelligible, and Asiadeh translated, smiling, that they asked whether he was a good doctor.

"I hope so," said Hassa, embarrassed, and prepared himself for having to prescribe a purgative for one of the cousins.

But the cousins were silent, sipped coffee, and looked out at the street, lost in thought. Then the eldest one sobbed, and two bright tears rolled down his bearded cheeks. He wiped them off and spoke sadly for a long time, Asiadeh listening with strained attention.

"In this town," she then translated, "there lives a wise man, and his name is Ali-Kuli. He is very old. He is a famous dervish from the brotherhood of the Bektashi. The people venerate him, for he is a saint and lives a godly life."

Then the guest spoke again, sadly and verbosely.

"Now God's wrath has struck the holy man," Asiadeh continued to translate. "He is ill and the craft of the dervishes is powerless. Doctors have seen him too, but they were unbelievers and did not help him."

"What's wrong with the holy man?" asked Hassa, suddenly interested.

The guest spoke, and Asiadeh looked at him, aghast.

"He is going blind," she said hopelessly in a soft voice, "there is no strength in him anymore. He spends his days half asleep. His face is the color of a dead man's. Hassa, I don't believe you will be able to help the poor man. God is calling him."

Hassa looked at Asiadeh, her sad eyes and short upper lip.

"I'll have a look at the holy man," he said decidedly.

They drove through the cobbled streets to the outskirts of the town. Asiadeh held Hassa's hand. "I'm afraid," she said. "How can one help a man whom God has marked?"

Hassa shrugged his shoulders. His wife thought him a barbarian.

"I can do things no philologue can do," he said.

Asiadeh looked at him doubtfully. Hers was the Orient's distrust against the world of technical skill. Her husband's work seemed to her as much an unimportant amusement without any practical purpose as her own. There really were only three careers: warrior, priest, and statesman.

They stopped in front of a low whitewashed house. In the courtyard an old man was sitting under the widespread branches of a tree, playing with a rosary. His face, the skin as white as alabaster with just a few hairs on it, was turned to the sky. On his head was a hat in the form of a kettle with an Arabic inscription on it, and Asiadeh read, deeply touched, the ancient adage of the Bektashi: "All which has being will pass, only He remains forever. His is all power, and everything is in His hands." The men kissed the old man's hand. He looked at them with empty, astonished eyes.

Asiadeh bent forward to the dervish and said softly: "Father! Trust yourself to the world of Western knowledge. God the Almighty can speak even through the hands of a doctor."

Hassa stood a little apart. He looked at the dervish's alabaster-white face and heard the foreign twittering sounds. He thought of Asiadeh, whom he loved, and whose respect he wanted to win. At last the dervish nodded and raised his hand.

"Come, examine him," said Asiadeh hesitantly. Hassa came close. He asked questions that perplexed Asiadeh, and heard that the old man had been treated for a long time and without any success for diabetes and diseases of the kidneys and eyes.

Hassa frowned and heard that the holy man slept eighteen hours a day.

The dervish undressed. Hassa looked piercingly through half-closed eyes at the emaciated body. "Ask him to raise his arms," he said, and noted that the hairs in the armpits had fallen out, leaving hardly any roots.

"I cannot really see anymore," said the dervish, and Hassa examined his eyes. "Bitemporal hemianopia," he said, and the dervish seemed to think he had uttered a magic formula.

Hassa thought about the case, and the tribe of Hassannovic stood around him and eyed him expectantly. The dervish put his on robes and sat down on the carpet again, indifferent and drowsy.

"I will let you know tomorrow whether I can help him," said Hassa. "I will have to sleep on it."

Asiadeh rose. It was quite clear that, where God had spoken, Western knowledge was powerless. The holy man would die whether Hassa slept on it or not, for God had willed it so.

"Let's go," said Hassa, and took Asiadeh's arm. On the way he was silent, in thought.

Back at the hotel Asiadeh sighed. "It is sad," she said, "very sad. But the hand of God is above all else."

"Yes," answered Hassa, "of course. Telephone the clinic, please. I'll have to ask a few questions."

Asiadeh went to the telephone and translated mechanically.

"Dr. Hassa here. May I speak to the director, please? My husband asks would anyone here dare to . . . one moment sir . . . one moment please! What was that? . . . yes, well, a— sorry, it's so difficult to pronounce . . . to operate on a tumor of the pituitary gland. You don't think so, sir? Yes, Dr. Hassa will come to see you."

Hassa rushed to the door, Asiadeh following breathlessly.

The director of the hospital wore a white coat, and Asiadeh translated without understanding what was hiding behind the long Latin names.

At last the director nodded, and Hassa shook his hand gratefully.

A little later they sat in their room again. Hassa was drinking coffee, excited and voluble.

"Do you understand," he said, "it's the Turkish saddle, the 'sella turcica.' That's where the gland is located. It's called the pituitary. It must be a tumor. We'll have to have an X ray. But the diagnosis seems to be conclusive. I will operate endonasally. After Hirsch's method. The statistics show that up to now only twelve point four percent of the cases have been lethal. But it's still one of the most difficult operations. Do you understand?"

He took a piece of paper and drew the anatomical diagram of a vertically cut skull. "There," he said. "That's the pituitary fossa, and here is the pituitary gland." Asiadeh tried very hard to understand this strange talk. "Turkish saddle," she said anxiously and raised her eyebrows.

Hassa gripped her waist and raised her up in the air. Holding her on his spread-out hands, he whirled across the room. "Turkish saddle," he cried, and his hands were strong and hard. At last he put Asiadeh down. The room was going round and round before her eyes. She sat down on the carpet and stared at Hassa.

"My God," she said, "the howling dervishes, the brotherhood that is called Mewlewi—they dance like that. And that's what you call pituitary gland?"

"No, that's the Turkish saddle." Hassa stood in front of her and spoke like a general facing an unruly regiment. "There is an eighty-eight point six percent probability that I will be able to cure your dervish. His illness is the rarest one in the world. But you will have to help, to punish you for mistrusting me. And because without you I won't be able to communicate with anyone during the operation. You'll have to wear a white coat and stand next to me. Can you do that? Or are you going to shriek onomatopoeically and sink to the floor in a faint?"

Asiadeh, still sitting on the floor, raised her head. "We've always been warriors. I'll be all right."

She rose and touched Hassa's face. He stood in the middle of the room and was now familiar and near. She looked at his hands, those hands that could do what no one else in Sarajevo could, and she grew timid and shy. "You really think you can conquer this Turkish saddle?"

"I hope so. If the diagnosis is correct . . ."

"*Allah barif*, God alone knows." Asiadeh was frightened. She looked down and saw suddenly, in a vivid waking dream, a band of riders in many-colored robes, sitting on soft Turkish saddles, chasing across the steppe. Hassa had a lance in his hand and his saddle was embroidered with golden letters. He raised his hand, and his lance pierced his enemy's face.

An alabaster-white face bent over the saddle and a strange voice called: *"Allah barif."*

"Allah barif," she said again and rubbed her eyes. The vision disappeared. Hassa stood at the washstand, washing his hands. Big bright drops were running down his fingers.

TWELVE

The sick man sat apathetic in the chair, and his face disappeared behind a sterile linen mask. The operating-theater nurse bent over the instruments. Asiadeh saw the slit for the dervish's nose and heard, as if from afar, Hassa's order:

"Nurse, solution of cocaine with ephedrine, and then Schleich's solution for infiltration."

She translated, and the room smelled of gas and iodoforme. She looked at the dervish's hands lying pale and helplessly on the arms of the operating chair, and the dry backs of the hands became the summer-green field near Amasia.

Sultan Orchan was riding across the field, accompanied by falconers, slaves, and Vezirs. A tubelike instrument was glittering in Hassa's left hand. The nurse bent over the sick man.

"Septum resection after Kilian," said Hassa, and Asiadeh saw another metal thing. Hassa cut, and a line of blood appeared on the linen cover. Asiadeh saw the blood, and her lips became dry and hot. On the linen the village Sulidshe rose up, and Sultan Orchan stepped into the house of the holy Bektashi, who had founded the brotherhood. The holy Hadshi-Bektash wore flowing robes, and Sultan Orchan asked his blessing for the army he was creating. A warrior with a broad, hairy chest stepped close to the saint, and the sheik laid the sleeves of his felt coat on the warrior's head, blessing him.

Meanwhile, Hassa asked for a speculum to grip the mucuous membrane. Asiadeh translated, and the nurse gave Hassa something long and glittering. Hassa was silent, and his hands were quick and very exact living things. A nurse held a bowl close to the dervish's face. Asiadeh's lower lip was hanging down. The dervish groaned softly, indifferently. Asiadeh wanted to close her eyes, but Hassa asked for a narrow chisel. She translated and opened her eyes wide.

The nurse held a small hammer in her hand. "Hammer," said Hassa, and the small instrument came down hard on the chisel. An instrument like a hook was put into the wound. Broad stripes of red blood covered the white mask, and splinters of bone lay in the blood-bespattered bowl. "Enough," said Asiadeh, and touched Hassa's shoulder. "Enough. Let the holy man die in peace." Her face was flushed, and a blue vein swelled on her forehead. Hassa pushed his stool back, and the nurse took the linen mask from the dervish's face. The face was pale and sunken. The eyes looked into the far distance, distorted with pain. "Enough," Asiadeh repeated, and looked at the blood-covered instruments. Hassa glanced around for a second. His eyes were absentminded and preoccupied.

"Yes yes," he grumbled. "The introductory operation is finished. Now we'll start the real surgical intervention. Tell them to be quicker about changing the mask. I'm going to make a trial puncture of the dura."

Asiadeh suddenly felt like a very small awkward child. The dervish sat in the chair, and the room looked like a medieval torture chamber. Hassa was the great magician and torturer. He chiseled at living bones and cut living flesh as if it were allowed to torture holy men.

Again the dervish's face disappeared behind the mask. There was a salty taste on Asiadeh's lips, and she had to blink rapidly. In the unreal and fluttering vision of her tear-filled eyes, she saw the warrior kneeling before the holy Hadshi-Bektash. The saint blessed the warrior and said softly: "Their name shall be Yanitshars. White be their faces, victorious their arms, sharp their sabers, piercing their lances. They shall forever return victorious and strong."

The room began to swim before Asiadeh's eyes. The narrow knife in Hassa's hand suddenly became curved and was trembling.

"It is a cyst," said Hassa. His voice sounded intense, and he held the knife in his hand as if it were a feather.

"May his saber be sharp, his lance piercing," thought Asiadeh. Her little hands became fists, and the dervish army of the Yanitshars flooded over Europe. The warriors wore the hat of the holy Hadshi-Bektashi, with a wooden spoon instead of a cockade. At night they sat in the courtyard of the Yanitshar barracks around the immense kettle in which meat was boiling. The sheik of the Bektashi wore a hat like a kettle with the white inscription and had all the details of ninety-nine regiments of heroes in his head. Asiadeh dried her eyes. She felt she had been standing for many long hours in front of this body that was bleeding to death, and at which Hassa was still cutting and cutting, and that she would have to go on standing there for days and weeks until Hassa had finished his gory work.

Now Hassa had a rubber tube in his hand and seemed to play with a rubber ball. "Suction," he said, and pressed the ball. The saint moved his fingers and moaned loudly. "Cotton wool," said Hassa, "for the drainage opening." He was holding a glass tube. Suddenly he raised his head and said to Asiadeh:

"The cyst could be attached to the bottom of the third ventricle. But the instruments are good and sharp." Asiadeh nodded but did not translate. The sentence, unintelligible as it was, seemed to be meant for her only and must be the expression of Hassa's inner confusion. The nurse rolled up the tampons. Asiadeh heard the dervish breathe heavily. Eight brothers of his order had once sat for days and nights in the barracks of the Yanitshars, imploring God's blessing for the ninety-nine regiments who wore the hat of the holy Hadshi-Bektashi, squatting around the kettles full of meat. And God's blessing was on the weapons until Sultan Mahmud's fury engulfed heroes and dervishes alike. Forty thousand men the sultan assembled at the Hippodrome in Istanbul. All forty thousand were executed, not one escaped the fury of the ruler. And since that day the holy empire was weak and defenseless. The last Bektashi fled to monasteries far away in the mountains, but when the sultan's favor was restored to them, they were like wolves with their teeth broken out.

"The cotton wool can be taken out in two days," said Hassa, and rose. "During the first day, a subfebrile temperature may occur. It won't turn into meningitis."

They carried the dervish away. Asiadeh walked beside him, looking at his white face. When she came back, she turned to Hassa inquiringly, her face flushed, her eyes red-rimmed with crying. Hassa was washing his hands, thinking that perhaps it might have been an intercranial tumor instead of a cyst, and that really he had been lucky, for the bone in the pituitary fossa had not been resistant at all.

They returned to the hotel. They talked of the flat in Vienna and the evenings in Grinzing when the sun was setting, and people were making their way to the little gardens overhung with vines on the outskirts of the town, where the young wine was served to happy people sitting at long wooden tables, singing and laughing under the stars.

They drank their coffee in the hall, and Asiadeh looked at Hassa's hands, these hands that knew how to handle lances and sabers, so different from the clanging weapons of the Yanit-shars.

"Will he get well?" she asked lightly, as if the dervish did not matter to her at all.

"Of course, if meningitis does not set in. If it does, he dies." Hassa's voice sounded lordly and conceited. Asiadeh raised her shoulders and bowed her head. She talked about her father, about the university and wisdom, which is so much stronger than brutal force. The face of the dervish, red with blood, was going round and round before her eyes, and a terrible fear attacked her. Suddenly she doubted that Hassa's knife could make the saint's eyes see, his muscles strong again. It was a sin to challenge fate like that. Hassa's dark blood-spurting magic could not have any power where God had so clearly shown his will. She wanted to get away from the place before the inevitable happened, and she lost her faith in her husband's power completely.

"The doctors here," she asked pleadingly, "surely they will be able to look after him now? Let's go to Dubrovnik tomorrow. It is so hot here, and I do so want to see the sea."

Hassa agreed. He could not guess why his wife wanted to get away so suddenly, but her eyes pleaded and her lips trembled, and it would be good to lie on the beach in Dubrovnik and look at the blue horizon of the Adriatic.

So they went as if fleeing from a scene of crime. For two weeks Hassa splashed about in the waves of the Mediterranean, they lay in the hot sand, and Asiadeh looked silently at the sea, the same sea that sent its waves against the shore of her homeland.

"I really should inquire how your dervish is getting on," said Hassa guiltily, and Asiadeh suddenly became very talkative and proposed an excursion into the mountains of Montenegro, to Cetinje. They drove across the Lovren. The blue bay of Catarro was deep down, the car hung on to a steep precipice, and Asiadeh was afraid of the way back, and of Sarajevo, where it was certain what news was waiting for them: that the holy man had died and Hassa's operation had been in vain.

"Let's just pass by," she said, when they were in the train, going home. "We don't need to stop in Sarajevo."

But when the minarets of the Arska Djamia appeared in the distance, she suddenly packed the suitcases, took Hassa's hand, and jumped on the platform.

"What's the matter, Asiadeh?" asked Hassa, but she did not answer, and they drove into town to breakfast in the hotel. Afterward they walked through the alleys of the bazaar.

In the garden of the Turkish coffeehouse sat the dervish Ali-Kuli, smoking a hubble-bubble pipe, surrounded by bearded men with pious sly eyes. The tribe of Hassanovic sat around the next table, sipping coffee from tiny cups.

The dervish rose, came toward Hassa, and bowed deeply.

"Woman," he said to Asiadeh, "you, who have the happiness to be the wife of a wise man, translate!"

He spoke very ceremoniously, and Asiadeh caught her breath.

"Wise man," he said, "you gave the sight back to my eyes, the color to my skin, the strength to my body, the growth to my hair. I will pray for your life to be bright, your bed soft, your way full of glory, and your wife worthy of you."

Hassa bowed, deeply touched. Bearded men surrounded

him. Solemn faces looked at him, and the tribe of Hassanovic stood next to him, glorying in his reflected fame. Asiadeh had to move back to the garden wall.

Nobody remembered anymore that she was the daughter of a pasha whose father had once reigned over Bosnia. She was just a woman, incapable of working the miracles Hassa's hands had performed, a woman who could not make eyes see, a body become strong, hair to grow—just born to be the humble slave of a worthy man.

At last Hassa managed to escape from the Asiatic gratitude surrounding him. He took Asiadeh's hand and left the coffee-house, smiling shyly. They went to the hotel, and Asiadeh was silent, lost in her own thoughts and feelings. Arrived in the hotel, she suddenly declared to Hassa's surprise that she wanted a bath. She locked the bathroom, and Hassa heard the sound of running water. But Asiadeh did not take a bath. She sat, fully dressed, behind the locked door on the rim of the bathtub, tears rolling down her cheeks. When she noticed that the tub was filled with water, she shut off the taps, then sat down on the floor and cried, long and silently, without really knowing why. Hassa had won, and it was both pain and joy not to be the daughter of a pasha anymore, but the wife of a man who could conquer death.

She wiped off her tears with both hands. The water in the tub was clear and steaming hot. She put her face on the warm mirror of water and held her breath for a moment. Yes, the Orient was dead. Hassa, an unbeliever, had saved a saint of the Bektashi brotherhood, and that showed he was more than just a man who was loved by a pasha's daughter. She rose and dried her face. Then she opened the door and came into the room on tiptoe. Hassa was lying full-length on the divan, looking up at the ceiling, not at all her idea of what a hero and victor should look like. Asiadeh sat down next to him and took his head into her hands. His brown face was satisfied and rather sleepy. Her eyelashes touched his cheeks and she sensed the faint scent of his skin.

"Hassa," she said, "you are a hero. I love you very much."

"Yes," said Hassa sleepily. "It wasn't easy to get away from that Asiatic crowd. They were jabbering away like a waterfall." He stretched out his hands and felt strangely excited by the slim pliant body lying next to him, submissive, weak, and thirsting. He drew her to him. Asiadeh's eyes were closed, but her lips were smiling.

THIRTEEN

It was a big flat on the first floor of a stately house on the Ring. Two old aunts, wrinkled faces and enraptured eyes, had looked after it while Hassa had been away. Asiadeh won their approval by dropping a deep curtsy, an art she had learned during the war when it had been planned to present her to a grand duchess.

The view though the windows showed a wide street and the green trees of the Burggarten. Asiadeh leaned from the window and breathed Vienna's mild air, the scent of flowers and faraway woods and green hills of Austria. She walked through the rooms of the flat, and the aunts, smiling happily, gave her the keys to cupboards, chambers, and cellar. Hassa ran though the rooms, and his eyes were those of a child who has rediscovered a long-lost toy. He took Asiadeh's arm and dragged her along the dining room with its dark, leather-covered, cool-looking chairs. He took her to the drawing room in the corner of the building, consisting mostly of windows and furnished with soft, light-colored easy chairs. Asiadeh was taken to the surgery with its white walls and innumerable metal things glistening in glass cupboards. In the waiting room lay journals straight out of the Ark, and on the walls were photos of people whose life Hassa had saved, as they themselves testified. The saved ones had proud petrified faces and looked down severely at Asiadeh.

Arrived in the bathroom, Asiadeh stopped, exhausted, and saw her own flushed, excited face reflected in the mirror. "Water," she pleaded, "please, water. Too much furniture all at once."

Hassa turned on the tap and gave her a glass. She drank appreciatively, and her face became serious.

"What water!" she said astonished. "The best after Istanbul!"

She saw Hassa's bewildered face and explained: "You know, we Turks, we don't drink wine. But we know all about water. My father can tell the differences between all the waters in the world. When my grandfather came to Bosnia, he had water sent to him from Istanbul in big earthenware jugs. This here is the best water in Europe."

She kept drinking in small sips, and Hassa thought her wild ancestors must have drunk like that from the well of their home after long wanderings in the deserts.

"In our country," said Asiadeh, putting the glass down, "there are only carpets, rugs, and divans in a room. The divans are set along the walls, and on them are cushions, and in some of the rooms there might be a little low table. We sleep on the floor, on mattresses. During the day the mattresses are hidden in wall cupboards. In winter we put a basin with glowing coal into the room to make it warm. I'm not used to all this furniture. I'm sure to bump against all these tables and cupboards, but it doesn't matter. Go on!"

They went along the long, dark corridor and Hassa opened the door to the bedroom.

"Here," he said proudly. Asiadeh came in. There were two

wide beds close to each other, a screen, a divan, and bedside tables.

"Here," she said humbly, and thought of Marion, who had disappeared, who had slept in this bed, dreaming of other men. Hassa closed the door proudly. He stood in the middle of the room and looked at the bed, at Asiadeh, at the little tables, and his face seemed sad. Asiadeh touched his chin, and he looked at her with his slanted, pleading eyes. He embraced her, as if trying to hide from something dark and musty, invisibly arising in the room.

Asiadeh bowed her head. There was Hassa's broad neck and the strong muscles of his arms. Suddenly she felt very sorry for him. This broad, strong Hassa, standing so awkwardly there in the middle of the room—how helpless and poor he was in a world of unsaid words and half-felt feelings! She caressed his cheek and thought that she would do everything to let Hassa stay the miracle worker forever, wise and strong in the world of visible forms. "Don't be afraid," she wanted to say to him, "I'll be a faithful wife to you." But she did not say it. She kept his neck in her embrace, and Hassa saw in her eyes the humble faith of the Asiatic woman. "Come," she said softly, "let's unpack."

At night they lay in the wide bed, close together, and Hassa played with her hair and spoke of his friends, of the café where he met his colleagues every day, of the Burg Theater with the marble gold-bedecked staircase, and of the life about to begin as soon as everything was unpacked and the flat aired.

Asiadeh listened. She looked up to the plaster ceiling and thought of Marion, who had seen the same pattern and yet dreamed of other men. She wanted to ask Hassa about Marion but did not dare. The bed was soft and warm, Hassa was wearing dark pajamas, and his cheek was lying on Asiadeh's knee.

"Stay with me, Hassa," she said, even though Hassa had no intention of going anywhere else. She raised herself up and looked at him, radiant with happiness. He was lying there, a little strange smile on his face, full of mysterious forces that ruled over her and her life. He drew her to him, and she felt like a small child in the arms of a great magician.

She closed her eyes and felt his hands, his body, his breath, close and warm. Happy fear overwhelmed her. Slowly and timidly she opened her eyes. Far far away was the decorated plaster ceiling, and Hassa's face had become taut and serious, with narrow dark eyes that seemed alien and cruel . . .

Later Hassa slept, his legs drawn up like a child, his cheek on her knees. Asiadeh did not sleep. She stared into the darkness. This flat was like an island, and she herself a castaway who had found safety from the wild ocean called life. Out there were mysterious cafés, men and women who thought like Hassa but who were no magicians and had no power over her senses and feelings. Out there somewhere was Marion, whose place she had taken, and of whom knew only that she was traveling around with a man somewhere in the world and deserved all the punishment God had prepared for unchaste women.

"Hassa," she said, and tugged at his hair. "Hassa." He turned and cleared his throat, astonished and sleepy. "There's so much air between us," said Asiadeh softly. "Be quite close to me, Hassa."

"Good," said Hassa, and went on sleeping. Asiadeh closed her eyes. She wanted this night to go on forever, for all her life. She wanted Hassa lying there next to her, like a sleeping child who would not have to go away into the mysterious world of alien people, words, and actions.

Then she slept, relaxed and quietly. Hassa's hand was on her breast, and she held it as if it were a talisman, a magic guard against the ocean that was throwing its waves at the shores of her island.

FOURTEEN

In the Ring Café the newspapers were rustling. The head-waiter was the first to recognize Hassa. He greeted him and called to the waiter: "The usual for the Herr Doktor—coffee with cream and the *Medical Journal*."

Then he stayed, still bowed, at the marble table. "Home again?" he asked, though this was obvious.

"Yes," said Hassa, "and married into the bargain."

"My very best wishes, Herr Doktor. The lady is a foreigner, we heard?"

"Yes, she is a Turk."

The headwaiter nodded as if it were the most ordinary thing in the world to marry a Turk. The he went on long-windedly about his brother, who had been in Turkey dur-ing the war, and that one really could look at it this way: The Turks were just ordinary people, the same as everybody else. Then he brought a stack of newspapers and journals. Absent-mindedly Hassa leafed though them. Out on the Ring the sun was shining brightly. Ladies with their little dogs were walking along the street, looking around, very sure of them-selves. The trees hung their branches across the street, and the dark building of the Opera looked like a fortress. The doors of the café opened. Friends and acquaintances came in, looked, and came to Hassa's table, hands stretched out in glad greeting.

"Servus," they said, and sat down. Hassa shook the outstretched hands and was overcome by the happiness of homecoming. There they were—the people who made up his "circle" and who seemed destined by a mysterious fate to sit with Hassa, talk to him, entertain him, think him nice or impossible, and yet follow his life with the passive curiosity of spectators. There was Dr. Halm, the gynecologist; the white-haired Natuschek, the inventor of a famous but completely useless diet; the orthopedist Sachs, who only worked in winter, during the ski season; the surgeon Matthess with his long legs and love of Chinese paintings; and the nerve specialist Dr. Kurz, who was the director of a sanatorium and thought love was a disease of the nervous system.

These friends sat at Hassa's table and asked questions, indistingushable from the waiter's questions. Then they shook their heads, half agreeing, half worriedly, and someone said, enviously: "So you've married an Angora kitten, you sodomite."

Hassa nodded and felt he was living a recurrent dream—surely he had heard and answered these words in another, unreal world.

More and more coffee cups appeared on the table. From a half-spilled glass a narrow strip of water ran across the marble top, formed bays and lakes, distended, and at last disappeared under Dr. Kurz's cup. Hassa told about his father-in-law who was a pasha and now a director in a large carpet store in Berlin, and of the palace on the Bosphorus, which he suddenly, inexplicably, seemed to know very well. He told of the strange courses his wife had taken at the university, and a bit timidly mentioned the wonderful cure he had performed on the world-famous dervish Ali-Kuli in Sarajevo.

The circle listened, astounded and jealous. Only when he uttered the words "tumor of the pituitary gland" did the faces relax and the thoughts turn to matter-of-fact professional channels.

"I had a case the other day," said Dr. Kurz, as if a tumor of the pituitary gland was nothing. "Kommerzienrat Danski suddenly started nervous hiccups. For full three days he kept hiccupping. What does one do in a case like that?" He stopped and looked conceitedly from one to the other.

"Hold his head underwater for half an hour and tell him to hold his breath," said the surgeon with the cruelty of his profession. "Success guaranteed."

"Swallow ice," said the orthopedist, and thought of glaciers during the ski season.

"I tried hypnosis," Dr. Kurz went on, "and will you believe it, the man woke up and went on hiccupping."

The doctors pulled their chairs closer together. Kurz said something about a psychic shock. "A vasomotorous irregularity of the diaphragm," said Matuschek loudly and passionately. The old headwaiter stood leaning against a marble column and looked contentedly at the doctors' table.

"A scientific discussion," he thought, "we are a top-grade café."

"You should go to a crammer who specializes in medical ignorances," said the gynecologist Halm. "You've forgotten how to think theoretically. It is simply an irritation of the diaphragm. And what controls the diaphragm? The *nervus sympaticus*. Ha! Ha! Ever heard of *lucus cisylbachi*? Well—there you are. There's only one thing to do . . ."

He never finished the sentence. A blond girl was standing at the table, looking with frightened eyes at the quarreling doctors and the bays and lakes disappearing under Dr. Kurz's cup.

"I'm Asiadeh," said the girl, and the hiccuping Kommerzienrat disappeared in the abyss of medical wisdom. The doctors jumped up from their chairs. Asiadeh shook their strange
hands. Furtively she looked at Hassa, who nodded imperceptibly. So these were the men whose hands she had to shake and
whose questions she had to answer, the men who were the parts
of that mysterious world in which Hassa lived.

"Yes," she said absentmindedly and sat down. "Vienna is
a very beautiful city." The doctors looked at her curiously
and asked questions. Asiadeh answered dutifully and patiently.
When the strange men smiled, their faces became distorted
with outlandish grimaces. She sat there among them with her
gray eyes and short upper lip, with the naive expression on her
face, and it seemed to them that the world was beautiful, worth
living in, full of alluring secrets, so very different from the
strange hiccups of Kommerzienrat Danski.

"We are going to the Heurigen tonight," said Dr. Kurz, for
he was a sensitive man who understood the soul of a woman.
"You have not been to the Heurigen yet, *gnädig* Frau?"

"No, but I know what it is. It is a place in Grinzing, and
when the sun sets, people go to the wine gardens and sing
songs."

"Nearly correct," Dr. Kurz praised her, and the men nodded. Yes, tonight they would all go to the Heurigen, to the
young wine of this year, to the green gardens and little vineyards in the suburb, to the narrow alleys that cover the hills
under the mild light of the moon. They rose. Home, quickly! A
glance into the surgery, a short talk with the wife or girlfriend,
and then into the car, along the rough street to the old vineyards in the silence of the night!

"All right," said Asiadeh, "let's go to the Heurigen." She

stood beside Hassa, slender, foreign, and quiet. Hassa gave her his arm, and they walked to the door. The eyes of all men in the café followed them.

"It's itching," said Asiadeh when they had reached the street, and moved her shoulder blades.

"What is?"

"The glances. The men look at me as if they want to kiss me."

"Perhaps they do."

Asiadeh stamped her foot. "Be quiet," she said furiously. "That's no way to speak to your wife. Come on. Let's go to the Heurigen."

Candles in glass holders stood on long green tables. Tree branches hung over the tables like petrified ghosts. Girls in gaily colored skirts went around in the garden, carrying jugs full of wine on big wooden boards. People sat there, faces flushed, illuminated by the fluttering candlelight. A slight warm wind blew from the vineyards, and people, trees, and tables seemed to dissolve in the mild light of the waning moon. There was a feeling of rapture, of pagan enchantment in the garden; it seemed that a ritual was being enacted here, a prayer for the benediction of the wine.

The jugs were emptied again and again. Tables and trees began to go round and round before the drinkers' eyes. The quiet garden had turned into an antique temple where candles in glass holders had been lit in honor of the invisible God. From far away came a song, a woman's voice, singing soft and melancholy. The words were drowned in the flood of trembling notes. People bowed their heads into their hands and seemed to hear in the sad notes a secret echo of their own dreams, thoughts, and longings. A fat man sat alone, leaning against an old tree. His face seemed turned toward all the suffering in the world.

Women sat embraced by their men, looking graciously around. Everyone was singing, and the girls kept bringing jugs of clear fragrant wine . . . Asiadeh was sitting on the hard bench between Hassa and Dr. Kurz. Doctors and women were all around her, and she was lost in the perplexing sound of their names. But even without names, without any questions, she knew at once and without any doubt which woman belonged to which man, who looked at whom with the eye of an owner or a stranger's flirtatious curiosity . . . Intently she studied the women's flushed faces, the blond, black, and ginger heads bending over the table and the hands lifting the wine-filled jugs to their mouths.

"Why don't you drink?" someone called to her across the table, and she shook her head, smiling. They were all nice people, but she could not drink. She sipped at a glass of water and said kindly: "I don't drink wine. My religion forbids it, you know. But you've got such very good water. The best in Europe."

She drank, and the girl in the gaily colored skirt put thick slices of sausage, ham, and bread on the table. Asiadeh looked at the white fat and pale reddish meat and felt a slight singing in her ears.

"Is that from the swine?" she asked, and people nodded and ate.

She opened her mouth and caught her breath in sudden fright. This was the moment she had feared and expected. They ate swine in Europe. She had never seen a live swine and did not know what the meat tasted like. But in her blood, in her veins and nerves, was a dark ancient fear, a hate and disgust of the meat God had forbidden Muslims to eat. Cautiously she nibbled at a piece of bread, and the blond woman who belonged to Dr. Matthess looked at her pityingly.

"Isn't it boring for you just to sit here without eating or drinking?"

"No, thank you, it is a beautiful garden."

The foreign woman smiled. Her hair was blond and her lips narrow and bright red.

"Have you got many children?" said Asiadeh, for she wanted to be nice to the foreign woman.

The blonde looked at her uncomprehendingly. "Children? I haven't got any."

"Oh," laughed Asiadeh, suddenly very gay, "so you are newly married too?"

The woman laughed and seemed very happy. "Counting it all, for ten years, but to three different men. I have been divorced twice."

Asiadeh blushed deeply, turning her head to the side. "Oh," she stuttered, "I understand, of course."

She emptied her glass of water and looked at the woman, full of pity. The poor thing! She couldn't have any children.

The delicate-looking girl sitting next to Dr. Sachs smiled at her. "Have some cheese," she said, and gave Asiadeh a slice. She seemed a nice quiet woman, but apparently one mustn't ask European women about children.

"Are you very busy with housekeeping?" asked Asiadeh, for surely that was a harmless question and could not possibly hurt anyone.

"No," said the girl, "my mother does the housekeeping."

"Oh—your mother lives with you."

Asiadeh looked approvingly at Dr. Sachs. Only a very good man would take his mother-in-law into his house.

"No, my mother doesn't live with me. I live with my mother."

Asiadeh did not quite understand. Perhaps these people were drunk. It was said that wine could work miracles. "And your husband allows that?"

They all laughed at that and talked, all together, all gaily and happily. Asiadeh did not understand everything, just that of these four women who sat at the table, painted and smiling, only two were married. But to make up for that, two had been married several times.

The ginger girl saw Asiadeh's perplexed, despairing face and bent toward her: "One can love another without being married, can't one?"

Asiadeh nodded. This did indeed happen, but it was impossible to love another without wanting to have children. That was quite impossible. Surely grown-up people must know that. The grown-up people laughed. Hassa laughed too, and his hand found Asiadeh's knee. She recoiled, horrified. This garden was no marriage bed, but perhaps Hassa was drunk. That did happen to Europeans, and then it was not their fault. The four foreign women who had many husbands but no children laughed shrilly, and Asiadeh suddenly understood that it made no difference to them whether they were married or not.

"I'll be back in a minute," she whispered to Hassa, and ran through the garden past the long tables. She bumped against a tree branch and felt alone, terribly alone in this labyrinth of drunken people.

She came out into the silent street. The people in the garden were masks in a nightmare. Women like these existed in the criminal quarter of Tatwala, or in the drunkards' alleys of Galata, but they did not have men who were masters of death and yet could not find other women. A dull, hollow pain filled

Asiadeh's breast. She walked along the row of parked cars and found Hassa's two-seater, got in, and crept into the soft upholstery, making herself very small. The street was dark and mysterious, like the life of these people who were kind and foreign, like shadows from a strange, unreachable world.

Asiadeh looked into the distance, at the dark outlines of the vineyards against the moonlit sky. From afar came the sound of singing. She heard the first line of the song:

"I'm coming back from Grinzing, bringing home a tiny little monkey . . ."

The words were enigmatic, unintelligible, like everything in this strange town. How could a Turkish girl know that in Viennese slang, "a little monkey" means being slightly drunk?

"Somewhere the real face of this world must be hiding," she thought confusedly. Somewhere in Grinzing tiny monkeys were jumping from branch to branch, tame and delicate, so they could be taken home. She looked around. No monkey was in sight. A deep sadness overcame her. The smell of wine and meat fat wafted at her; a strange weakness made her close her eyes and put her head on the cushions. Half an hour later the frightened Hassa found her. She stretched her hands out to him and whispered: "Hassa, I have lost my way, and I'm afraid of the monkeys. Save me, Hassa!"

FIFTEEN

"Have some caviar, John."

The lights were dazzling, and the cold buffet with its display of delicacies glowed in all colors of the rainbow. The black caviar grains were soft and tender, the red lobsters looked like meditating philosophers, pies rose like fortresses, oysters swimming in ice carried all the scents of the ocean in their pale shells.

Obediently John took some caviar, squeezed a lemon on it, and ate. The humming in his ears grew louder.

"Gale force nine," said Sam Dooth and chewed a pie with obvious enjoyment. "Strange, isn't it, that big ships rock just as much as little ones." After that Rolland pushed his plate away and rushed to the exit. "You dog," he said in a foreign language, and the Greek understood perfectly well. He smiled and took more caviar, but Rolland was already on deck. The ocean was gray and the horizon kept going round and round before his eyes. Wind-lashed waves beat against the boat like clouds dropped into the sea. A steward came and put a rug around his legs. "Coffee? Whiskey? Cognac?" "Dog," said Rolland, and the steward nodded understandingly, for it was gale force nine.

John Rolland had a stale, sour taste in his mouth and felt he was being hurled into a never-ending abyss. With the greatest difficulty he managed to light a cigarette, only to throw it away immediately. Just one draw and something horrible would have happened, something he never could have lived down.

John Rolland looked angrily at the packet and thought fiercely that it was all the fault of the wrapping, which showed a silly camel standing in the desert. He could be sitting quietly in the bar of his hotel, and the floor under his feet would be solid and horizontal.

Six days ago he had opened the packet, as he had been doing every day, his eyes again following the stupidly smiling face of the cigarette-camel. And suddenly the mask of the camel grew, sand was whirling under his feet, the dry desert wind was beating against his face, he saw the soft trembling heels of the desert animals and felt the hard dusty fur. With sudden tenderness he had caressed the cigarette pack.

"Perikles," he had said, "look for a desert with camels and mosques. I'm going on a journey, and you are coming with me."

Then he had dropped off to sleep, and the next day Sam Dooth had stood before him, holding two tickets to Casablanca, and his wise Greek eyes had been smiling.

John Rolland moved his feet under the rug and saw the agent coming on deck, smoking a cigar and looking very satisfied.

"How can you be happy," said John Rolland bitterly, "when everybody knows that thousands of people have to drain the cup of bitterness on this earthly valley of tears? You don't understand *Weltschmerz*."

Sam Dooth nodded, took a seat, and ordered mocha.

"*The Chinese Wall* is running on Broadway for the fourth week," he said. "I have every reason to be happy."

"I've written it," breathed Rolland, "and I could die of grief when I consider the fate of pregnant women in India."

"Yes, that's the usual thing to think of at gale force nine," said Sam Dooth, sipping his mocha. "This is the eighth time I'm crossing the ocean."

Rolland felt deeply insulted. He thought of getting up and telling his agent that all Greeks were amphibious, that Ulysses had been a pirate, to say nothing of the Argonauts. He thought of telling Sam Dooth that his, own ancestors had always been people of the earth, had conquered three continents but were all for the freedom of the seas, that it was subhuman to cross the ocean in a nutshell of only forty thousand tons, and that he would never call him Sam Dooth again, only Neptomanides. Instead he rose from his chair, looked at his agent with glazed eyes, and said, smiling: "Sam dear—I'm going to lie down. My last will and testament is with the reception clerk at the Barbizon Plaza."

He walked away, stumbling a little, keeping a secure grip at the rail of the staircase, and opened the door to his cabin.

Then he was lying on his bed, eyes closed, his body continuously sinking into an abyss and being hurled upward again. He folded his hands over the cover and thought of the time when he was six years old and rocked on Sultan Abdul-Hamid's knees. Abdul-Hamid had pinched lips, small sly eyes, and an immense hanging nose, his hands were steeped in blood, and all the world was afraid of him. But John Rolland sat on his lap, the bloodthirsty sultan caressed his cheeks and made him recite a Persian poem—how did it go?—he remembered only one line:

"*Taze bitaze, un binu*"—Fresher and fresher, newer and newer . . .

"I am neither fresh nor young," thought John Rolland, closing his eyes. Minutes passed, but during these minutes the bloodthirsty sultan was overthrown, a new sultan girded himself with Osman's sword, and John Rolland lived in a palace among eunuchs and women. Sometimes he wore a red and blue uniform and shook hands with dignitaries.

Then he was sitting on a big carpet, reading books, writing poetry, while a slender slave served him and introduced him to the secrets of love. His body sank into an abyss again, and Sam Dooth gave him orange juice and grinned wickedly. Again minutes passed, but during those minutes the sun had risen in the east and sunk into the deep red in the west. The gale force had gone up to ten. Sam Dooth was sitting in John Rolland's cabin, humming a little Greek song about the dock worker Dshordadshaki, who seduced a widow and ran off to Saloniki with her money.

John Rolland got up for a few minutes, feeling sorry for the widows in India and all the pregnant women in America. Then he wanted to write now, immediately, an educational film about camels, and to take a well-known cigarette firm to court for assault and battery. But by that time the gale force had risen to eleven, and John Rolland thought of the nice quiet room he had left in New York and was filled with *Weltschmerz*.

He heard the raging waves of the ocean and tried to think of the still waters of the Bosphorus, but it didn't work.

And then there was pale sunlight in the cabin.

John closed his eyes, opened them again, and was astonished to see that it was the moon, while he had thought it was the sun. He slept and thought he could write a film called "Dry

Land." Suddenly he was wide awake. The boat was motionless, like a soldier on guard. John went to the window and saw a greenish-gray strip of land, a town with white square houses, minarets, mosque cupolas, and a dark face on the beach, looking longingly at his cabin.

"Africa," said Sam Dooth, coming into his cabin. "I've booked rooms at the Splendide Palace in Rabat. Later we'll go to an oasis, I've forgotten the name, but the hotel there is called the Mediterranean. HC, of course."

John Rolland shaved and saw through the window the face of a chimera-camel passing by. He rushed on deck. The wind blew in his face, and the big palm trees waved their branches to him.

"Come to Africa," he said, gripping the agent by the hand. He went down the gangway and, drawing a deep breath, stepped onto the soil of Casablanca.

Three hundred small steps, a narrow corridor, and a weather-beaten guide with a tangled beard touching the stones of the Hassan Tower with timid tenderness. Deep down lay the town of Rabat. The guide said: "This town is like a white maiden on the breast of a black slave."

John Rolland was silent. He looked at the white town, the ocean, and the gray line of sand on the horizon.

"This tower," the Arab told them, soberly looking into the far distance, "was built by Hassan, the same who built the Giralda in Granada."

He fell silent. There was dust in the folds of his robe. John looked at the sand, the old wrinkled face, and the bare stones of the tower.

"Here, on this spot," said the Arab, "the khaliph ordered Hassan to build a second Alhambra. The master spent his days and nights here, on the flat roof. But one day the khaliph wanted to interrupt the meditations of the wise master and climbed the three hundred steps to the tower—and he found the wise Hassan embracing his wife. Thus, mosque and palace remained unfinished."

The Arab stepped to the rim of the tower and pointed down. "Here, on this stone, Hassan's limbs were shattered."

John Rolland looked down. A thick vein swelled on his forehead. Suddenly he spat into the abyss and shouted passionately in Arabic: "Son of a she-dog! To seduce a khaliph's wife!"

The guide heard the Arabic swearing and stood petrified. Sam Dooth gave him a tip and, discreetly pointing at his head, said, "Careful! The young gentleman is not quite all right." He took John Rolland down; they went into the town and wandered around in the narrow alleys of the bazaar. Camels passed by, their heads moving like cars of wheat in the breeze.

In a coffeehouse Rolland ordered two cups and drew on a long hubble-bubble pipe. He was silent and bitter, his teeth biting into the amber mouthpiece. Sam Dooth began to be afraid.

"Let's go to the hotel," he said, and John nodded.

In the evening he sat in the hotel bar, wearing a dinner jacket, drinking a Hennessy, telling his neighbor, a French businessman, that he was an American, spoke only English, and was traveling for pleasure.

"This here seems to be a wild country," he said conceitedly, "the natives look as if they never use their bathtubs."

"Quite right," said the Frenchman, "they haven't got any. They are indeed very dirty."

"Do these natives speak French, or have they got a language of their own?" asked Rolland ingeniously.

"Oh, they've got a language, all right, but it's so barbaric that no one can learn it." The Frenchman was touched by the foreigner's ignorance and felt it his duty to enlighten him.

"You know," he said, smiling, "before we came here, they were practically cannibals. Real barbarians. Only two hundred years ago a monster was reigning here. His name was Khaliph Mulai Ismail. Can you imagine: he left twelve hundred sons and eight hundred daughters! A whole self-made tribe."

The Frenchman laughed loudly, and John Rolland laughed with him. "It must have been difficult not to get confused with all those children. The birthdays alone . . ."

"But these people do not celebrate birthdays. They're just savages. This khaliph had his eldest and most beautiful son put between two boards and slowly sawed in half by two Negroes from Timbuktu."

"Terrible! Like a sandwich," said John Rolland. "It's a good thing that there aren't any khaliphs anymore."

"There are a few left. But they're quite unimportant now. Just for show. By the way—tomorrow is Friday. The savages will have a sort of parade. Come to the palace courtyard. It will amuse you."

"I'll come," said Rolland very seriously, and looked at Sam Dooth, who was munching almonds, looking very apprehensive.

At half past ten John Rolland came into the immense courtyard of the white palace. Sam was walking behind, carrying a camera, feeling worried. It would have been much better for John not to visit any palaces or khaliphs. But John was stubborn and kept probing around in the wound that should have healed long ago.

Around the sun-flooded square, a row of noblemen was standing. In the middle was a company of guardsmen on horseback. Fat Negroes with shining faces, blue lips, red trousers, and snowy-white turbans sat on noble Arab steeds, as if turned into stone.

"Negroes from Timbuktu," whispered John, and thought of the prince who, once upon a time, had been sawed in two by those Negroes' ancestors. A trumpet call cut through the air. Steel glittered in the hands of the Negro guards. Swords and flags were lowered. Slowly the door of the inner palace opened. The nobles sank to their knees. Red fezes touched the grass of the courtyard. Two officers of the Imperial Sherif Guards came riding from the palace. Behind them came two Negroes, leading a white stallion, stepping quietly and nobly, a gold-embroidered saddle on his back. The horse came forward with slow, solemn steps. Behind the horse—bowed shoulders, long beards, flowing snow-white robes—the ministers of the Sherif Empire. And then—a great coach, richly gilt, with closed crystal windows. Behind them a narrow dark face, two black eyes, and delicate hands, playing with a pearl rosary—His Majesty the Khaliph and Sherif.

A wild shout from the black officers. The rows of the riders closed.

Above the mosque the prophet's green flag unfolded slowly.

Suddenly, from the crowd of spectators, a man broke out. He raced across the green courtyard, gesticulating wildly. A plump man with a camera was running after him. The raving man stopped at the gate. He was shrieking in a unintelligible foreign language, and his gray eyes had become quite white.

"Your Highness," cried the fat one, "Your Highness, calm down!"

But two long, very strong hands gripped his collar, shook him wildly, and the crooked lips were covered with foam. Gray, raving eyes came close to the fat one's face and a very strange foreign hoarse voice cried:

"Away! Away! At once! There are no khaliphs anymore! Tomfoolery! Mosques! Camels! Cigarettes! Away, quickly!"

He jumped into a taxi, his fat friend following. "Where to?" the fat man asked brokenly.

"To the airport," John Rolland replied.

And all at once the raving maniac became a helpless child. He put his head on his friend's shoulder, and his whole body trembled with convulsive sobs. "All this doesn't exist anymore," wailed Rolland, and cried for the vanished empire, the khaliphs on the Bosphorus, the long line of imperial princes who had lived before him, the princes who wrote poetry, lived in forbidden palaces, and had put him into this strange cold world so that he would once more remember the imperial Selamlik on the Bosphorus by seeing the bright vanished glory of coats of the Negro Guards, the slow steps of the ministers, and the golden coach of the foreign khaliph.

"We're flying to Paris," he said, recovering. "There aren't any mosques and monarchs there."

"May I report most humbly—I mean, because of your health. There's a big beautiful marble mosque in Paris. Apart from that, the shahinshah lives there, the dethroned emperor of Persia. And there should also be some relations of the expelled and vanished prince Abdul-Kerim, who has disappeared."

"Then we don't." John Rolland adjusted his tie and thus ended any similarity between himself and the expelled prince. "Then we'll go somewhere else. To a normal, healthy country where they haven't any ghosts or Negroes. I want to have a good time in Europe—do you understand? A good time."

"Perhaps Berlin," Sam Dooth proposed, and John nodded, tired and indifferent.

"All right," he said. "Berlin."

The taxi stopped at the airport.

SIXTEEN

In the evening John Rolland strolled along the Kurfürstendamm, looked at the glowing lights of Berlin, and ordered
a cold punch in the restaurant Kempinski.

"I'm going to start a new life, a really respectable, healthy
life," he told Sam Dooth, and Sam nodded. He had heard this
same sentence before—many times.

So they started a new life. At one o'clock they left the Bar-
berina nightclub. John Rolland was stumbling about, trying to
convince a taxi driver that the only way to live was by being a
total abstainer. The taxi driver listened sadly, looked at Sam
Dooth's dark face and Rolland's Eastern profile, and took them
to the restaurant Orient in the Kaiserallee. There he turned
them out, and they disappeared behind the red draperies of the
entrance.

It was now half past one. The hall had carpets on walls and
floors, and it was crowded. A young man was sitting at the
piano playing fox-trots, one-steps, tangos, and even a Viennese
waltz. Heads, looking like bloated radishes in the dim red light,
moved in time to the music; waiters were gliding about like
puppets in a Turkish shadow play. The whole hall looked like a
dark red jaw filled with false gold teeth. Then bills appeared,
spread out on plates, like applications for clemency from the

host to the guests, and slowly the hall became emptier and emptier. Only a few half-drunk patrons stayed sitting there silently, their faces pale, like heads in a gallery of waxworks. The man at the piano went on playing, but no one was listening anymore. No one noticed that the noisy fox-trots became softer and softer, then slowly changed into a strange, exciting foreign melody. In this nocturnal smoke-filled hall it sounded like a hymn, and to John Rolland the notes of this hymn became the walk of a bayadere and the matte blue of a Persian miniature.

He felt thirsty, ordered a cocktail, and looked at Sam Dooth. "Indo-Chinese scale," he said, and winked. Sam Dooth called the waiter, and five minutes later the musician sat at their table. John Rolland poured wine into one of the many glasses and spoke English in a very patronizing way.

"Your music," he said, "it runs in upward and downward scales. Strange, these flat sounds. They should be played on a flute."

"Yes," said the musician, and left the wine untasted, "it is quite a different polyphony. The tonal system is constructed on the triad. Tonic-subdominant—dominant. The excessive use of seconds reveals the origin of the whole harmony."

John Rolland became very sad when he heard these words.

"I'm drunk and depraved," he thought. "Here I am in Europe and going to nightclubs instead of trying to improve my mind by attending to matters of culture."

The strange musician hummed a song, his fingers drumming the rhythm on the table. John Rolland listened, wide awake, and said: "At each repeat the song must start one second higher. The cadence chords then determine the natural transposition."

He sang, and the musician listened, astounded.

"Drink," said Rolland, and pushed the glass toward him.

"Thank you," said the musician politely, "but I am a Muslim. A Tsherkess from Istanbul. I was in the Imperial Guards."

That made Sam Dooth pay the bill at once, and John could not get out quickly enough.

A taxi took them back to the Eden Hotel, and at the threshold of his room, Rolland again vowed to begin a new life tomorrow. Sam Dooth looked thoughtfully at the floor and nodded.

At noon John Rolland woke up. His head was heavy, and he had a vague memory of having heard some exciting music. "This is Europe," he thought. "Berlin is the town of work and culture. I must prove myself worthy of it."

He dressed and said indifferently to Sam: "Heptomanides, I am going to a museum. You stay here. Museums are not in your line. But I need inspiration and cultural penetration."

Then he stood on the street, undecided, for he did not know where to find a museum and was even a bit afraid of the cool darkness in large halls.

He turned to the left, where he saw a big church, and went in, feeling he was performing an act of culture. He looked at the Roman columns, very satisfied with himself.

"Fourteenth-century, isn't it?" he asked the sexton.

"No," said the sexton, "this is the Kaiser-Wilhelm-Gedächtnis-Kirche. Beginning of the twentieth century."

Quickly John Rolland left the church. He walked along a wide street, noting with satisfaction that it was called after the great philosopher Kant. That made him feel spiritually elated and transported into higher culture.

"A beautiful town," he thought, and stopped in front of a window. There were many-colored carpets and rugs with soft rounded patterns. Between them lay yellowed Persian manuscripts with pale miniature drawings: almond-eyed princes drinking from golden cups and in the distance a frightened deer, one leg raised elegantly.

John Rolland looked attentively at the display. "Very good," he thought, and knew that he would not lose his way in this world of manuscripts and miniatures. He thought of the barbarian who was sitting there in the shop, and who probably knew as little about Persian miniatures as he himself knew of the Roman architectural style. A vague feeling of revenge arose in him, and he decided to shame the barbarian who was selling these miniatures just as the sexton had shamed him.

An old, sad-eyed man rose as he came into the shop.

"Show me some Persian miniatures," said Rolland in English. The old man nodded, and landscapes, hunting scenes, and banquets were unfolded before John's eyes.

"This here," said the old man, pointing at a band of angels in a light, cloudy sky, "this is copy after great Buchari, school of Achmed Fabrisi."

"Not for me," said John Rolland, biting his lips. "I would like a landscape with a slight Chinese influence but still full of Persian feeling. Rather like Djani did them for the sheik Ibrahim-el-Gülshani."

The old man looked at him piercingly. "Sorry," he said in his broken English, "we not got it. Not much of fifteenth century. But here from time Abbas the Great. Look—yellow autumn trees, in sunset. Could be Mani, such delicate colors."

John looked at the page, lovingly caressing the prophet Jonas wearing the robe of a Persian prince.

"I'll take it. But it is a decadent art, this Indian school. I'd like something more healthy, more positive, the way Shud-sha-ed Dauleh painted. You know what I mean?"

"I know very well, Your Imperial Highness," said the old

man in Turkish. "I know exactly what you want, but I have not got it."

John Rolland raised his head. The old man was standing in front of him, bowing deeply, and the shop door was closed. John Rolland made a hasty movement, as if to flee. He looked around: carpets and rugs, miniatures, the musty smell of the shop—reality and dreams, past and present, in a sudden vision that swam before his eyes.

"Your Highness," said the old man, "it is my fault. Punish me. I should have known—one day Your Highness will come and ask for what I frivolously gave away. Women have neither intelligence nor patience. But I am an old man, and I should have known. I should have kept her."

Shapes and colors were whirling before John Rolland's eyes. What was the old man talking about? What did he want? Why were his hands trembling, his eyes dismayed?

"My fault, Prince," he repeated. "Asiadeh has married, and I have allowed it. Execute me!"

Rolland's voice suddenly took on the timber of a ruling monarch. He forgot the slim passport in his pocket, he forgot the name of Rolland. He felt unmasked and recognized. "Who are you?" he asked in the soft Turkish spoken at his ancestor's palace.

"Achmed-Pasha Anbari. Asiadeh is my daughter."

"Oh," said Rolland, and remembered a confused letter to an exiled, vanished prince.

"What has happened to the woman the emperor chose for me?"

Achmed-Pasha stayed bowed down. He was all humility and joy, for he was talking to a prince of the holy House of Osman. He told about Asiadeh, of the strange man, and his sentences were long and reverential. The prince frowned, and the carpets on the wall represented the palace on the Bosphorus.

"Shame!" said the prince, "shame!" and he felt something had been taken from him that was his by right.

"Shame!" he repeated fervently, and beat with his hand on a rug. "For that thou hast sat at the high portico on the carpet of our favor, for that we have raised thee from the dust and inundated thee with our benevolence! To the desert with thee, into exile!"

But suddenly he remembered that his name was John Rolland, and he was a scriptwriter in New York. The whole thing was absolutely ridiculous.

"All right," he said forgivingly, for the old man was about to fall on his knees. He gave him his hand, and the old man kissed it reverently. "Let's go and have something to eat," said John Rolland suddenly, for he had enough of the musty air in the shop, of the twilight among those rose-colored carpets and the gentle miniatures. "Let's go."

The pasha looked at him aghast. "What great honor," he said, thinking of the poison the prince would put into his food, and of the death he had so richly deserved. But the prince did not think of poison; he went to Kempinski and ordered a meal strictly after the culinary rules of the old empire, with no pork or alcohol, for suddenly he knew how to behave.

"I am not a prince anymore," he said while they were eating, "I am an author, that is to say: an artist."

"A royal profession," asserted the pasha. "Many of your illustrious ancestors were great artists."

"I am not a great artist," said Rolland seriously. "Every man is the mortal son who carries the eternal Father within him. Art is meant to express the invisible Father's breath through something that is visible and tactile. If a man cannot achieve more than to understand and show the son—and this is the only thing I can do—then his art remains on the surface and has no meaning. And if he strives, using abstract ideas only, to show forth the Father, then he does not create a work of art but metaphysics. To show forth, by using words, the immortal living in us—that is magic. The Word must have knowledge of the matter, in the same way Adam had knowledge of Eve. But my word doesn't have that power."

"Because it is a foreign word, spoken in a foreign language," said the pasha, and his brow became sadly furrowed. "I believe the languages of Europe are gradually losing the power that lives in a word. They are becoming a technical thing, a simple exercise of the brain, an emasculated medium of information only. We in the East are more animalistic, we still feel the power of the word, and that is the difference between East and West."

"No," said Rolland, and shook his head. He spoke slowly and impressively and suddenly saw himself sitting in the hall of an Oriental palace, surrounded by a crowd of wise men.

"In the consciousness of the West," he said, "the individual is of primary importance. In ours it is the knowledge that we are irrevocably united with the universe. The West is isolated from the universe, the bond between them is torn. The West is trying, by its conceit, to become an individual cell, isolating itself, drawing trenches around itself. The East is bisexual, it lives and acts in unity with the universe. That is why there is something unfinished and yet illimitable about the art of the Orient, while the art of the West, with its rigid borders, is a personal one. If I were not a debased man but allowed to create, my soul would first have to emerge from the cosmic ocean that surges within me. For the Western artist it is the other way around. But fundamentally all this does not matter, for we are all but transparent masks of the Invisible One."

"Your Highness is not debased," said the pasha seriously. "Your Highness has no faith in the Father. Your Highness must consider: In the world of the Orient it is the father who reigns, in the world of the Occident it is the son. Every artist should strive to find the Father in each event."

"I cannot," said Rolland, "for I am a coward. I am afraid of the world of visible forms. If I were to create pure art, it would be lust translated into aesthetism. But real art is something sublime. It is real magic, in which the word attracts the invisible breath and preserves it, forcing it to become a body and manifest itself to us humans. That is why a real artist can create like God. In the beginning was the Word."

Rolland fell silent and looked about him as if in a dream. In the large room of the restaurant Kempinski, he saw chewing teeth, faces bent over plates. A wave of disgust came over him; he wanted to be alone again, away from this satiated, masticating world. Then he thought that this wish was the opposite of what he had just said, and felt a desperate thirst. He wanted to drink so that the inner forms of the visible world would become obliterated and he could be alone again, alone and without desire in the great hostile desert. He suppressed this violent desire, for he was a prince of a holy house, and a pious pasha with tired, pleading eyes was sitting at his table.

So he kept on talking, more or less mechanically, and the pasha, looking at him, thought of the disaster that had befallen the House of Osman, and of his daughter, who could have helped the prince but who was now far away, and he was overcome by shame and grief.

The prince's face was the transparent mask of the Invisible, and the pasha saw more in this mask than the prince knew or suspected of himself.

"He should have a wife, a good wife," thought the pasha, but did not dare to say so, for Rolland's face was again cold and haughty. He was drumming his fingers on the table and said: "You have all betrayed and left me. The house, the empire, the rule. And the oldest servants of the throne give to other men women who belong to me."

The pasha was silent, thinking of blond Asiadeh, thinking that if he were a prince, he would take the wife who was intended for him with weapons in his hand. But he was no prince, only an old man who sat in a shop in Kantstrasse, and there was no woman intended for him anymore.

"Let's go," said Rolland. He went out onto the street, and the old man stumbled along by his side like a mourning ghost. He spoke again of Asiadeh, of her husband, of the town of Vienna, where they had wonderful water, and Rolland listened to him indifferently, for women were troublesome noisy toys of less worth and use than a bottle of good whiskey. At the corner of Kurfürstendamm, he bade the pasha goodbye and went slowly to the hotel.

The street was wide and clean. Rolland looked at the faces of the passersby, and they seemed satisfied and well fed. He felt a great musty emptiness rising up inside him—he wanted to crush these people, to strangle them, these people who dared to be alive and satisfied, when the old empire had fallen to pieces. He thought of the pasha, of his sad eyes, his bowed back, and a feeling of loneliness engulfed him. He wanted to go back, to talk about Persian miniatures, and about the Invisible, who manifests himself through the transparent masks of terrestrial beings.

But he did not go back, for the old empire was in ruins, and the dead should be left to repose in peace. Instead he went to the hotel, saw Sam Dooth reading a newspaper, clapped him on the shoulder, and said, surprising himself:

"Get up, Perikles, we're going to Vienna."

SEVENTEEN

The car was gliding along the winding main road. To the left, in the valley, rose the towers of whitewashed village churches. Green meadows were shining in the summer sun. Well-fed cows were standing by the wayside, looking with round soft eyes at the car. Children with dusty feet sat under trees, playing with dry branches. On the right, gentle hills swept up. The bright colors of Indian summer were spread over the earth, and the sun was near, mild, and familiar, an old friend. Asiadeh drove slowly up the Semmering, her foot pressing the accelerator as if it were a fragile toy. Just one pressure, and the car shot forward like a raging horse breaking lose. A slight movement of her foot, and the car became slow, like a good obedient domestic animal. Asiadeh gazed at the landscape, the green meadows, church towers in the valley and crucifixes on the curves of the road. It was a strange feeling: being able to direct a confused heap of steel, wheels, lamps, tubes, and tires by a nearly imperceptible pressure of the foot. She drove leaning against the soft leather, her eyes, hands, and feet united with the engine. Sometimes Asiadeh smiled, and her furrowed brow became smooth again. She turned corners carefully, her foot on the accelerator. But quicker than any car, her thoughts would stray back many miles to Vienna, to the flat on the Ring, to Hassa sitting there, dripping with sweat, worn out in the glare of the summer sun.

This was how it had been:

These days the curtains of the house on the Ring were always drawn. Asiadeh would go to the beaches and cafés, come home, and meet strange people sitting in the waiting room, leafing through journals. In the little drawing room with the bow windows lingered a faint smell of medicines, and in the next room Hassa was rattling about with his instruments.

Sometimes his loud voice could be heard:

"Twenty-two!" he shouted. "Can you hear me? Twenty-two!"—"Fourteen," answered a patient, and again the instruments rattled. Then Hassa came out sweating in his white coat and kissed Asiadeh quickly. But the look in his eyes was so far away that she was afraid he might say "Twenty-two" and make a diagnosis. But he didn't. He would just sit down for a minute, holding Asiadeh's hand in his, and then disappear again into the surgery.

"Say 'E'!" he shouted, and a high plaintive voice said "Eeee." Asiadeh went into the big living room. Books and journals were piled on the writing desk, the philological journals with their colorless covers looking like old offended virgins.

Feeling quite guilty, Asiadeh opened one of them and learned that the diaspon of the polystadiality in the Georgian language stretches from the amorph stage to the flectic one. This might sound unintelligible to nonphilologues, but Asiadeh understood it and was amazed that this unheard-of diaspon left her completely cold. Bored, she glanced quickly at a few more pages. On the last one was an announcement that Professor

Shanidse had discovered palimpsests with hammetic texts on the shore of Lake Wan. Exasperated, she closed the journal. Since she had been married, the mysterious forms of strange words had lost their charm for her. They now sounded coarse and unpolished in her ears and did not bring any pictures of slit-eyed nomads and faraway steppes anymore.

The telephone was ringing. "Yes," she heard, "you can come today. Let's say at six-thirty." She had heard enough. The surgery would not close till eight o'clock. So she trotted off to the café and read journals, waiting for Dr. Sachs or Dr. Kurz. At half past eight Hassa came, and they had the choice of driving to the Prater or the Kobenzl. The trees were rustling in the Kobenzl, the Big Dipper could still be seen in the twilight, and Asiadeh was drinking buttermilk, listening to Hassa talking about his patients, or the theater, or politics. They sat there till night fell. Asiadeh looked at the lights of the town spreading out below and thought that real life was wonderful but rather earnest too, and quite different from the way one imagined it.

"When we have children," she said, "we will take them with us to the Kobenzl. They will sit between us and eat cake. I want five children."

"Yes," said Hassa absently. "I'm sure we will have children— sometime." Then he was silent. To tell the truth, he was afraid of these children who would sit between him and Asiadeh. "Yes," he repeated, and took her hand. He loved her very much . . .

They drove back into the witches' cauldron of the town. "Shall we go to the Semmering over the weekend?" asked Hassa. Asiadeh nodded. She had never been to the Semmering.

Saturday came, and at six o'clock the baritone of the opera

phoned and insisted he had fibrositis. He came dashing in, and there was no fibrositis, but the baritone clutched Hassa's sleeve, his protruding eyes rolled, his stomach heaved, and Hassa had to go to the theater to pour cocaine down the baritone's vocal cords during the intermission.

"We'll go first thing in the morning," he told Asiadeh, "and we'll stay till Monday evening." He looked ashamed, like a little boy. Then came the night, and Hassa had to get out of bed, for somewhere a child was choking with diptheria. "Bronchotomy," he said, and Asiadeh was not at all surprised when he telephoned at seven o'clock and said: "Just go alone. I'll come later by train. Give Kurz a ring, ask him to come along so it won't be too boring for you."

Asiadeh telephoned Kurz. Yes, he had time. The hysterics could wait, and so could the manic depressives.

So that had been that.

Asiadeh looked at the pictures of the Madonna at the roadside and thought of Hassa, of the strange sick child, and of life, which was beautiful but earnest. Behind her sat Dr. Kurz. He too was thinking, for he was an educated man with a highly organized brain that was meant for thinking. He thought of the cows, for they were standing by the roadside, he thought of the churches, for they were near, he thought of the mentally ill, for they were his bread and butter. He looked at Asiadeh's neck and thought of that.

"A beautiful neck," he thought, "and such blond hair! Hassa is lucky with women. But only in the beginning, he can't keep them. Strange that she always calls her husband just Hassa. So deep down in her subconscious she feels he is a stranger. She's got a beautiful bosom. Perhaps Hassa won't come after all. Fantastic, the practice that man has. And all he's got is technical skill. I'll order champagne in the evening and talk a lot about Hassa. Praising him, of course. That always works. She'll trust me. That's the main thing. Apart from that she's homesick. Probably a hidden father-complex. That'll have to be seen to. Well—that neck! I'm sure Hassa is not up to her standards. If she has any temperament, perhaps I can even tonight . . ."

Thus thought Dr. Kurz, for he was an educated man with a highly organized brain that was meant for thinking. The car stopped in front of the Südbahn Hotel. From the window s of the great hall one could see the angular contours of the mountains and the wide deep valley.

"Beautiful," said Asiadeh. She went out on the terrace, and suddenly a wild zest for life overcame her. The air was cool and dry, the blue mountains enclosed the horizon. Infinity was confined in this valley. It must be wonderful to stay here, separated from all everyday cares by the steep wall of the mountains.

Down in town Hassa was sitting at the bedside of the sick child, listening to the rattling in the throat; down in town the panting baritone was pacing up and down in the waiting room, for by now he had firmly convinced himself that he had cancer of the throat; down in town the telephone rang, the housemaid took the receiver off and answered that the *gnädige* Frau had gone to the Semmering. Down in town an elegant foreigner asked the commissionaire where and what the Semmering was. But Asiadeh did not know any of this, and if she had, she would not have been interested.

"Let's go for a walk," she said, and Kurz followed. They went along the small street up to the hotel Panhans. The wood on their right was somber and threatening, full of ancient darkness.

"You know," said Asiadeh, "I keep thinking these mountains are walls, or ruins of old fortresses."

Kurz looked at her attentively. Then he began to talk in a soft, earnest voice. He talked and went on talking, impressed by his own deep thoughts. "This woman inspires me," he said to himself, and did not realize that Asiadeh was not listening.

They went down into the valley. An old church stood on a small hill.

As they came closer, Asiadeh read the weatherbeaten letters at the entrance: *"Maria Schutz steht allen Feinden zum rutz."* She looked at it for a long time and felt a sense of forbearance. "Maria's shelter stands, despite all enemies." A whole world arose behind the little church with its old inscription. Perhaps this church had seen the victorious Turkish army. Perhaps the Osman archers had ridden through these mountains on their long-maned horses, and villages had erupted into flames. Perhaps on this little square in front of this church portal, pyres had burned, soldiers had warmed themselves during the night, thinking of the loot awaiting them behind the walls of Vienna. The church door was closed, but the inscription looked down, mute and serene, for it had been victorious over the foreign enemy, the grim general, the whole House of Osman.

Asiadeh looked around. Deep peace lay over the landscape. She sighed. "You are a happy people," she said, "you have a beautiful country."

Grief and a little jealousy rang in her voice. But Kurz did not notice that. He saw only her upturned lip and the strangely set eyes. He went on talking, and Asiadeh sank deeper and deeper into her thoughts, for only now she realized fully that she herself had become part of this green and beautiful country and should be glad that the power of the House of Osman had been shattered before this little church. For the first time she realized that she was not a Turkish woman anymore, that none of her children or children's children would ever be Turks. Lost in thoughts, she went back to the hotel, Kurz at her side.

"In the afternoon," he said, "there's a five o'clock tea dance in the hall. There are always many foreigners. May I have the honor?"

Asiadeh nodded.

At five o'clock she sat with Kurz in the hall at one of the low tables. The band played a strange, yearning melody. Dancing couples were gliding over the parquet floor, and Asiadeh caught stray sentences repeating the same sweet nothings in all languages of the world.

Kurz bowed, asking her to dance, and on the floor the rhythm of the odd melody cast its spell on her. It was pleasant to dance in the bright hall, seeing the blue mountains in the distance. Men and women moved past them, closely embraced. Asiadeh caught covetous glances and heard the breathing of strange mouths. Kurz's hand hardly touched her waist. It showed he was an honorable man who knew how to behave toward a friend's wife. Yes, it was a beautiful country, and a beautiful hotel, and life itself was beautiful and not really so very earnest.

"Enough," she said suddenly, and left Kurz standing like a tailor's dummy. Quite out of breath, she went back to their table and sat down. Kurz's face bent toward her, and Asiadeh quickly emptied her coffee cup. Hassa should be there now, she wanted to whirl with him across the hall, to feel his strong hands, see his slanting eyes gazing into hers, smiling, entreating . . .

At the other end of the hall, a tall, slender woman rose from her chair and came toward them around the dance floor. Asiadeh saw brown hair gleaming like a chestnut, drawn severely back into a coil, a delicate oval face with haughty eyes and a narrow nose. The noble curve of her lips was repeated by the thin brows on her high, smooth forehead.

Slowly the stranger approached their table. Asiadeh looked up to Kurz, who was suddenly blushing furiously, his eyes blinking in astonished embarrassment. His mouth was half open, as if he was trying to decide whether to smile or to sneeze. The stranger was standing at their table, proud and beautiful. Her lips opened to show small, glittering teeth. "Good afternoon, Dr. Kurz, how nice to see you again."

It was a soft, melodious voice. Kurz rose. Drops of sweat showed on his brow. The strange lady was still standing there, a haughty, superior smile on her lips.

Kurz cleared his throat. "May I . . . may I introduce . . ." His voice sounded hoarse.

Asiadeh was amazed. He looked like a man who had suddenly thrown himself into ice-cold water.

"May I introduce . . . Frau Dr. Marion Hassa . . . Frau Dr. Asiadeh Hassa."

He stopped and did not look at all like a doctor who could cure nervous diseases.

Asiadeh closed her eyes. Just for a moment. Somewhere in her breast was a sudden searing pain. Her mouth was dry. She felt herself being hurled into a whirling abyss. Deep deep down the band was playing. Wild sounds smote her ears. She opened her eyes. Smiling grandly, Marion had taken a seat at their table.

"I'm so glad. What a coincidence." The voice still sounded

soft, but not melodious anymore. "Is Alex here too? Or has he stayed in Vienna?"

"Who, please?"

"Alex, our husband," Marion laughed.

"Oh—no. Hassa is in Vienna. I always call him Hassa, you know."

She got up. Quickly she crossed the hall and felt pricking needles in her back. So that's how it was. "Our husband." Frau Marion Hassa—Frau Asiadeh Hassa. She was lying in a stranger's bed. She had a stranger's name. She was sitting in the same drawing room with the bow windows where this slim Marion had sat, and Hassa had kissed these proud, haughty eyes. There really was a woman called Marion whose place she had taken. Asiadeh ran across the yard, her eyes staring, her brow furrowed.

"The car, please."

The attendant opened the garage. The car started. Asiadeh's hands gripped the wheel as if it were Marion's neck. She drove, wildly sounding her horn, and looked full of hate at the two frightened children who jumped aside just in time.

"Somebody should drop a bomb on this hotel," she thought, and sped up again. The grey asphalt spiraled before her eyes. She sobbed shortly and wiped her tears away. The Turks were a mild and weak people. Not a stone should have been left on the other in this country, not one meadow, not one cow. A desert it should become, gray and empty, like the steppes of Turkey. The axles of the car squeaked. Asiadeh put the brakes on. The wheels dug into the dust of the road. She changed gear. "Go! Go! Away! Away!" she thought. "What does it matter that the water in the radiator is beginning to boil." Down on the next curve a four-seater appeared. Asiadeh did not notice it. She gripped the steering wheel and opened the throttle. Now!

But she did not go. She looked at the instrument panel and felt a sudden blow on her breast. Glass tinkled. She looked up. There was a car with a bent push-rod and broken lamps. She had no idea how she had driven into it.

Two people were sitting in the car, looking at her with astonished, frightened eyes. Asiadeh jumped out of the car and ran to them, her gray eyes glittering with fury. She saw two faces, a fat one and a narrow one. "Scum!" she cried, and did not know that she meant Marion. "Haven't you learned how to drive? Can't you see what you're doing? Every idiot has a driver's license these days! You're drunk! You should be reported to the police, you scoundrels!"

She was standing there in the middle of the road, spitting insults, quarreling with Marion. The two gentlemen crept slowly from the car, bowed, and smiled.

"Don't stand there grinning like fools!" shouted Asiadeh, stamping her foot.

The gentlemen bowed again. "Please excuse us, Madam," said one of them in English, "we are inconsolable that you drove into us. We will be only too happy to compensate you." A well-cared-for hand stretched out toward her, holding a hundred-dollar bill.

"Foreigners, are you?" cried Asiadeh, beside herself with fury. "Coming to our country, driving into ladies! You should be deported! Why don't you go back where you came from, you vagabonds! What are you doing here anyway?" It was obvious that the foreigners did not understand a word. They stood there, embarrassed, shifting their weight from one foot to the other. At last the fat one said to the thin one in a foreign language that Asiadeh understood only too well:

"Look, John, what a beautiful bosom that girl has! And what hips! Give her a kiss, perhaps she'll calm down."

At the sound of her native language, Asideh became a raging tigress. She snatched the hundred-dollar bill from the slim man's fingers, tore it into little bits, spat on it, and threw the pieces into the stranger's face. Then she jumped into her car and drove away without a word.

The two men followed her with their eyes. "A woman with temperament," said John at last. "She'll be a handful for her husband."

"Beautiful bosom," repeated Sam, "she's still quite young. What was the matter with her, anyway? She must be mad. Only mad people tear up hundred-dollar bills."

Sadly he got into the car, John followed, and they drove on very carefully. Half an hour later they arrived at the hotel. The five o'clock tea was over, the hall was empty.

"Is a Frau Dr. Hassa staying here?" asked John. The clerk at the reception desk bowed.

"Yes sir, room twenty-eight."

"Let's go to the bar first," said Sam. "You should have one to get some courage." John nodded.

After the third whiskey Sam said: "Speak English to her at first—mustn't frighten her, you know. Be polite and pleasant, women like that." After the sixth whiskey he looked down bashfully and growled: "If you like her, take her away at once. If the negotiations come to a deadlock, call me. After all, I'm your agent. Now go, I'll be waiting here."

John rose and walked up the staircase, his face proud and serious. He knocked at the door. "Come in," called a melodious voice.

John Rolland came in. A woman rose. Haughty brown eyes, nobly curved lips. "Frau Dr. Hassa?" asked John, and bowed. The woman nodded. John gave her a penetrating look and smiled graciously. Then he took a seat in an easy chair and lit a cigarette.

"Do you prefer a conversation in English or in Turkish?" he asked indolently.

The woman looked astonished.

"English, of course," she said.

John smiled and crossed his legs. The woman was beautiful but obviously had no idea of the situation.

"I am Prince Abdul-Kerim. I have come for you, for you please me." Six whiskeys in one afternoon were really too many.

"Please?" said the woman, all blood draining from her face.

John laughed. "You did not expect me. My palace is gone, but I still exist. I find this foreign world boring, and I have run away from my agent. We can leave today."

"My God," said the woman, and bit her lip, "what do you want?"

John frowned. "Don't you pretend to me!" he said severely. "Do I have to order you to come?"

"I'm coming, I'm coming," said Marion, teeth chattering, "I only have to make a phone call to my maid."

Her trembling hand found the receiver. "Kurz, for heaven's sake, come to me, quickly." She put it down. "I'll go and pack my suitcase," she said pleasantly. "I'll be ready in half an hour."

Then she ran from the room. John put out his cigarette and waited.

A gentleman came into the room, looked darkly at John, and bowed. "Dr. Kurz," he said. Then he sat down, took on a professional manner, and asked very softly:

"What were the objects of your first conscious thoughts?"

"The crown," answered John honestly, slightly drunk.

"Oh," said Kurz, frowning.

"A whiskey," whispered Marion at the same time, rushing into the bar.

"Just imagine," she told the waiter, completely bewildered, "there's a stranger coming into my room, speaks English, says he's a prince and wants to take me away. My divorced husband was a doctor, so I understood at once: megalomania."

"Terrible," said the waiter.

The fat man who had been sitting peacefully asleep in the corner suddenly cleared his throat and cried, "Waiter!" He ran across the hall and exchanged a few words with the commissionaire. Then he became very agile and ran up the stairs. When he opened the door of number twenty-eight, he saw Dr. Kurz tapping John's knee, a conciliatory smile on his face.

"Do you often dream of railways or planes?" asked the doctor, and John answered: "No, I never dream."

"Oh," said the doctor worriedly, and his eyes became quite small.

"Come on," cried Sam in Turkish, "quickly, before it's too late!"

As John jumped up, the doctor jumped up too. "Oh!" he said, and took Sam's arm. "I presume you're the nurse? Typical megalomania. Tending toward manic-depressive condition. To whom may I send the invoice?"

"What invoice?" said Sam angrily.

Dr. Kurz became very dignified. "Fifty schillings, please, for medical assistance."

"Twenty is enough," hissed Sam, and shoved a note into the

doctor's hand. Then he grabbed John and dragged him out of the room.

"I understood immediately," said John in the corridor, and winked slyly. "This doctor is the husband of my fiancée. She wanted to gain time until she's finished packing. I suppose she is ready now?"

"Shut up," whispered Sam, and took John to the car.

Only when they drove out of the courtyard did he say in a very superior voice: "Get that into your head, John—if an author enters into any negotiations without his agent, he ends up in the loony bin. The doctor is quite right, you've got megalomania. You think you can negotiate without me. Tomorrow I'll go to the right Asiadeh and get it all sorted out without you. Even for a marriage you need an agent."

He spoke like a father for a long time, and John became smaller and smaller.

"Sam," he said at last, very dejectedly, "believe me. As soon as I saw her, I took a dislike to that woman." Sadly he shook his head and spat out of the window as the car traveled toward Vienna.

Meanwhile, another car with a shattered front window stopped at the house on the Ring. Asiadeh ran up the stairs and found Hassa standing in the corridor, hat in hand, ready to go.

"Hassa," she cried, sobbing, "I have insulted your friend Kurz, I have crashed the car, I have torn up a hundred-dollar bill and spat on strangers, and it's all Marion's fault." Tears streaming down her face, she buried her head on Hassa's shoulder.

Hassa looked at her trembling shoulders and gray eyes, red with weeping. This wild girl loved him, there was no doubt about that, even when this love was strange and incoherent full of odd ideas and impulses.

He caressed Asiadeh's hair and said softly: "There is no Marion, there never was a Marion, there's only Asiadeh."

She looked up gratefully.

"Yes," she said, "there's only Asiadeh, and she has forgotten to note the number of the car she has driven into. Don't be angry with me, Hassa, I'll never drive again."

EIGHTEEN

S am Dooth walked slowly along Ringstrasse, biting his cigar. He stopped in front of the cinemas and shook his head disapprovingly. Vienna was a reactionary town—not one single film by John Rolland was showing. "Summer season," he grumbled angrily, and walked on. The streets were sinfully wide, the houses shamefully low. It had been a stupid idea, going to Europe. They should have gone to Mexico or Cuba. John should keep away from women. Women had always meant trouble to the House of Osman. Sam stopped and shook the ash off his cigar. Six years ago he had discovered Prince Abdul-Kerim ragged and starving in a hovel on the Bowery. Sam's clever Greek heart had seen a chance at once. He fed the poor boy and gave him a new name: John Rolland. But behind the white starched shirt, behind the slim passport, there lived still the delicate soul of an Osman.

"He is a drunkard," thought Sam, "and he'll stay that way until he has found peace." He frowned and was glad that love of mankind and a sense of business went hand in hand. "If he goes on drinking for another three years, he'll see pink elephants. The Osmans have never been very robust, and then that's the end of filming." Sam thought of John with the same tender solicitude a farmer's wife has for her best cow. "Perhaps a good wife might help him," he went on thinking "a wife who is humble and quiet and company for his evenings. He should be able to talk about home with her sometimes. That should give him inspiration. He's mad, that's what he is."

Sam Dooth shrugged. He never thought of home. Then he stopped. A brass plate with the inscription "Dr. Alexander Hassa, Ear, Nose, and Throat Specialist" blinked at him. He went up the wide staircase and asked for Asiadeh. The maid took him to the drawing room with the bow windows.

Sam Dooth was an experienced agent and a good business-man. His heart was well balanced and his head clear. But now he stood in the room as if rooted to the ground and blinked in utter confusion.

The temperamental lady who had torn a hundred-dollar bill to bits looked at him, smiling. "Ah . . ." said Sam Dooth, and looked around fearfully. But there were no heavy objects any-where near her.

"Madam," he said, and the prepared speech stuck in his throat. "Madam, please excuse me for disturbing you. But we traced your address through your license plate. My friend and I are desolate to have caused you displeasure."

"You can speak Turkish to me," said the blond lady, looking angrily at him. "You have already said kind words about my bosom and my hips in this language."

Sam looked sad. Any minute now she would take a brass plate and throw it at him. Or scratch his eyes out. Women who tear up hundred-dollar bills are capable of anything.

"Hanum," he said in his softest Stamboul Turkish, "even though my sins be more numerous that the grains of sand in the desert, your generosity can cause them to vanish like mist in the rays of the sun. Do you remember, Hanum, that when the sultan surprised the great Saadi committing a sin, Saadi cried: 'Oh Sultan, behold the sin, and you will forgive!' "

Sam Dooth was a clever man. Very likely he had been born on the aristocratic hill of Phanar after all.

Asiadeh clapped her hands happily. "Hassa," she cried, "come here!"

The door opened, and the white-coated Hassa came in.

"This one here," said Asiadeh, "is one of the two foreigners I ran into yesterday. And spat at. He is well brought up, for he is from Istanbul, and he asks me humbly to forgive him. Shall I forgive him, Hassa?"

"Forgive him," said Hassa. He saw a fat, black-haired man standing there blinking in the drawing room, and he did not know that this fat man wanted to take his wife from him and to destroy his house and peace—all for the sake of a man whose name was John Rolland, and who was threatened by delirium tremens.

"Herr Doktor, honored Hanum"—Sam Dooth was all humility—"my friend and I would be very happy if you would be our guests tonight. It is so seldom that we meet countrymen in Europe."

Asiadeh looked questioningly at Hassa.

"You go," said Hassa. "Today is Thursday. I'm at the Medical Association."

Sam Dooth was amazed. These European men were very stupid indeed. And God punishes the stupid ones and helps the clever ones. A blond woman, a beautiful woman, and he let her go out with two strange men. No need to have a bad conscience.

He bowed and left. Matchmaking was an ancient and honorable profession. The first mention of matchmakers is on Assyrian cuneiform tablets. In the holy palace of Byzantium, matchmakers from all over the world fought for the honor to put the Basilisa into the emperor's bed.

Whole provinces were given as a reward. The Great Osman of Istanbul despatched matchmakers to all four points of the compass. Princes and pashas sent him women. To be a match-maker was indeed an ancient and honorable profession. Sam was very proud.

It was evening, and Asideh was smiling, her eyes blazing with gaiety. She stood in her dressing room in front of the mirror, holding her lipstick like a scepter. Indeed the Turks were a noble race. They knew how to behave toward a lady, even when this lady had driven into their car and insulted them. She touched the lipstick to her lips. Tonight she would speak Turkish—all evening. It did not matter who the strangers were, as long as they were countrymen, clumps of earth from home. She opened the perfume bottle and touched her temples with the stopper. Tonight she would talk of Anatolian villages and little boats circling the islands of the Marmara Sea, steered by vigorous helmsmen. She would feel the dust of Asiatic hills and sense the narrow alleys of faraway towns, protected from the heat of the sun.

She took a little brush and drew it over her soft eyelashes. She would bathe in the sound of familiar native words, and the strangers would tell of yellow-eyed camels coming from the desert.

"That's it," she said, and looked at her rosy fingernails. She would be nice to these strangers whom she had insulted but who had the dust of her homeland on their feet.

She left the house. In the hotel hall, Sam Dooth rose. Next to him, looking with light, empty eyes into the far distance, was John Rolland. His eyes met Asiadeh's, his hand pressed her rosy fingers. The hooked nose of the Osmans scented the fragrance of her body, and he said calmly: "Hanum, I am your slave."

They were sitting in the restaurant, silent waiters serving them. Rolland's hands were sliding over the dishes; glasses clinked. Asiadeh spoke of her father, who lived in Berlin, of her brothers, fallen in the war, and of their house on the Bosphorus.

"Is it a long time since you left Istanbul?" she asked.

John Rolland looked at her. His eyes grew dim under half-closed lids. "A woman," he thought. "What a woman! Tears up money and can defend herself. A real Osman, best Istanbul polish. One should not disown a woman before one has seen her. I was a fool. But now I'm clever. Prayer is better than sleep. And a woman is better than wine. She will be mine."

"Yes," he said, "we've been away a long time from Istanbul. But we know: The people live well, the homeland is thriving, the army is strong. There is no sorrow anymore in Istanbul."

"And no Osmans," Asiadeh added.

"No." John's voice sounded very indifferent. He too had the best Istanbul polish. "There are no more Osmans. Only Turks. The Osmans were like old wolves with fallen-out teeth."

"Well—they did have their good points," said Sam, for he was afraid of John's indifferent voice.

"A good point does not mean a claim for eternal gratitude," said John. "Everything was measured and weighed. The limit had been reached."

"I was engaged to a member of the House of Osman," said Asiadeh. "A servant must not speak badly of his fallen master."

"I was never a servant of the House of Osman." Rolland's

eyes opened wide. "But you yourself, Hanum, preferred to marry a Viennese instead of an Osman. That shows the limit had been reached."

"He had disowned me." Asiadeh's voice was very cool, and Sam Dooth suddenly remembered he had to make a telephone call and perhaps send a telegram.

He went and instructed the hall porter to have a bottle of whiskey on the side table of John's bed. He was a clever man, and he looked after his friend.

"I met your father in Berlin. He asked me to give you his greetings." John spoke softly, and his hands hung weakly from the arms of his chair.

"You have seen my father? You know him?"

"Of course I know him. I have known him for a long time. The first time I saw him was at the Babi-Sadat, the Gate of Happiness. It was when Memed-Rashid kissed the coat of the prophet for the first time. That is quite a long time ago. It was on the fifteenth day of the Ramasan. We came in through the Emperor's Gate. The emperor wore the uniform of a marshal, and behind him came his grand vezir. We went to the Hall of the Holy Coat. The whole hall was draped in black cloth, and on it were verses from the Koran, embroidered in golden letters. In the middle, covered in gems, stood the chest that holds the coat of the prophet. But these remiscences must be boring for you. It was all a long time ago, and you are a modern woman."

"Go on," said Asiadeh, and put her knife and fork aside. Blood rose in her cheeks. Yes, there had been a time when her father had walked at the emperor's side through the Gate of Happiness to the Hall of the Holy Coat.

"The coat of the prophet was swathed in forty gold-embroidered robes. The hall was lit by candles. It was very hot, and it took a long time to undrape the coat from the forty robes. The emperor was a sick man. He stood there, supporting himself on his sword, his eyes closed. He prayed. Then he kissed the prophet's coat, and after him all the others, one after the other. Your father was in the thirty-eights. He was a young general then. To the right of the coat stood the Imperial Seneschal. On both of his hands he held a velvet cushion, and on this cushion lay silken scarves. After each kiss he wiped the coat with one of these silken scarves, and each dignitary received a scarf. Then came the palace servants, carrying a silver jug. The seam of the coat was rinsed and the water poured into small flasks. Each of us received one of these flasks, sealed with the imperial seal. It was a beautiful day, the day I saw your father for the first time."

Asiadeh sat there, staring down at the table. She was sitting in a big, brightly lit room. A headwaiter in white tie and tails was bowing at the next table. A selection of hors d'oeuvres was trundled past on a trolley. The prophet was a ghost, haunting the room, unreal, mysteriously conjured up by the stranger's words. A dark hall with black hangings, and a sick emperor leaning on his sword. The pictures blurred and merged—the sick man sat at the table, and red wine was poured on the coat instead of water.

"Was that the only time you saw my father?"

"No. I saw him again ten years later. In the mosque of the standard-bearer Eyub."

"If my father was the thirty-eights in Memed-Rashid's retinue, where were you?" Asiadeh's voice sounded very naive.

"I? I was the seventeenth."

They were both silent. At the next table, a guest took a long time to order his dinner.

"You are a confidence trickster," said Asiadeh softly. "But it does not matter. I like to talk about the olden times."

"I am no confidence trickster." John's voice was sad. "Why do you think I am?"

"Because . . . well. It's really quite simple. You are most certainly not older than forty. At the time when my father was the thirty-eighth in the emperor's retinue, you must have been less than twenty. And you say you were the seventeenth?"

"That does not mean I am a confidence trickster." He did not sound at all insulted. He was silent for a while and then said in a hard, cutting voice: "Imperial princes ranged before the retinue and military personnel."

"What do you mean?" Asiadeh's eyes were wild with terror. Suddenly the big hall had turned into a prison cell. "What do you mean?" she repeated, and then was silent. She did not need an answer. She saw the narrow face, light-colored empty eyes, the nose. She saw the dry, malevolent lips and the square, angular forehead. The face was a mask, motionless eyes stared at her, piercing her like spikes.

"No," said Asiadeh, "please, no."

She drew the back of her hand over her lips. Rolland did not say a word. His stony face was that of a statue, strayed from an ancient world into this light-flooded hall.

"Your father gave me your address," he said at last. "The emperor assigned you to me. I did not think of you. Not in Istanbul, not in America. Now I see you. Now I think of you. You shall be the mother of princes."

Asiadeh was silent. Steadfastly unsmiling, she looked at Rolland. So there he was. The exiled one, the lost one. Pines were growing in his palace. She had seen their branches and tops over the broad wall. Many times a fat eunuch, probably his seneschal, had been sitting on the terrace. He was the seventeenth, allowed to kiss the prophet's coat after Memed Rashid, and the narrow-shouldered Wacheddin had assigned her to him. She belonged to him, every fiber of her body was his. For him she had once learned Persian poems and Arabic prayers, for him she had listened to the sound of barbaric words.

"Your Highness," she said, and then could not go on. The present was confused, a wild dream. Somewhere far away Marion's haughty laughter sounded—and died away. The house on the Bosphorus, home, the blood-red sunsets of the Golden Horn, all that was reality again, embodied in the strange man who had narrow, evil lips and staring eyes.

Suddenly she wanted to get up, take the slackly hanging hand, press her lips to the angular shoulder. "Your Highness," she repeated, and inclined her head. "I am your slave. I follow wherever you go."

She raised her eyes, overcome by a wild, raging, even painful happiness. John's lips smiled.

"I thank you," he said. "Your father has brought you up well. Come to the hotel tomorrow at five o'clock. We will prepare everything." He rose and escorted her to the door.

She walked along the Ring, and the asphalt felt like a soft carpet. Happiness—the One—the Unthinkable—here it was, suddenly. It had pale eyes and narrow lips and spoke in the soft dialect of Istanbul. Suddenly it was hers—inseparable, like a limb—happiness.

Only when she reached the house did she remember that she was married, and her name was Frau Dr. Hassa. Frightened, she looked around. There she stood, rooted to the ground, and shook her head, completely at a loss. There really was a man called Hassa, to whom she was married. She turned and walked quickly toward the park.

NINETEEN

She walked about in the avenues of the park. Sand and gravel crunched under her feet, trees fluttered shadows on the grass. Lovers, closely entwined, sat on lonely benches. Soft whisperings stopped short when Asiadeh passed by. She walked on, her head bent. Dark branches arched over the avenues, and the gravel under her feet glistened in the moonlight.

Then she stood on the bridge, leaning on the railing, looking down into the dry emptiness of the riverbed, at the crooked earth bathed in silver. She walked along the avenues, around and around, the same circles, again and again.

Hassa, she thought, once he was sitting in his car, kissing her, thinking he was superior to her. Then he stood humbly on a rainswept street in Berlin and asked her forgiveness. When had that been? Yesterday? Centuries ago? He saved a holy man of the brotherhood of the Bektashi and had made her a woman on a hot summer night in the wide bed of a Serbian hotel. Asiadeh stopped. The moon shimmered through the branches, mild and soft, like Hassa's soul. He had stood beside her, his eyes frightened and entreating, in the bedroom with the wide double bed, where Marion had once slept, dreaming of strange men.

Yes—she had promised to be a good wife. She had lain beside him thinking of Marion, who had left him, and for whom the doors of hell were waiting. Asiadeh did not notice that she kept walking in the same circles through the avenues, filled with whispers of love.

Hassa was an unbeliever, a heretic, helpless in the world of feelings. His hands were strong, his fingers skillful, and he was content in the narrow world of his love. She saw him in his white coat, smelling of medicines, or in the café, telling his friends simple stories about his patients, the theater, or politics. Her heart, her whole being, was filled with love and warmth for him. Unthinkable: no Hassa in her life anymore.

Asiadeh lit a cigarette. The little flame threw a bright glow on her face. She smoked while she walked and became desperately afraid of the prince who had so suddenly appeared out of nowhere and who now claimed her.

Once upon a time her ancestors had come from the desert and become the slaves of the prince's ancestors. She had to thank the prince's ancestors for the favors they had shown her ancestors, for every breath of air, for every movement of her limbs. She would today be a farmer's wife, a wild woman of the steppes, if the prince's ancestors had so desired it. The cigarette glowed; she looked at the lengthening ashes and thought of the searing heat of the desert from where the ancestors came to conquer the world. The great Orchan, the choleric Murad, the cruel Selim who marched to Egypt and threw the prophet's coat over his broad shoulders. All the greatness of the empire was embodied in this man with the slack hands who was calling her. She must go to him, she must become a servant in the empty House of Osman, humble and submissive, as it was women's duty before God.

She threw the cigarette away. In helpless fear she crunched

the stub. Perhaps she should find another woman for Hassa, a woman who was not under the spell of a lost empire, a woman of his own kind who could wait in cafés while he was treating baritones, and who would not run away when Marion came to the table.

She looked around. All at once she was afraid of this strange town, the foreign world into which she had been forced, a world that she did not understand, a world that bored her. Yes, she knew it quite plainly, she was bored, bored in the room with the bow windows, in the café with the doctors, bored by visiting people whose thoughts and feelings were so different from hers, her father's, and the prince's, whom she had never seen before and who was yet closer and more familiar to her than Hassa with his patients, his friends, and his conversations.

Hassa should emigrate to Cairo or Sarajevo, he should wear a fez like his ancestors, he should live the way Asiadeh was used to, treat dervishes and visit mosques—then she would stay with him. Abruptly Asiadeh stopped. Her thoughts were in turmoil. An empty bench stood in the shade of a big tree. Asiadeh sat down.

"My God," she said softly, and her hands felt like ice. Hassa was her husband, she loved him, no one had forced her to submit to him. And now—now there she was, like Marion, sitting on a bench in the park, thinking of a strange man, while her own man was lying in his bed longing for her. She wanted to go to the prince, it was her duty, but Hassa's shadow would follow her, would pursue her in the nights when she would be lying with the prince, during the day when she would be talking with him. Everywhere his shadow would haunt her, she would see his eyes, she would read the mute reproach in his face, hear the curse he would send to her.

Asiadeh hid her face in her hands. There was no way out of

the blind alley of her misery. She knew quite well: She would not dare to leave, she would not dare to look into the mirror if she left Hassa.

She stared at the trees, completely lost. Duty and shame, honor and lust had suddenly become muddled in a tangled bundle, and she did not know anymore whether duty drove her to the prince or love kept her with Hassa.

But one thing she knew: There must be a difference between haughty Marion, who left her husband, and Asiadeh, who sat thoughtfully on a bench in the park and stared into the night. But perhaps to Marion the man she had gone away with had been what the newly found prince was to Asiadeh.

She sighed. There was no difference between her and Marion the aduletress. Hassa would not take a third wife. His days would pass, lonely and sad. Alone, shunning all mankind, he would walk along the streets, cursing the women who had sworn to be faithful to him only to go away with other men.

Asiadeh rose, her face deeply flushed. She was ashamed. Slowly she went to the exit. Yes, there was a difference between a princess of Istanbul and Marion, who betrayed her husband.

Deep in thought she walked along the Ring. This was where her future lay, here in the dust of this wide street. For decades she would sit in cafés, drive up the Kobenzl in the evening, and kiss Hassa. She would lose her home and her identity, her soul would dissolve in the world of Europe, but she would not leave her husband, she would remain a good wife who could look anyone in the face—except into Abdul-Kerim's wan, lonely face, Abdul-Kerim who had called her and whom she had not obeyed.

She came to the house. Slowly she went up the stairs, slowly she opened the door. In the bedroom the lights were still on. Hassa was lying in bed, sleepily and indifferently leafing through the philology journals he had taken from Asiadeh's table. He looked up and smiled.

"It's late. Did you have a nice evening? I've been trying to read your journals but couldn't understand a word. What on earth is polystadiality?"

"A hypophysen tumor, translated into philological terms. It doesn't matter if you don't understand it. Yes, thanks, it was very nice." She paused. Suddenly it seemed very strange to her, that she was speaking German to her husband while thinking and dreaming in another language. She suppressed a slight feeling of unease and came to Hassa's bed. He was lying on his back, looking at her.

"You're very beautiful tonight, Asiadeh, very beautiful."

She sat down on his bed, bent forward, and kissed his brow. Hassa's hands stretched out toward her. He caressed her, and she felt the scent of his skin, the strength of his muscles, the familiar signs of his love. She undressed and again sat on his bed, legs drawn up, head on her knees.

"It was very nice," she said, "we talked of the olden times and of our homeland. But for a woman the true homeland is the bed of her husband."

Hassa drew her to him. She clasped his head in her hands, her body clung to him, her lips were gliding over his skin, she embraced him as if seeking help and protection in his strong arms.

Hassa became completely awake. Asiadeh's hidden passion swept over him. Her eyes were humble and enchanted, her body thirsting and longing. She was his, her clear skin, the blond hair falling across her face—all of her was his. She was kneeling in the bed, her head pressed against Hassa's breast. Slowly she was rocking backward and forward, moaning like a nocturnal lonely animal.

"I love you, Hassa, only you," she said, and Hassa clasped her body, threw her on the white sheets, saw as if for the first time her serious eyes looking up at him, her soft lips pressed together. Hassa forgot his patients, his Medical Assembly, his tiredness. He only felt the moist warmth of her mouth, the submission of her delicate body. Later she sat in bed, her hands around his neck, silently staring at nothing. She was smiling and looked at him, tenderly pleading. "Hassa," she said, "do something for me."

"Yes, Asiadeh."

"In the dining room, Hassa, there is a bottle of cognac in the sideboard. I'll get it for you. Drink a glass of cognac, or you'll go to sleep, and I don't want you to go to sleep. I want to see your eyes open." She ran through the flat in her bare feet and came back with a bottle under her arm and a glass in her hand. In her pajamas, her blond hair in tangles, she looked like a boy, a small page, excitedly doing his first service.

"Drink with me," said Hassa.

"No, I don't need cognac to become intoxicated."

She filled the glass, and he drank slowly. She filled it again.

"You're seducing me." He laughed. "This is a sin. The Koran forbids alcoholic drinks."

"There is an amendment," she said very seriously, "by the great scholar Sheik Ismail of Ardedil. There are times when alcoholic drinks are allowed."

Hassa drank. Asiadeh sat cross-legged on the bed and looked at the bottle. "I'm quite awake, Asiadeh, but I'll go on drinking if you order me to."

"Yes," she said, folding her hands on her lap. "You shall never be unhappy because of me, Hassa." Her voice was pleading. "I will do everything to make you happy—always."

Hassa was astonished. "Thank you," he said, touched. "You shall be happy with me too. Am I good to you?"

"You are very good to me. But what makes a woman happy? A woman is happy when she sees her husband's eyes smiling and knows that it is because of her. I will never do anything to distress you. I am not Marion."

Now Hassa filled the glass himself. He got out of bed and sat next to her, smiling and in very good humor.

"Marion," he said, "Marion is an idiot. I did love her very much once, but now I don't love her anymore. I love you. Marion is getting from bad to worse. Perhaps I should be sorry for her, but I'm not. Fritz has left her. She really couldn't expect anything else from him. Now she's alone, for all she's so beautiful, and I've got Asiadeh. I'm happy."

"Thus God punishes the unchaste." Asiadeh smiled, her little tongue gliding over her lips, but she took note of the fact that Marion was alone now. "Have you drunk enough, Hassa?"

"Yes."

"Then listen to me." She inclined her head to one side, and looked down, pious and innocent. "We have now been married long anough, Hassa. It is high time for me to have a baby."

"Ugh," said Hassa uneasily, and squinted at the bottle. But Asiadeh pushed it away and sat there, darkly silent.

"A baby?" said Hassa and crept under the covers.

"Yes, first one, then another, and then others, with God's help."

"You're quite right, of course," said Hassa, "but do you know how much it hurts when a woman is having a baby?"

Asiadeh nodded. "My mother had the same pains, and my grandmother too. And my great-grandmother. It can't be as bad as all that."

"Yes, of course." Hassa did not know himself why he was so terribly afraid of becoming a father. He was simply afraid of children, in the same way he had been afraid of school when he was a little boy. He did want children, but not yet, later, at some other, not clearly defined, time.

"Well, it's like this," he said, embarrassed. "If I have children, I want to be certain that they will always be all right. But I want you, too, to be all right. Only one in three patients actually pays, and eight in ten operations are on the National Health. If we have one child, we'd have to sell the car; if we have two, we'd have to let one of the housemaids go; if we have three, we'd have to move into a smaller flat. You should be well off, and the children too, and therefore we should wait until things are better. Then I'll promise you quintuples."

Hassa was quite exhausted by his long speech. Asiadeh looked at him searchingly.

"I have lived without a car and servants and was quite happy. You don't want any children because you're still a child yourself—that's all. You know, Hassa, that I am always there for you—happy to be there. But I'm not only your lover . . . first of all I'm your wife."

Hassa tried not to hear these last words. "When you did not have a car and servants, you were not my wife. But now you are, and I have to look after you."

"Be that as it may." She was still sitting there, legs crossed, hands folded. "All that time I was still the daughter of a minister of the crown, and the fiancée of a prince."

"Your prince," laughed Hassa, "he's probably now an extra in Hollywood, playing eunuchs in Oriental films."

"You're a very stupid child," cried Asiadeh, gripping his ears and shaking his head. "You want to be my husband and my baby all at the same time. If you make me angry, I'll pour all the

cognac into your mouth. Then you'll have a headache tomorrow and won't be able to treat your singers."

"And if you make me angry," said Hassa, and put his hands
around her cheeks, "if you make me angry, I'll drag you into
the surgery and take your tonsils out. Then you can't talk for a
week and have to stay in bed. And it'll serve you right too."

"You're a brute." She laughed and let go. He fell back into
the pillows. She put the lights out. "Sleep," she said, and Hassa
slept, quietly, for he could not see into the future.

Asiadeh did not sleep. Thoughts were chasing one another
in her head, going round and round. Life seemed an enigma
with no possible solution. In the villages of Anatolia, in the
steppes of Turkestan, in the camps of faraway nomads, a
woman went once a year into the shrubs or into the black felt
tent. The men sat around the fire and prayed, and the woman
lay on the ground to give birth to a child. Then the men came,
cut the cord, and the child was there, kicking its feet, stretching
the little lips to its mother's breast. There was no servant in the
nomads' tent, and their car had four legs, a long snout, and was
called a camel.

She sighed. It was impossible to understand why a camel
should be more important than a child who kicked its legs and
called for its mother's breast. She closed her eyes. For a
moment she saw Marion's curved brows and the pale spiky eyes
of the man to whom she had been assigned. Then she slept.

TWENTY

"It is good that you are punctual, Hanum," said John Rolland, standing at the table on the hotel terrace. "Please be seated, Hanum." He moved his chair to the side and was extraordinarily polite and talkative. "You must know, Hanum, that with my friend I can talk only about the visible world. He is mute and deaf for the world of feeling. I will love you very much, Hanum, I have a great store of love that I have never wasted on anyone before."

Asiadeh did not reply. How strange that this man called her Hanum and had an unused fund of love.

"We will go soon," said Rolland, and there seemed to be a glimmer of tenderness in his dim eyes. "I have had a message today. My firm has ordered a film script from me: 'The Mistress of the Desert,' or something like that. They want me to collect impressions on location and therefore send me to Gadames in the Libyan desert. I would like not to go alone. Come with me. For two months we will sleep in tents, drink camels' milk, and live the life of the nomads. That will be our honeymoon. Then we will go to New York, and there you give birth to the first prince. Then we'll move to California, to a bungalow. You know, when the empire was shattered and the whole world collapsed, I believed that life had come to an end.

I don't remember anymore how I got to America. I was starving there. You know—to be starving is a very disagreeable experience. But I hardly noticed it. I thought there simply was no place in the world for me anymore. Later Sam picked me up. After that I was not hungry anymore, but there was still no meaning in my life. All that will be different now."

John talked, intoxicated by his own words. Yes, a man without a homeland had to dream, work, have headaches, and think of death. And women were noisy toys, worth much less than a bottle of good whiskey. But this one—who was not just a woman, no noisy toy—was a gift from heaven, of the lost homeland, to Prince Abdul-Kerim, a suddenly appearing support in the ocean of foreign life. The first Osmans had been nomads, wandering all over Asia before settling down. That was their mistake. A nomad has no homeland. The nomad's homeland is his tent. Wherever he puts it up—that's where his home is. Asiadeh would be his tent. "We will go away in a few days, Hanum, straight to Libya."

Asiadeh looked away. Libya, she thought—black nomad tents. And the first prince is to be born in New York. She made a tremendous effort and looked into Rolland's lean face. It seemed wonderfully beautiful. "Prince," she said, "I wrote to you from Berlin, offering you my humble love. You answered and disowned me forever. I have found another man, and he needs me. It is unfair of you to destroy another man's home after you have renounced your own. I cannot follow you."

She spoke softly, looking straight into his eyes. John blushed violently. His eyes widened and glittered.

"I wrote to you but did not know you. It is not unfair to destroy other houses. All the present is built from the ruins of the past. Fatih Mohamed destroyed Byzantium and built Istanbul. Without the ruins of Byzantium there would never have been an Osman Empire. Who is your husband? An unbeliever who does not value what he owns. I'm sure of it. You will always be strangers to each other. And I, I love you."

So spoke Rolland, who did not know about the night in the park, or what had happened later when she was sitting on Hassa's bed, when Hassa was drinking cognac and talking of Marion.

Asiadeh smiled weakly. Really, life was too difficult for a woman from Istanbul.

"I am not your subject," she said in a hard voice. "You have formally disowned me. I am now an Austrian, the wife of an Austrian, and later, God willing, the mother of Austrians. It is too late, Prince. Warriors destroy other people's houses, but they do not ask their women to help them. And my husband is not an unbeliever. He is a master of life and death and comes from a pious family in Sarajevo."

She fell silent. Rolland's face had become gray and his cheeks hollow, his temples wrinkled, his eyes dim, proud, and alien. Asiadeh looked at him, and his whole life passed before her eyes.

He was an exile, a beggar. Like a rudderless boat, he drifted about in the world. Once he had been living in the confined spaces of the palace on the Bosphorus, virtually a prisoner who did not know anything about the world outside. He was naked in this foreign world, a naked man, asking for clothing. All the weakness of the old tribe was in him. Suddenly she was full of love and pity. She bent toward him, took his hand, and said:

"Abdul-Kerim, I cannot, I must not. Canst thou not understand? Perhaps I love thee, Abdul-Kerim, but now I cannot come to thee."

He looked at her, mutely questioning.

"Wait." She did not know anymore what she was saying. She

was gripping his hand, feeling herself driven by a mysterious alien will. "Wait," she repeated and, overwhelmed by a sad, blinding vision, cried in passionate despair: "Perhaps my husband will disown me. Then I will come to thee, Abdul-Kerim. I cannot destroy my house."

Now Rolland laughed. He took his hand away and sat in his chair, straight as a ramrod.

"Marvelous, Hanum. The holy House of Osman must wait until a dog of an unbeliever has the idea of disowning his wife. You love me, you do, you want to come to me. I can read the signs of loving in your eyes, your hands, your lips. You loved me when your boat passed my house on the Bosphorus. You loved me when you wrote to me from Berlin, and you love me now, sitting here in front of me. It is your duty to love me. But you are a coward, Hanum. You are just a coward, and no Osman should be anything but brave."

Asiadeh did not answer. It took great courage to be silent now.

John rose. "I am your slave, Hanum," he said in the polite rhythm of the Istanbul palace.

"Go with a smile, Prince." Mechanically Asiadeh's lips formed the prescribed sentence. She remained sitting there, her shoulders drawn up, her eyes looking into the far distance.

Abdul-Kerim went across the hall and up the hotel staircase. Even on the stairs he became again John Rolland, an alcoholic scriptwriter who was about to collect impressions for his next film in Libya. He came into his room. Sam Dooth sat in an easy chair, looking up curiously. On the side table stood a virgin whiskey bottle. Last night John Rolland had not been thirsty. Now he went to the table, took a tumbler, filled it with whiskey, and drained it in one go.

"Oh," said Sam, and knew everything.

"I am a dog." John filled his glass for the second time. "My ancestors conquered two continents, and I cannot even conquer one single woman." He sat down on the bed. The glass trembled in his hand. "I don't need a woman," he said abruptly. "I don't need a home. I need whiskey."

He drank again, and Sam said again, "Oh." The he drank too, in small sips, and not from a tumbler.

"Now John will become quite mad," he thought.

"What'd you need that special woman for?" he said. "There's millions of them. I'll get you a slave in Africa. Let's go to Libya. Europe is no place for you."

John stared into his glass. "Let's go to Libya," he said suddenly. "If you're a drunkard, you don't need a woman, or two continents, or a palace on the Bosphorus." He began to undress. "I'm going to bed, Sam. Go! Send a telegram to the pasha in Berlin and tell him he brought his daughter up badly. Very badly."

Sam got up and shook his head disapprovingly. Impossible to imagine how John's ancestors had ever managed to conquer Byzantium.

"Go to sleep," he said. "It is not my job to look after a prince's harem, but I'll take the matter in hand because I am a good fellow and forgive you the destruction of Byzantium. The whole thing is quite ridiculous. I'll straighten it up within three days."

He left, and John threw himself on the bed.

Sam Dooth went to a café near the Opera and sat there for quite a time, sipping Turkish coffee. Nobody who saw him sitting there would have guessed that he was working feverishly.

Sam Dooth was a clever man. It was his ambition to show John that a Greek succeeds where an Osman fails. Holding a ten-schilling note negligently in his hand, he looked very bored when the headwaiter bowed before him. And he learned all about Hassa: his age, past, habits, and circle of friends. After which he put the ten-schilling note back into his pocket and thanked the headwaiter politely. Then he strolled to the table where the surgeon Matthess was quarreling with the orthopedist Sachs about the differences between surgical and orthopedic treatment, and introduced himself: "Sam Dooth, film agent from New York."

The doctors were visibly flattered, and Sam sat down. With a superior smile he told them that his firm planned to make films about medicine for the use of schools.

"I came to Vienna because we want to make the scientific part under the supervision of Viennese doctors."

The doctors listened, greatly interested, and felt they were being drawn into the whirl of the Great World. It was impossible to put one's finger on the exact spot at which the conversation turned to doctors in general, from there to laryngology, and finally to Dr. Hassa's private life.

After they had talked for an hour, Sam Dooth rose and thanked them in a significant way. "We'll get together about the films," he mentioned.

The following morning he went to the phone booth and dialed Hassa's flat. "The maharajah of Travenkor here," he panted into the receiver. "There's a terrible humming in my ears. When can I see the Herr Doktor?"

"Herr Doktor is in the hospital and will be back in three hours' time."

Gratified, Sam put the receiver down and went to Hassa's flat. He found Asiadeh alone, squatting on the couch in the corner of the drawing room. He bowed. Asiadeh's lips were slightly swollen, her cheeks pale.

"God preserve this house!" he said ceremoniously.

"While you do everything to destroy it!"

"I serve my master," said Sam emphatically. His eyes became big and dark. "Many Osmans have gone to their deaths by the hands of murderers, but only very rarely was the murderer a woman."

"I'm no murderer." Asiadeh jumped up and ran about in the room. Her lips trembled. "I did not call you! I too do my duty. I'm the wife of my husband."

Sam looked at her calmly and declared that duty had two sides: fear of responsibility and lack of imagination. If the Turks had stayed the Arabs' faithful mercenaries, as their duty told them, they never would have gained their great and greatly feared name.

Asiadeh came to a stop in the middle of the room, her mouth open. "But I don't want a great and greatly feared name for myself! Leave me alone!"

Sam smiled sadly. "Abdul-Kerim's brother, father, and grandfather died in very sad circumstances. He is searching for a helping hand, and you throw him into an abyss. You are no better than those who drove his ancestors to their deaths."

Asiadeh cowered on the cushions, crying silently with open mouth.

"I can't," she said, tortured. "Can't you see that I can't?"

She wiped off her tears and said suddenly in a hard voice: "Effendi, if a woman who has herself chosen her husband and has sworn to be faithful to him—if such a woman leaves her husband without any reason except that she prefers a rich foreigner—what do you call such a woman? There are very bad words that describe such a woman, Effendi. The law says: 'In this visible world the woman should be stoned, and in the Great Beyond be exposed to eternal ruin.' A man from the

House of the Khaliphs should have mercy for a woman and not drive her to ruin."

Sam jumped up. This Turk was obstinate.

"Hanum," he cried, "you are a saint. I bow deeply before your moral integrity. I honor it. Not another word. But I too have my duty, and I will do it."

His hands became fists, his face flushed.

"Stay here—but know with whom you are staying. Dr. Hassa is a man who is ashamed of his ancestors and repudiates them. A man whose scientific training ends with pouring cocaine down singers' throats. Every doctor in Vienna is laughing at him. When he was a student, he had a mistress. When she was expecting his child, he left her. His first wife left him, disgusted with his stupidity and obstinacy. He had to leave this town for years because the children in the street were pointing their fingers at him. Do you know who his father was? A Balkan racketeer who gathered his riches from the blood of his brothers. And for this man you sacrifice John Rolland. Truly, women are not human. They have only the outer shape of human beings."

The tears had disappeared from Asiadeh's eyes. She stood there laughing. Her eyes glittered, her whole body was shaking with laughter. She inclined her head sideways and said in a broken voice: "Oh yes, and apart from that, he was in jail because he had robbed a bank. He keeps giving out counterfeit checks and was found not guilty of murder only because of lack of evidence. That's that, and now will you please take your hat and go!"

She turned and left the room.

Furiously Sam wobbled across the Ring. The battle was not finished yet, not by a long way. He ran to the telegraph office. Frowning, he wrote out a long telegram, mixing citations from the Koran with pleadings and good advice.

Meanwhile, Asiadeh walked about in town. She passed streets, shops, cafés. All men in the cafés had Rolland's eyes, and the dummies in the windows of gentlemen's attire had princely figures and Osman noses. The Ring Hotel looked like a malevolently lurking animal, and she made a wide detour to avoid it.

At home, dinner was awaiting her. Hassa ate his soup and talked of Backhendln and of a strudel that only his mother knew how to bake. Asiadeh listened attentively and told him about baklava, a Turkish honey dish served with coffee.

In the afternoon, while Hassa was in the surgery, the maid brought her a telegram: "Know all. Service to ruler first commandment. Achmed-Pasha." Asiadeh folded the telegram again. That was all she needed! She felt like a fortress in the frontline, shelled by heavy artillery.

"I'm going for a walk," she told Hassa, and he nodded. "Listen," she said, "what would you do if I never came back?"

"I could never laugh again." Hassa looked at her timidly.

"But I'm coming back, quite certainly I'm coming back. At home, in Istanbul, somebody always had to accompany a woman to make sure she really did come back. But nobody need watch me. I'm coming back."

She went to the telegraph office and sent two identical telegrams, one to John Rolland and one to Achmed-Pasha: "Cannot. Asiadeh."

Then she strolled about in town. On the terrace of the café on the Stephans Platz, she saw Marion. She was about to turn away when she remembered that she had nearly—very nearly!—done exactly what Marion had done, and that she had despised her for it.

Suddenly she felt pity and sympathy for Marion. Smiling,

she nodded at her, and Marion returned the greeting, amazed, if a little grandly.

Asiadeh went home, passing the hotel.

Up there Sam was packing suitcases.

"We'll go to Rome, John. Women always meant trouble for your family. From Rome we go by plane to Tripoli, and then to Gadames, and do some work. You'll have to write a good film or they won't pay us."

John nodded. "Don't put the typewriter into the suitcase, Sam. I'll start working on the train. What do they drink in Italy? I've never been there."

Sam closed the suitcases. "Italy is nearly as beautiful as Greece," he declared weightily. "They drink wine there. But in Tripoli they have liquors made from dates. Very good. So let's get on with it, John."

They left the hotel.

TWENTY-ONE

T he aquaplane lay in the port of Ostia like a bus at its stop. The pilot, his face strained with concentration, was testing engine and propellers. Everything was okay, the propellers whirred, the engine trembled steadily.

John took his place at a window and pressed the long tube of the ventilator. The other travelers were in their seats too; it reminded John of a dentist's waiting room. The doors closed. White waves beat against the thick glass of the window. Suddenly they became smaller and flatter and then sank down, down, as if at first they had clamored for attention, wanting to say goodbye, but then had been tamed by the whirring propeller.

Before Rolland's eyes, the Ostia beach spread out with its bathing cabins, the Beach Hotel, and the enormous Halls of the Littoria. Abruptly the plane rose.

"Bismillahi, Rahmani, Rahim—in the name of God, the all-merciful, the all-forgiving," whispered Rolland, and was astonished to find this sudden fear of God in his heart. He opened the ventilator tube. Air beat on his face, blowing his black hair from his forehead. So now he would have to spend many hours in this seat next to the window, pressed into a box that hovered between Europe and Africa. Silently he sat there, pressing his face to the window. The noise of the propeller drowned any conversation.

It was good just to lean against the window, quiet and alone, weakly surrendering to the thoughts that had driven him from New York to the desert, then again to the strong severity of towns, and were now chasing him across the sea to the faraway coast of the barbarians. Deep down the wind was tearing the soft folds of the clouds.

White rags were drifting across the flat, unmoving blue of the sea, and the plane's shadow was gliding over it like a big bird.

Training his eyes, John looked to the left. There, behind the wide line of the horizon, Istanbul was hiding. Ahead, clouds covered the coast of Africa.

The Mediterranean was spread out before John's eyes—a magic ring, embracing past and present. He felt that, from the beginning of time, all centuries were mirrored on this blue surface, and that these centuries had become part of him, united with him, ruling him.

He was a nomad, an exile, chasing after an unknown aim. His home? He did not know anymore where his home was. The waters of the Bosphorus? The same waters were down here, before his eyes. The palace? There were better houses in the world, richer and more beautiful, and all open to him.

What he had lost when he had crossed the great water and come to Manhattan's stony splendor was his serenity, his security, his mystic aim in life. He was empty inside, completely empty. The rooms where he lived, the streets he passed, the houses he saw: They were just soulless structures meaning nothing to him. Life was a drab succession of eating and working, for he was expelled from the enigmatic ring of fate, to which he belonged, and for which he was born.

Sometimes it overcame him—while working, in a restaurant, during a conversation: a silhouette, a word, a profile, quite without coherence—and the emptiness arose in him, attacked him, strangled him like a malevelent insatiable nightmare. And as the pain would become unbearable, he would flee into the outward aim of life: into the new name, the new passport—but with the vague knowledge that these were worthless trimmings only, easier to throw off than a new shirt, a new suit. Then he would hate his new life, the straight narrow avenues of New York, the majestic line of the skyscrapers. Then the faraway lines of his lost world would flutter before his eyes, then he breathed the salty air of the Bosphorus and the dry intoxication that came from the desert with the sand that crunched under his feet.

Again John pressed his forehead against the window. Down, far down, the blue shape of Vesuvius disappeared, the Bay of Naples stretched into the soft green of the coast.

"I race from one pain to another," thought John, and remembered the white houses of Morocco, the wide courtyard of the khaliph's palace, and the tearing pain that had engulfed him at the sight of the white-swathed ruler with the dark dreaming eyes. This world of insatiable longings—it too was filled with masks and demons. Every touch of the Western world drove him back to the lost glory of the past. Every touch with a fragment of the old world, every memory of the past brought on new pain, new tortures of helplessness and inescapable fate.

John sighed. It was good to sit in a big plane, suspended between these two worlds that kept creating new pains and new tortures.

Most of his fellow travelers were asleep, and the two pilots looked bored; one of them was leafing through some journals.

Sam Dooth slept, his face covered with a newspaper. On one wall was a poster showing a hotel and a road through green meadows that looked like the ones on the way to the Semmering. John saw before his inner eye the girl who had driven into his car and stamped her foot. He felt a strange warmth and again opened the ventilator, greedily breathing in the cold sea air. Suddenly it was good that Asiadeh was in the world, a being who, like himself, was cast between two worlds and yet could remain gay and steadfast in the loose sheath of terrestrial happiness.

"I should just take her," thought John tiredly, and felt the accustomed emptiness rise up in himself. His limbs became heavy. It really did not matter whether he was here, above the Meditarranean, in New York, or in the desert.

John stretched out his feet. He was genuinely astonished to see that it was not Asiadeh sitting opposite him, but a strange sleeping gray-haired woman.

Outside, on the horizon, the yellow stripe of the barbarian's coast appeared. John pressed his hands to his temples. Behind the yellow stripe was the great desert, with minarets that would drill into his soul like lances. A stranger he was in New York, and a stranger he would be here, in this world of sand.

Gracefully gliding, the plane descended. The ancient castle and white square houses of Tripoli appeared. Then the plane touched water, waves, and foam glittered in Africa's sun. John's face stiffened.

"Where have you booked?"

Sam Dooth rose and took fat wads of cotton wool from his ears. "In the Grand Hotel," he croaked.

They went across the landing stage to the waiting car. Before them rose the tower of the Karemanli Mosque. Disdainfully,

John looked away. There was no home for a wanderer between two worlds . . .

In the big hall of the hotel stood black servants wearing snow-white trousers. On the terrace, protected from the blazing sun, colonial officers were lunching. The palm tree-lined promenade went up to the ancient castle, and along it wandered camels, donkeys, Arabs, and veiled women. Sam Dooth vanished quickly toward the Government Palace.

John was alone in the big hall, with its vaults and pillars, which made it look vaguely like a temple. He rose and went to the reception desk. The hall porter was a dark-skinned man with big, sad eyes.

"This is a beautiful country," said John.

"Very beautiful," said the hall porter. "Will you travel farther inland?"

"Yes."

"You will see many things. Go to the oasis Zliten. There is the grave of the holy Sisi Abdessalam. Or into the Djebel Mountains. The people who live there in underground caverns follow the law of the holy Ibad. In the oases of the Sahara you will see new wells and new houses. Water is flowing over the desert, and it begins to blossom. Even in Djarabub there is a new well."

"Djarabub?" said John. "I used to get my dates from there."

The hotel porter looked astonished. Dates from Djarabub had once been the tithe of the oasis to the House of Osman.

John blushed. "But I'm not going to Djarabub, I'm going to Gadames."

"That's where the tribe of the Tarki live, and where the women rule the men. Once it took three weeks to get there. Now it's just three days."

"When did it take three weeks?"

"Well, in former times, under the Osmans."

"Oh," said John, and his eyes became small slits. Then he asked for a telegram form and wrote:

"Asiadeh Hassa, Vienna. Going to Gadames, where women rule the men. If you want to rule, come."

Sam Dooth appeared, dripping with sweat and smiling broadly. "Tomorrow the desert bus goes to Gadames. Everything beautifully organized. Hotels all the way. Marvelous roads." He looked at John's blanching face and giggled.

They lunched and dined on the hotel terrace; they walked about in the town and saw the narrow bazaar alleys and natives sitting on their doorsteps, drinking tea. The sea lay quiet, like a sheet, the hot desert wind—the Gibli—blew from the Sahara, and little grains of sand crunched under their feet. Negroes with robust faces and upturned lips passed by on horseback, their daggers glittering in the setting sun.

The bus waiting for them the next morning was a double-decker, had a dining room, a bar, and a radio. John sat down at the bar. A waltz sounded from the radio. Palm trees grew along the road, camels ran across it, and a white-robed man with sun-glasses waved to them.

Small square buildings, decorated with many-colored flags, rose on gray hills. Sand was crunching under the wheels of the bus. The country was flat and plain. A yellow sky arched threateningly over the yellow sand, the yellow sun hung over the land like a glowing torch. From time to time ghostly oases, palms, and wells appeared on the horizon—the Fata Morgana, unreally luminous in the burning air. Far away rose the jagged fallow rocks of the Djebel. Scorching heat flooded over the desert, all visible forms dissolved in the parched sands. From time to time strange hills could be seen by the roadside, or a puddle of water—a water island in the sea of sand.

Mehari—slender riding camels—passed by, with the dread of the great desert in their eyes. Veiled men stood at the outskirts of oases, and the radio played a waltz.

Then came the night. Suddenly, without warning, the sun disappeared. Stars hung in clusters over the desert. The bus stopped in front of a small hotel. Weakly John fell into his bed, and the last things he saw at the window were the long shadows of palm trees and a veiled child, looking up fearfully at the stranger.

And again day came, again the yellow sun hung over the desert. On the hills stood desert policemen who looked indifferently at the slowly passing bus. High up in the sky hung a government plane, yellow and unmoving. John looked at it and thought of the Mediterranean, the sea that divides and unites two worlds. Up there in the sky the pilot looked at the bus and thought of the wind that came up each midday, and of the government of Libya, which had sent him to a faraway oasis because a sheik had fallen ill and needed medicine.

And in the Castello, the ancient building on the seafront, the government thought of the sick sheik, of the pilot and the bus traveling to Gadames.

Many things the government of Libya thought about: Somewhere in the Tunisian Sahara, typhus was raging. The pilgrim caravans were knocking at closed borders. The men of the Tarki tribe wore their hair in long plaits, an ideal breeding ground for typhus lice. The government of Libya had to think of everything: how to get the men of the Tarki tribe to cut off their plaits, how to stop child marriages in the oases, and how to get water from the dry sands of the Sahara.

Paper flooded the government's desks, and the government knew everything: that in the oasis Mitsurata a woman had had an illegitimate child and wanted to declare it legitimate, that

Negroes from inner Africa wanted to settle at a well near the Egyptian border, that in faraway oases trachoma raged, the curse of Africa.

The government knew of white, yellow, brown, and black peoples in the desert, and it knew of the American company that wanted to make a film in the desert. And it also knew of John Rolland, who was traveling by bus across the Sahara, and knew that his real name was Prince Abdul-Kerim. All this the government knew, and the telegraphist of Gadames, the officers of the garrison, the hall porters of all the hotels—they all knew that Abdul-Kerim, prince of the House of Osman, was traveling to Gadames, that the government knew about him and honored his silence.

All this the government knew, all of what was happening in the oases of Libya. But of what was happening in Vienna the government did not know, and did not care either.

It was a matter of supreme indifference to the government of Libya that a woman bought a large book called *The Wonders of the Sahara* in a big shop on the Graben, and that this woman then sat at home in the drawing room with the bow windows, bent over the atlas, her finger following the road from Tripoli to the rocks of Djebel, across the oasis Nablus and the castle Tguta. The woman bent deeply aver the atlas when her finger found Gadames, the pearl of the Sahara. Later the woman leafed through the book, and a telegram lay in the wastepaper basket, crumpled and torn.

All this the government of Libya neither knew nor cared about, and John Rolland did not know it either. He sat near the radio in the bar of the double-decker bus. Dry wind beat on the windows, dead sand whirled in the desert air, a scorching sun was hanging in the yellow sky. Once the regiments of the House of Osman had battled here in the wilderness of the

Sahara, but it was better not to think about that, for the stones were dead and mute, and the palms of Gadames appeared on the horizon like green moss, stretching their branches up to the yellow sky.

The bus drove around an old well and stopped abruptly. A man with a veiled face and laughing eyes came from a hole in the wall and took their suitcases. John followed him, and Sam followed John. Palm trees grew around a square. In the middle stood a long, low, reddish-pink house, with beautifully soft outlines: Hotel Ain-al-Fras.

John went in, and the servant took the suitcases to their rooms. As John passed the reception desk, the clerk asked: "Mr. John Rolland?"

Astonished, John nodded.

"A telegram for you, sir."

He put it into his pocket and went into the small garden, where the earth smelled of fire in the scorching heat of midday. There he read: "Am only a woman, don't want to rule over men. Asiadeh."

John folded the telegram and left the garden. The room was yellow, like the sand. Somewhere was a town called Vienna, and somewhere was a woman called Asiadeh, but everything was distant and flickering, like sand wafted about by the desert wind.

TWENTY-TWO

D r. Kurz was making the rounds in his sanatorium. Everything was as it should be: corpulent Romanian ladies sat in the recreation room playing bridge; a nervous author was leafing through newspapers and complaining about a headache; a crowd of elderly patients was sitting on the balcony, passionately arguing about schizophrenia and diabetes; in the long avenues of the garden, melancholics were sitting on the benches, quarreling about suicide. Kurz smiled amicably and understandingly. He prescribed vinegar massages for the melancholics and a modern diet for nerve cases. For women who suffered from depressions, he prescribed entertainment and male company. He had done that for years with very good results. Women were like children, only much easier to treat. As an expert nerve specialist, he had had his experiences: Any woman could be conquered, but not every one was worth the trouble.

Dr. Kurz finished his rounds and returned to his study. Oh yes, one could have any woman. It was like a mathematical equation with several unknown factors. Kurz sat down at his desk and spoke into the telephone: "Nurse, I am now busy with scientific research and not to be disturbed by anyone."

Then he crossed his legs and lit a cigarette. The scientific research was called Asiadeh.

"A beautiful women," thought Kurz, "a desirable woman." His fingertips pricked agreeably. The instinct of an experienced nerve specialist told him that a crisis was developing in Hassa's marriage. Hassa himself had no idea, of course. Husbands never did. But Kurz sensed a marital crisis by imperceptible signs of everyday life. By Asiadeh nodding her head, by small suppressed smiles, by the trembling of her lashes—by all that Kurz noticed, the secret signs of an inner conflict. Another man? Kurz shook his head. No other man was anywhere near Asiadeh. "The woman is just bored," diagnosed Kurz contentedly. "Without knowing it, she is longing for an adventure."

Kurz picked up the telephone. Eight times he dialed a number, eight times he smiled at the invisible person at the other end, and eight times he repeated:

"My dear chap, I'm having a little party on Saturday. No, nothing special. Hassa will be there, and Sachs and Matuschek. Yes, the *gnädige* Frau too, of course. Yes, dinner jacket. I'm looking forward to seeing you." On Saturday at half past eight, Asiadeh came into Kurz's brightly lit flat in the Rathaus quarter. Hassa was by her side, the stiff collar pressing on his neck, the starched shirt arching out on his breast. Asiadeh saw highly polished furniture and an open cupboard with a battery of bottles.

The big room was filled with blue cigarette smoke that, notwithstanding the bright lights, turned the guests' faces into those of mysterious veiled strangers. Words hovered in the air like little gray birds. "A cocktail," cried Kurz, and Hassa took the glass. Women were sitting in wide easy chairs, their shoulders naked, their eyes glittering. Asiadeh looked into the mirror: She too was painted, and her shoulders were exposed to people's glances. Outwardly there was nothing to distinguish her from those women who had several husbands and were drinking cocktails.

The men stood like statues with glasses in their hands. Their words sounded unreal, foreign, ghostly. A woman with a severe profile, her eyebrows drawn together as if in pain, sat in a corner talking about the theater, making it sound as if she was telling secrets.

"It really was too much," she said, "did you see the show?" "No," said a young man, making a sweeping gesture, "but there's a book about it. Have you read it?" "No." It was not clear to Asiadeh whether these two were talking to each other. The guests looked like disciples of an unknown sect, performing an ancient ritual. Their movements seemed to have some magic significance. They emptied their glasses silently, they swam in a haze of tobacco smoke, silhouettes in a shadow play. Sometimes they all fell silent at the same time and looked at each other, conspirators at a midnight meeting.

"The stock exchange," said a man with a big bald pate, and raised his finger meaningfully. "The pulse of economy, the barometer of public life. That is something one must have experienced. In Paris or in London." He paused, his finger still raised. No one was listening.

"Yes," said Asiadeh timidly, and went to sit in a corner. Maids in white aprons were offering plates of sandwiches, many-colored and angular, like pieces of mosaic. Asiadeh nibbled at one while a doctor at her side told her about Geneva. "Consilium," he said, and looked around like a victor. "Switzerland is only beautiful in winter," someone breathed.

"Do you know St. Moritz or Arosa? I was staying at the Tschuggen Hotel last year."

"No," said Asiadeh, and was ashamed that she had never stayed at the Tschuggen Hotel. "I'm afraid of snow. Cold is the messenger of death." Two eyes looked at her pityingly through the tobacco haze. An immense crystal bowl was brought in, filled with cold punch—a big frangant cauldron. The guests stood around it like swimmers before the start. An enormous silver spoon glittered in Dr. Kurz's hand. The guests' faces became flushed, their voices louder.

"The problem of the Mediterranean has not been solved yet, not by any means," someone said, sounding very superior.

A little man polished his glasses and cried imperiously: "The woman of today will tomorrow be the woman of yesterday."

And people laughed, feeling frightened.

After her eighth sandwich, Asiadeh rose and walked around the flat. Men and women were sitting in dark corners, closely huddled together. A man wearing a creased shirt sat alone on a divan, holding his head. Two women had squeezed Hassa into a corner. He held a glass of punch in his hand and raised it to Asiadeh. She nodded gaily.

Dr. Kurz stood next to her.

"How are you, *gnädige* Frau?" He pretended she had never run away from him on the Semmering.

"Very well, thank you." Asiadeh thought of the Semmering and had a very bad conscience.

She walked along with Kurz and stood suddenly in an empty room, where a puzzling picture confronted her.

"A genuine van Gogh," said Kurz. "Do you sense the dry intoxication of the lines?"

Asiadeh did not. She saw a canvas covered with many-colored spots and nodded reverently.

"You'll be able to see it better like this." He switched off the lamps, leaving only an indirect light to shine on the picture. Asiadeh sat down on a soft chair. She raised her head and again stared at the canvas. Nothing. The picture just bored her. The room was empty, but a whiff of perfume lingered in it. Loud laughter came from the next room. "What do you do with yourself all day long, Asiadeh?" Kurz's voice had an intimate ring.

"I read about Africa."

"Africa?" Kurz was really interested. Women who read about Africa could not possibly lead a happy married life.

"Yes." Asiadeh became suddenly very animated. "About the Sahara. It is a strange country. It must be very beautiful. Have you ever heard about Gadames?"

"No." Kurz was genuinely astonished.

"It is an oasis in the heart of the Sahara, around the holy well of Ain-ul-Fras. Only seven thousand people live there, but they have many castes. There are the noble Ahrar, the Berber Hamran, the black Atara, and the Habid, the former slaves."

"Really," said Dr. Kurz, "a faraway oasis in the desert. So that's what you read about. Do they have women there too?"

"Oh yes, there are women. They live on the roofs, and all roofs are joined together. No man is ever allowed on the roofs, and no woman is allowed on the streets. And they live in rooms between roofs and streets, so that's where men and women meet. A strange world. Sometimes I feel I've been there."

"A strange country," Kurz repeated. He was standing in front of her in the semidark room. Suddenly he bent forward.

"Asiadeh," he said, "not only in Gadames. Here too people are separated from each other by roofs and streets. Much more strictly than in Gadames. There is no road from one soul to another. Loneliness is the fate of man. There in the Sahara, or here in the petrified wood of the big town."

He bent very close to Asiadeh and whispered:

"The woman is lonely in her marriage bed, and the wanderer is lonely in the world of everyday. Seldom only, very seldom, like the stroke of lightning in a miracle . . ." He did not go on. He gripped Asiadeh's head, he pressed his lips on hers. She recoiled violently. He drew her up to him, his hands clutching her body. He pressed her head to his chest, and his hot breath touched her neck.

Suddenly Asiadeh threw her head upward. Kurz looked into wildly glittering eyes. Asiadeh's hand grabbed his throat. With one savage jerk she jumped up, her knees digging into his stomach. The raging eyes turned into slits. Suddenly she whistled, short and sharp, like a bird of prey. Her teeth caught something soft and strange. Terror-stricken, Kurz tried to move back. He dragged at the small wild body that was hanging on to him as if with talons. He tore at her shoulders, petrified with fear. Without uttering a word they fought in the semidarkness of the perfumed room. There was nothing human in Asiadeh anymore. It was with the hatred of a savage animal that she bit into the strange thing in her mouth. She felt a salty taste. Kurz staggered and nearly fell.

Abruptly she let him go. She stood, head bent forward, wiping her lips with her handkerchief. A wide ribbon of blood ran over Kurz's face. He sank exhausted into an easy chair, looking green and completely shattered.

Asiadeh left without a word. She came into the brightly lit next room, her eyes still like slits in her white face.

A big glass of punch stood on the table. She took it up and emptied it straightaway. For the first time in her life she tasted alcohol—she felt a thousand fiery lances drilling inside her body.

So these things really did happen—in real life! One of her husband's friends looked at her with the eyes of lust. She stepped in front of the mirror. She felt soiled, all of her, her body and her soul, soiled and dirtied. The other guests' faces were turning cartwheels before her eyes. Someone laughed—it seemed the howl of a hyena at midnight. She walked on, her bloodstained handkerchief in her closed fist.

Hassa was sitting on a divan in the next room. "On the other hand, one could have a general narcosis," he was saying, "but of course only with the head hanging down."

She beckoned to him. He stood up at once and followed her. She did not say a word. She thought she could guess what would happen if she spoke. Hassa was standing there, broad and strong in his wonderful readiness to protect her. She forgot the prince and the faraway oasis in the Sahara. Hassa was there, her husband. Something terrible would happen, but she could not stay silent any longer.

"Hassa," she said, "my lord and master. Your friend who invited us to this house broke the bond of hospitality. He enticed me into an empty room and tried to rape me. I think I have bitten his ear off. Go, Hassa, kill him."

She spoke hastily in a hoarse voice. Hassa looked at her, frightened and astonished.

"What's the matter, Asiadeh?" He saw the bloodstained handkerchief in her hand. "What's that blood?"

"I think I've bitten his ear off. You must kill him now, Hassa—go—kill!" Her voice sounded husky, greedy for revenge.

She stood there, delicate and lonely, her hands hanging down, and repeated, in dark ecstasy: "Kill him, Hassa, kill him!"

"You've bitten his ear off? My God, what a wild girl you are!" Hassa did not know what to think, so he just grinned.

"I should have bitten into his throat, but I'm only a woman. Kill him, Hassa, he has insulted me."

Hassa's grin became wider and wider. He had had a lot to drink that night. The idea of his wife biting his colleague's ear off seemed absolutely grotesque to him.

"I'll go. But don't look at me like that, it makes me quite afraid of you."

He walked through the rooms of the flat. The perfumed chamber where the van Gogh hung on the wall was empty. At last he found Kurz in his white surgery, his shirtsleeves rolled up, trying to put a bandage on his ear.

"Your Angora kitten has scratched me a bit," he said, embarrassed.

Hassa shook his head. "Nerve specialists have no idea of bandaging," he said disgustedly. "Come here, I'll do it for you."

He washed and bandaged the wound professionally.

"That's a wild woman you've got there," complained Kurz, obviously appeased. "She really ravaged me. How can I face my patients now?"

"Serves you right," said Hassa, playing with the surgical scissors. "You shouldn't molest strange women."

"What do you mean—molest?" Kurz's voice sounded quite indignant. "What has she told you? We were standing in the van Gogh room, and I explained the picture to her. Perhaps I was in a rather gay mood. While I was talking, I put my hand on her shoulder or touched her face—I don't really remember. Suddenly she springs at me—I can tell you, like a wildcat, like a little fury. You don't really believe that of me, Hassa, do you, that I'll try to seduce a women when there are twenty people in the next room. Ridiculous. Really—I and other people's wives! Ridiculous! I've got enough on my plate with my hysterical patients. By the way—tomorrow I'll send you a case—a rich Polish woman with nervous complaints. Probably reflex-neurosis."

Hassa laughed. Kurz was a harmless creature, and Asiadeh had her harem ideas about behaving in society. Orientals were just different, that was all. He felt quite sorry for Kurz.

And while Hassa dressed the wound and talked about the reflex-neurosis of the rich Polish woman, Asiadeh was sitting on a broad divan in the next room, and a man with a vague face told her all about modern English writing: "The whole tragedy and the whole absurdity of life is contained in Galsworthy," he said.

"Yes," answered Asiadeh, and looked at the closed door. There, behind the wall, something dreadful must be happening. Why could she hear no cries? Perhaps Hassa had strangled him, or beaten his skull in with a hammer, and the enemy had sunk down without a sound. Any second now there should be a dreadful cry. Or? Asiadeh's heart stopped beating—or it was the other who was the victor, and Hassa was now lying in a pool of blood in the perfumed room? But that was impossible. Hassa was stronger than Kurz, and certainly more courageous. And surely God was on Hassa's side.

The door opened, and Asiadeh's breath stopped.

"Since Oscar Wilde, the literature of England has become earthier and more meaningful. One feels the striving for reality, and therefore the preference for biographies and reports."

"Oh!" said Asiadeh.

Hassa and Kurz stood in the door, side by side. Kurz's left cheek was bandaged. "A little mishap." He gave an embarrassed laugh. "I slipped with a glass of champagne in my hand, the glass broke and cut my ear. Nothing, really. Colleague Hassa gave me first aid."

Asiadeh rose and walked toward them. Kurz was suddenly small and unimportant. Hassa stood before her; he took her arm and led her to the window. She looked up to him and felt her lips trembling. "You did not kill him, Hassa? You let your wife be insulted? But you are my husband, Hassa. Must I take my revenge into my own hands?"

"You already have, my child." Hassa spoke jokingly, a bit diffidently. "You are a good woman, and I can trust you. But we're not in Asia here. If I killed every man who wants to be nice to you when he's had a few, I'd become a mass murderer. After all, we are all civilized Europeans, aren't we?"

Kurz came to join them. His voice sounded humble.

"*Gnädige* Frau," he said, "I am terribly sorry. I think I was a bit befuddled, and you a bit nervous. Please do forgive me, I had completely forgotten that you are a lady of the harem. Here in Europe we are not so fussy when we are in a happy mood."

Asiadeh did not answer. She looked into the big mirror: There were her legs, her arms, her naked shoulders. There was her face with soft lips and gray eyes. All that belonged to Hassa, the unbeliever, who could not protect his wife. Shame and sorrow overwhelmed her. What could a woman expect when she had a civilized husband who surrendered all of her to strangers' glances?

"Next time I go to a party," she said, "I will be covered in veils and hide my face. Perhaps I will be safe then. Come, Hassa."

They went. Kurz saw them to the door. "I am a nerve specialist for Europeans only," he thought, "my learning ends at the gates of Istanbul."

Without speaking, the two got into the car and drove away.

"You do have rather a temperament, haven't you, Asiadeh?" said Hassa. "Remember when you boxed my ears?"

"You think I should have made love to your friend?"

"But my dear child, one doesn't bite, not anymore."

Asiadeh did not reply. Hassa was suddenly terribly alien and far away. The trellises around the park were like ghosts surrounding threatening darkness. The broad Ringstrasse was framed by sinister, brooding houses. And the men and women who lived in these houses were wild and unfeeling in their confused minds.

Asiadeh thought of her father, who would have thrust a knife into the strangers' eyes that had seen her, and cut off the lips that had kissed her.

"Are you angry, Asiadeh?" Hassa's hand touched her arm. "We won't ever go to Kurz again if you don't want to."

"No," said Asiadeh. She was ashamed of her husband, ashamed of the world she was living in, of the way of life she could not understand. The car stopped, and they went up to their flat. Hassa was no coward, Asiadeh knew that. His hands were strong, his glance straight. Why did he not strangle the enemy, or at least punish him in some way? He would never laugh again if she betrayed him, yet he did not revenge her. He simply did not want to. He had no urge to throw the enemy on the ground, to see blood spurting from his eyes—those eyes that had dared to desire his own wedded wife.

Asiadeh looked at Hassa with half-closed eyes. There he was lying in bed, looking at her guiltily but without understanding.

"Don't be angry anymore, Asiadeh. We will not invite Kurz again, that's all there is to it. It really was disgusting—embracing other people's wives. I'm quite glad you defended yourself. That'll be a lesson to him. You are my brave wild girl."

Hassa laughed, satisfied with himself, and closed his eyes.

But Asiadeh was sitting up in bed, her knees drawn up, staring at the bedside lamp. She did not think of Kurz anymore. There were probably many men like Kurz. A burning pain tore her breast. She put her head upon her knees and thought long and intensely, frowning deeply. She thought of men who were uncivilized, yet knew perfectly well the meaning of the word "honor." She thought of Marion, who suddenly was not a stranger anymore. She thought of her father, of the oasis Gadames, and of this alien world she had to live in, which she did not understand.

The pain became unbearable. Pearls of sweat appeared on her brow. One thought was in her head, and one thought only. She did not think of her father anymore, or of the prince, or of Marion and the alien world around her.

She sat in her bed, mouth slightly open, her frightened eyes staring at the lamp. She moaned softly, like a child, and the same thought kept revolving in her brain, did not let go, pierced and tortured her. So she sat, lonely and groaning. Hassa was asleep beside her. The lamp was burning, and she thought the same thought over and over again. Until daybreak she pondered whether it was right to have children by Hassa.

Then she slept. The enigma had not been solved, but she smiled, and the first rays of the rising sun fell on the carpet.

TWENTY-THREE

L inked in a mysterious way are the destinies of us human beings. The magic ring of events bridges oceans and continents, uniting us mortals. An old pasha in Berlin deciphers with tired eyes the designs on old carpets, speaks a few words, and the life of a man called John Rolland, who lives in New York, is thrown out of balance.

A Viennese doctor sees the neck of a beautiful woman, and the woman loses her faith in the world of the West. Events take their course as parts of an enigmatic design. The dead and the living, past and present, are joined together in a whirling dance, imperceptibly merging one into the other, thus becoming the fate and determining the actions and thoughts of living creatures.

Nothing is lost in the world of thoughts orbiting the earth; thoughts conceived hundreds of years ago keep on living, live an unreal life in the dust of libraries, in the yellowing pages of old manuscripts. Then suddenly they take on the form of actions, changing into worldly events—and the shadowy dance goes on, the dance around the world, like a wedding ring around a finger.

Many hundred years ago the brave warrior Usama ibn

Munkyz rode across the fields of Egypt and the villages of Palestine. For many decades he shed blood in honor of the prophet's green flag, in battles against the unbelievers who had come from lands across the sea, threatening the peoples of the prophet. He fought the Frankish knights before the gates of Jerusalem, the holy town. At Edessa he fought, at Akka, wherever the half-moon and the cross met in the Holy Land, his steed appeared, covered by his coat of mail, and across the wide field his war cry would sound:

"In the name of God! Here is Usama ibn Munkyz! Come on, you Frankish knights!" But when the great Saladin made peace with the Franks, the warrior Usama, sent by his ruler, journeyed through their castles and towns. He saw foreign customs, heard the foreign language, and was mightily astonished. Years passed. The warrior Usama became old and tired. He returned to the town of Damascus, to the court of the ruler. He buried his sword, and with his hands, trembling with age, he took up the pen. For his ruler and his children he wrote the great *Book of Instruction*, in which he collected not only the memories of campaigns and battles he had fought but also all he knew about these strange people, the Franks, who had come across the sea to battle against the peoples of the prophet.

For many decades his book was read by Arabic knights who went to battle against the Franks. Then *The Book of Instruction* fell into oblivion. Centuries passed. Unnoticed, the wise volume lay in dusty libraries. No one ever remembered the learned warrior Usama ibn Munkyz. Then came the day when Western scholars discovered *The Book of Instruction* in yellowing piles of old manuscripts. Laboriously the eyes of trained scholars deciphered the old script. The book was published, and from the rubble of the past, the warrior Usama rose up again, and with him his descriptions of life in the country of the Franks.

Negligently Asiadeh leafed through the Arabic writing she had found accidentally in the ocean of books in the big library. The attendant smiled when Asiadeh handed her the book. Funny—a beautiful girl wanted to know about the instructions of a forgotten Arabic warrior.

At home, squatting on the divan, Asiadeh opened the book. At first the ancient Arabic language was strange and foreign. She read about hunts, knightly duels, and strange events that had fascinated the old warrior. Then abruptly she stopped. Across the next page was a big heading: "About the Customs of the Franks."

Asiadeh read, smiling and shaking her head: "Praise be to our Lord and Creator! Anyone who has had the opportunity to gain a deep insight into the Franks' way of life will praise and glorify Allah for creating him a Muslim. Thus he will look on the Franks as animals only who, like all animals, have just one virtue: immense courage on the battlefield.

"The Franks know neither self-respect nor jealousy. It may happen that a Frank walks along the street with his wife. Another Frank meets them, takes the strange woman's hand, leads her away, and begins to talk to her. And the husband stands and waits until the conversation is ended. But if it goes on too long, he leaves her to stand with the strange man and walks away."

"Very interesting," thought Asiadeh, "even then . . ." Excitedly she read on. "I witnessed the following event: Whenever I visited Nablus near Jerusalem, I stayed in the house of my friend Muis, where all Muslims stayed. The windows of his house looked out on the street. Opposite was the house of a wine merchant, a Frank, who often had to go on journeys. One day he returned to his house and found a strange man lying in bed next to his wife. 'What are you doing here?' asked the wine merchant.

" 'I was traveling,' said the stranger, 'and came in for a bit of a rest.'

" 'And why are you in my bed?'

" 'I saw the bed prepared for the night, so I lay down.'

" 'But my wife is lying there with you.'

" 'Well—it is her bed too,' said the other, 'I cannot forbid her to lie in her own bed.'

" 'By the truth of my faith,' cried the merchant, 'if you do that again, we'll have a serious quarrel!'

" 'That was the strongest expression of his fury and jealousy!' "

Asiadeh put her head on the back of the divan and laughed. A mad people, these Franks. Brave on the battlefield but completely without any manliness in affairs of jealousy. Centuries had passed since the wise warrior had studied the Franks' customs—but unchanged were the souls of men, unchanged the reasons that let them allow their women to walk along the streets unveiled. Hassa was a Frank. Just once more and he would really quarrel with his colleague who had kissed his wife. She read on. The thick volume did not seem at all outdated anymore.

"Another instance: Once I visited the bath in Tyros and took a closed cabin. As soon as I had finished my bath, my servant rushed in and cried: 'Master—will you believe it—there is a woman in this bath!' I ran at once into the great hall. Really— there, standing next to a Frankish knight, her father, was a young woman.

"I did not trust my eyes, and said to a friend:

" 'For Allah's sake! Is this really a woman? Please go and assure yourself of this outrage!'

"My friend went close to the young woman and, before my eyes, assured himself that this really was a woman. Then the Frankish knight turned to me and said:

" 'This is my daughter. Her mother died, and there is no one who could wash her. So I have taken her here and washed her myself.'

" 'You did right,' I said, 'may Heaven reward you.'

"But in my heart I thought: 'Behold now, you believers, the great contrast: Quite obviously the Franks have neither a sense of honor nor jealousy, yet they shine by virtue of their immense bravery, even though it springs from the fear of losing honor. May God condemn them.' "

Asiadeh closed the book. Not so very long ago she herself had been for the first time in a bath, awkward and trembling, and strange men had seen her half-naked body. No, Hassa was not a degenerate. He was only a Frank, just like the old knight of whom Usama had made fun. His forebears had lived in Sarajevo and protected their women, but no trace of them was left in Hassa. He was a part of this world into which he had been born, and to which he wanted to belong. It was not his fault that Asiadeh understood the warrior Usama and laughed at the Franks, who walk on alone when strange men talk to their wives.

Asiadeh frowned. There was an abyss between her world and Hassa's, and there was no bridge across. It was not Hassa's fault that he was like all other people around him, and it would be unfair to punish him for it.

Asiadeh sighed. No, Hassa was not the man who could be the father of her children.

She looked at *The Book of Instruction*. As if in a dream, she saw herself walking into the future together with the warrior Usama, her father, and the prince from the House of Osman, who was in an oasis and called himself John Rolland. It seemed an unreal allegory, this vision of the eternal round dance that goes on through centuries and encircles the globe like a wedding ring on a finger.

Strangely, unfathomably linked indeed are our thoughts and dreams. Here are five pictures:

In the café Watan in Berlin, the old pasha is sitting, a cup of coffee in front of him and getting cold. With tired old eyes he looks at the Indian professor behind the counter and thinks of the prince, who is too weak to take his promised bride to him, and of his daughter, who lives with an unbeliever and is still not pregnant.

On a low stool in his surgery, Dr. Hassa is sitting. The rich Polish woman in front of him is complaining of reflex-neuroses. He is treating the Kilian points and is thinking of Asiadeh, who is sitting in the next room, reading an unintelligible Arab book, laughing loudly. He is thinking of her very lovingly, and with some concern, for she is twenty-one years old and has to be educated in the world of European customs and manners.

On the terrace of the Ring Café, Marion is sitting, her beautiful face suntanned, her eyes haughty and proud. She looks at the leaves, already beginning to fall from the trees, and she thinks that the summer has gone; she thinks of Fritz, who has left her. She thinks of her wrecked life, and of Hassa, who has a beautiful young wife whom she met on the Semmering on the day that madman came into her room, calling himself a prince, wanting to take her away. She smiles sadly, shaking her head, and thinks that a madman who imagines himself to be a prince is happier than she with her beauty and youth and her wrecked life.

A few streets away, Am Graben, Dr. Kurz is sitting in the bridge room of a café. The room is full of smoke. People's faces are pale, and the women are rather overdressed. Dr. Kurz puts the cards on the table and bends sideways to Dr. Sachs.

"I don't know," says Dr. Kurz. "Colleague Hassa does have a beautiful wife."

"Very beautiful," confirms Dr. Sachs.

"But so very foreign," says Dr. Kurz. "I can't understand Hassa. You can't talk about anything with this woman. Just a wall—that's all she is. Another world! You can say what you like, colleague, Asiatics simply are different from us. There's nothing we can do about it, no education, nothing. Am I not right? When this woman sits there and just stares in front of her, I'm sometimes quite afraid for Hassa. You can never tell what might suddenly come up from the depths of this strange mentality. Might as well marry an Eskimo or a Negress. The harem of some pasha or prince—that's the place for that woman. By the way, I had a case the other day. On the Semmering. A megalomaniac tried to tell me he was a Turkish prince. That would be something for Frau Dr. Hassa. Ha-ha-ha-ha!" Dr. Kurz laughed—and outside the gates of Gadames, in a wide stony field, sat John Rolland, who knew nothing of all these thoughts that whirled around him, nothing of the people sitting in faraway countries, secretly, invisibly linked with him.

He sat on a low stone. The stony field of the Sahara stretched out before him, sad and lonely. Hot wind blew over the dead stones, the scorching breath of a phantom giant. In front of him arose the stone idols of el'Esnam, the mystic Gate to the Sahara. Ancient, weatherbeaten, enigmatic, as if placed there by the hands of a cyclops. To the right stood the poor tents of the Tarki tribe. Virile lean men, swathed in robes and veils, sat at the tents' entrances, looking at the foreigner with indifferent disdain. The scorched earth smelled of fire. Far away a caravan was passing on toward the Tunisian border. Seen from afar, the camels looked like sand blown up by the wind. They were bringing gold dust from Timbuktu, perfumes from Ghat, ivory and ostrich feathers from the far south.

A slender woman, her face unveiled and her bosom bare, came from one of the tents toward Rolland. Her big dark eyes looked into the far distance, into the flat lonely plain of scorching sand and stones. She breathed in deeply and said: "It is beautiful here, stranger. Nowhere in the world is it as beautiful as here."

"Yes," said Rolland, and raised his eyes to the brown-faced woman with the naked breast. "Thou art a woman from the Tarki tribe, where women rule the men?"

The woman nodded. "Many centuries ago," she said, "there was quarreling in our tribe between men and women. The women left their men and went away, taking weapons and camels. The men went after them. There was a horrible battle, and we, the women, won. Since then we rule the people, and as a sign of serfdom we have thrown the veil over the faces of our men."

The woman fell silent, with a superior smile on her lips.

Then, abruptly, she went on: "Thus we tell the foreigners. But it is a lie. There was no battle hundreds of years ago. It is just no good for a man to be without the protection of a woman. Poor and naked is a man without a woman. Without support he is roving around in the desert. He steals and murders, and no one wants to see his face. He finds home and support only in the tent of a woman, and therefore the honor is hers."

"Yes," said John, "poor and naked indeed is a man without support."

He rose and walked across the stony field, the hot wind whipping his back. In the oasis the streets crossed and re-crossed one another, narrow like graves. The roofs hung over them in chaotic clusters. Negro women with three blue stripes on their temples slid past him, still bowed under the sign of erstwhile slavery.

At the square-shaped well Ain-ul-Fras, the palm trees shook their branches. An old man, eyes weeping with age, sat at the water clock. "Ain-ul-Fras," he said, "the holy well, called after the mare of the prophet. This water clock has been here for four thousand years and has never gone wrong." John shuddered—here, at the end of the world, time was measured in centuries.

He returned to his hotel room. Sam Dooth was already in bed, fast asleep. The typewriter stared at John like a fierce monster with four rows of teeth. John undressed. Darkness fell. An unearthly quiet lay over the oasis. With wide-open eyes John stared into the darkness. He was a wanderer between two worlds, forever driven by the load of his unrest, like a man from the Tarki tribe who roams around in the desert, stealing and murdering.

Suddenly—a sound. Softly at first, then louder and louder, terrifyingly weird sounds came from the desert, rustling and weeping, as if all the demons of the Sahara were trying to squeeze past the hotel gate. John sat up in bed. The weeping, now far away again, changed into a wild howling.

"The Rul," thought John, "the night phantom of the desert,

the dreadful rustling made by millions of grains of sand suddenly cooling." He shuddered. He had heard of the horrible
desert demons when he was a child. His nurse had told him,
or his mother—he did not remember. In the olden times,
before the prophet appeared in the world, the desert gods
ruled the Sahara. When Mohamed's multitudes conquered the
world, they drove the desert gods away, and these became
demons. Until midnight the prophet's word rules in the world
of sand. But then the ancient demons rise up. Howling and
weeping, they slink through the land, attack strangers, lead
wanderers astray until they hear the first morning prayer. Then
the holy words drive them back into their caverns.

John was trembling. Hastily he jumped from the bed and
dressed. The emptiness of his room had suddenly become oppressive. Something invisible, something immense and ancient
grasped him and drove him out into the magic voices of the
night.

He left the hotel. The moon was shining on the palm trees,
and their shadows looked like petrified giants. Panting, John
ran through the empty oasis, past the holy well, past the slave
market with the barred cells. He was running aimlessly, without knowing why or where to, until he found himself on the
moonlit square again, in front of the ancient water clock. On
the right rose the Djama-el-Kabira, the great mosque. John
came to a halt. The faraway demons' voices fell silent. He
brushed his forehead with his hand. The mosque's gate stood
open, and it seemed the Gate of Eternity. Driven by an unfathomable impulse, he entered.

The mosque was lit by small oil lamps. The pillars of the
colonnades stood like slaves turned into stone. John shuddered. He had not been in any house of God since the day he
had turned his back on his homeland.

He slipped off his shoes.

An old man was sitting on a barbarically patterned carpet, reading the Koran. In the flickering light of the oil lamps, he looked like a dancing mummy.

The mummy rose and bowed.

"I want to pray," said John.

The old man moved his pinched lips. "Here," he said, and pointed at the pulpit, "that is the kibla—the direction of prayers. If thou prayest, I pray with thee, I am the imam of this mosque."

John did not listen. He knelt down. Everything around him had vanished, lost in the valley of forgetfulness; his forehead touched the floor. His lips whispered half-forgotten words. He prayed for an hour or more. Time was measured in centuries. Then he sat cross-legged on the rug, looking at the fluttering light without thinking, his soul dissolved in the calm of the old mosque.

The old man looked at him curiously. He also had finished praying, the holy book was lying on his knees, but he did not read anymore. "Peace be with thee, Prince."

John flinched. Was this a dream? Reality? He rose. "Thou knowest who I am?"

"We are a small town, Prince. We know all there is to know about the foreigners who come across the desert in the car of the devil incarnate. Tomorrow I would have come to thee, to greet thee and remind thee. For thou hast been here a long time and livest like a dog without prayer. But Allah had mercy on my old age and sent thee here. Praise be to him."

John looked into the old imam's eyes.

"Once," he said softly, "this oasis and all the land around belonged to my ancestors. And now here I am, lying lonely in the dust before God. The world has disowned me, and I am like a splinter of wood from a ruined house."

The imam did not reply. His eyes were cast down, his red-painted fingernails glittered in the light of the oil lamps.

Fear overcame John. "An outcast am I who cannot find peace. A stranger am I in a strange world."

"Abdul-Kerim," said the old man, and raised his rugged beard. "Thy ancestors sat at the Bosphorus and ruled over us. They sent their warriors and destroyed our houses. And now thou art lying in the dust before God. I am a simple man of this desert, and thou a prince from a destroyed house."

He sobbed, short and evilly. His hand glided over his rugged beard. "The world of the unbelievers," he said disdainfully, "what is it? Nothing more than the sands of the desert. Who is afraid of that? Our caravans travel to Timbuktu, to the Coast of Gold, to Ghat, and to the black rulers of the Sudan. We are simple people and never had a palace on the Bosphorus. But for a year or even two, our caravans travel across the great sand. At night our women weep on the roofs of Gadames. Sad songs are sung in the desert. The men are in Timbuktu, or on the Coast of Gold, or in the jungle with the heathen. But the homeland? Here each of us carries his homeland in his heart or in his head. It is always there. A man can lose a foot, an arm, an eye—everything—but not his homeland. Thou livest in the stone houses of strange towns, but nothing is strange in God's world."

"Peace," said John angrily, "but where do I find it?"

Astonished, the imam looked up at him. "In the house thou art going to build for thyself."

"Another man is master in my house."

The old man was silent, his lips slyly compressed. "I am a poor man from the oasis of Gadames," he said at last. "But the world is full of miracles. I was going to see thee tomorrow, but even tonight Allah has sent thee to me. And only today a uniformed man brought me a piece of writing that concerns thee. I read it to the congregation, and everybody was astonished at Allah's miracle. Great is the power of the Lord. Only one hour it took for the writing to come here to the tents of peace from the country of the unbelievers. I cannot understand the meaning of it, for I am a simple man."

A piece of crumpled paper lay in John's hand. He smoothed it out and read:

"Radio Austria, Vienna. Gadames, via Tripoli. To the wise Imam of the Great Mosque. In the Name of God. Prince Abdul-Kerim from the House of Osman is staying among you. Visit him. Protect him. Watch over him. Tell him: Peace be with thee. His house is being built. I am guarding it. God willing, he will move into the house. Asiadeh, daughter of Achmed, from the house of Anbari."

John folded the telegram. "In the name of God," he said, "I am like a man from the Tarki tribe. Poor and naked is a man alone. The home is offered to him by a woman. Therefore the honor is hers."

He bowed and left the mosque. Thoughtfully, the imam followed him with his eyes. Then he prayed long and fervently: "For the prince and the house that is being built for him, for the caravans traveling across the desert, for the men at war, for the oasis Gadames, and for all pious believers in East and West."

TWENTY-FOUR

"And therefore the knowledge that you, honored Hanum, are not near to me, and consequently cannot throw things at me, nor tear up hundred-dollar bills—that knowledge gives me the courage to write to you. It is now four months that we are roaming about in deserts and oases with Rolland and lead the pitiful live of uncivilized homeless nomads. For John has finished his work very quickly, and the producer decided to shoot the outdoor scenes on location. So we make pilgrimages from one place to another in the company of actors and directors, like strolling players. This life depresses me, the more because my ancestors were—contrary to yours—not vagabond warriors but Greek patricians, quiet, respectable, and respected people. I have lost twenty pounds and cannot get accustomed to date liqueur, but that, honored Hanum, will probably not interest you very much. We are at present on the borders of human civilization, and the outdoor scenes are being shot at full speed. The stand-ins tumble skillfully from camels, and so far the leading lady has been kidnapped eight times by savages, unfortunately always over-exposed.

"Man's life, Hanum, is always in God's hand, but I am afraid that here God's hand is overdoing it a bit. Yesterday I found a scorpion in my bed, which turned my thoughts toward the Hereafter. If this kind of thing goes on, I will renounce all active life and finish my days in pious meditations as a solitary hermit and asket on the holy mountain of Athos. The custody for our friend Rolland's fate I leave to you, oh most honored lady.

" 'We emr bil urf'—Act according to your customs, says your Holy Book. But lately I have become afraid that John's customs hardly deserve this title, and if I did not love him like a son, I would leave him to his fate. For in really bigoted fervor John visits every single mosque in this country and spends an exaggerated amount of time lying in the dust before Allah's face, which behavior creates an understandable annoyance among the other members of our expedition.

"But yesterday something happened that made me seriously doubt his sanity. I would really prefer to see him drunk, even though I myself am not partial to an excessive partaking of alcohol. So yesterday, after we had finished the dialogue between the kidnapped lady and the wild robber, we went for a walk in the oasis together with other members of our crew, hoping against hope to find some useful extras. For you must know, oh Hanum, that the people in this country are very stupid and have no idea how to act if they are supposed to be Arabs. Well—we met a ragged native, girded with a dirty green loincloth. John spoke to the poor colored chap, and we thought it was about hiring him. As far as I could tell from scraps of conversation, the vagabond declared to be a descendant of the prophet, just returned from a pilgrimage to Mecca.

"Following which—I blush as I'm writing this, Hanum—following which John embraced the unwashed savage, sat down with him in the shade of a palm tree, and began a conversation about the wonders of the holy town Mecca. And all that before the very eyes of members of our expedition. Think of it, Hanum! A citizen of the United States of America embraces a wretched native!

"We all turned away and left immediately, for it was dreadful to witness this scene. Assistant Director Mooney declared John must have gone mad. But the others decided never to shake hands with John anymore, as he was obviously no gentleman. I had quite a time convincing them that he was too drunk to be responsible for his actions. Thus I just managed to save his reputation. But strictly between you and me, Hanum, he was not drunk at all, but completely sober.

"As you, honored Hanum, by virtue of your marriage and inclination, have become a European, I dare to ask you a great favor: Please admonish John, ask him not to keep on wriggling in the dust before the face of Allah, and to stop these undignified embraces of native saints. For I believe you have a certain influence on my friend and partner, because the other day he stated, after eight liqueurs, that he will be the father of your children. And after the twelfth liqueur he was saying something about a house you are building for him. But I do not know what he was talking about.

"I should add, incidentally, that John has, quite unnecessarily, taken to riding a camel, and sometimes he will even wear native robes, which is very undesirable for a member of New York's Club of Film Authors. There, too, you should show yourself as an example to him, for the last time I saw you, you had—as I see now, perfectly correctly—decided to stay with your honorable European husband (please give him my regards, Hanum, may God send him many patients) instead of this Asiatic touched very superficially only by European culture— which is what he has now shown himself to be.

"Our work here, Hanum, will be finished soon, and I may

tell you that my poor friend has decided to spend the rest of the winter season in Vienna before returning to America. But I will of course do all I can to protect you from his Asiatic molestations, if you will graciously grant my entreaty to send him an energetic word of warning. For to tell the truth, drinking, for which I sometimes have to tell him off, is more harmless than keeping the degrading company of Koran readers, native singers, or ragged descendants of the prophet— at least in the eyes of any citizen of the United States of America.

"I close my letter, Asiadeh-Hanum, with the conviction that we understand each other, for we are both people of Western culture: You an Austrian, and I a citizen of the U.S.A. I salute you hurriedly, for I hear John in the next room planning a pilgrimage to the holy Sidi Abdessalam with one of the native scholars. I have to put my foot down with a firm hand, even though the thermometer shows halfway to boiling point in the shade.

"Yours sincerely, Sam Dooth."

Asiadeh folded the letter and sniffed at the rustling paper with the air of a connoisseur, for she thought she could detect the smell of scorched earth. The many-colored Libyan stamp showed the desert, the sun, and a slow-moving camel.

"Halfway to boiling point," she thought, astonished, and looked out the window. It was snowing. White flakes were falling on the asphalt, the trees were bowing to the house in greeting, their branches weighed down under their snowy burden.

It was quite inconceivable that there could be a place where the sun was hanging down from the sky like a yellow torch and sandstorms were whirling over the desert.

Asiadeh caressed the letter. No, most certainly she could not send any word of warning to John Rolland, neither by letter nor in person when he came to Vienna. Why should he not throw himself into the dust before the Lord and have wise conversations with dubious descendants of the prophet?

Four months had passed since John Rolland had sat before her with his proud face and slackly hanging arms. During these four months the leaves had fallen from the trees of Vienna and had rustled under her feet, reminding her of desert sand. Then snowflakes had fallen from the sky, and the whole world had become white.

During these four months Achmed-Pasha had visited his daughter for one week and looked at her disapprovingly, for she had disowned the prince and was still not pregnant.

During these four months Hassa had one day packed their suitcases and taken Asiadeh to the Tyrol Mountains. He had held long wooden planks and sticks in his hands, and Asiadeh had only a vague idea of what they were to be used for. In the Tyrol, Asiadeh wrapped herself up in furs, and her teeth chattered when she looked out at the snowfields.

She sat in the hotel room next to the glowing stove, looking anxiously out of the window. Out there, on the wide field, Hassa put his wooden boards on the snow, took the two sticks into his hands, and rushed in mindless, death-defying speed across vales and mountains. He wore a scarf and a soft round hat and looked virile and beautiful in the strong assurance of his movements.

Asiadeh watched him and was proud that he was her husband for as long as she wanted him. But she still sat next to the glowing stove, teeth chattering, thinking of the house she had to build for the prince. Not one single stone was ready yet. For Hassa was a good and beautiful man, but most certainly not a house.

After that the months had gone quickly and monotonously, and only for one week there had been a dull feeling of war. Asiadeh remembered it very well: It had been in the middle of December. Hassa had come from the hospital with smiling eyes and a frozen nose. "Soon it'll be Christmas," he had said, his face glowing like that of a little boy. "Soon I'll go and get a Christmas tree and decorations."

"No, don't," said Asiadeh, "I don't want that."

Hassa's eyes became round with amazement.

"Christmas," he said, "do you know what that is? A fir tree with many-colored paper chains and glass balls, and under the tree lie the presents. When I was a little boy, Father Christmas with a long white beard used to come as well. I thought he was real. Don't you really know what Christmas is?"

"I know perfectly well what Christmas is. It is the Christians' most important religious festival, but you know that your wife is a Muslim, and you really should be one too. We can't celebrate Christmas."

"But my dear child." Hassa was completely bewildered. "Look—Christmas is Christmas. Can't you understand that? We have always celebrated it, all my life."

"All right," said Asiadeh, "you buy your Christmas tree, and I'll go to Berlin for a week to see my father. There's a mosque in Berlin, and it is a long time since I have been to one."

Hassa became furious. He walked up and down in the room. He told about his childhood. He insulted the world of Asia and even said that Marion, bad as she was, had never objected to Christmas.

"Why should she?" said Asiadeh. "She was no Muslim."

But Hassa did not listen and went on talking about the Christmas tree until his first patient arrived and he had to go to the surgery.

After the last patient had gone, he went to the café, full of wrath, and told Dr. Matuschek about his trouble.

"Can you understand that," he said, completely at a loss, "she doesn't want a Christmas tree. And she'd find a marvelous fur coat under the tree. Can you understand that?"

"A savage," Dr. Matuschek said, laughing.

The next day the whole café knew that Hassa's wife had forbidden her husband to buy a Christmas tree. As soon as he heard this, Dr. Kurz came to Hassa's table with outstretched arms and asked pityingly: "My poor man, what will you do then on Christmas Eve?" The headwaiter helpfully suggested a small café somewhere in town, kept open for poor devils with nowhere to go.

Hassa was beside himself with anger and embarrassment. But Asiadeh remained as hard as a rock. Therefore Hassa went to Dr. Sachs' on Christmas Eve, and Asiadeh crouched alone on the divan, bundled up in warm shawls.

For one whole week Hassa went about the flat sulking silently. But on New Year's Eve he forgave his wife and gave her the fur coat as a token of reconciliation.

"But when we have children," he said severely, "we must celebrate Christmas. The children cannot grow up like savages."

"Of course," said Asiadeh, for she was a peace-loving woman, "of course, when we have children . . ."

Then came the Fasching—the season of balls, masked balls, paper streamers, confetti, music, fancy dress . . . Hassa was ensnared in the whirl of the great balls taking place one after the other, or even several of them on the same night. He bought a ball-calendar and brooded over it with furrowed brow.

"The Opera Ball," he whispered, "the Ball of Vienna Town,

the Feast of St. Gilgan"—the whole glory of the old town unfolded before Asiadeh's astonished eyes.

On one night all the seats had been taken from the auditorium of the Opera to make a dance floor, and in the boxes, jewels glittered on white hands. She saw the Gothic severity of the city hall disappear behind festive decorations and fairy lights, she saw the hall where worthy councillors of commerce wore the clothes of country bumpkins, and lawyers' spouses squeezed their soigné bodies into brightly coloured dirndls.

All this amazed her, for somewhere it was halfway to boiling point in the shade, and John Rolland was lying in the dust before Allah's throne and talking to wise scholars about the holy Abdessalam.

The door creaked. Hassa had come home from the hospital, smiling, obviously in very good humor. As he caressed Asiadeh's hair, she raised her head and looked into his eyes.

"Day after tomorrow is Gschnas," said Hassa. "We'll go, of course."

Asiadeh laughed. The word "Gschnas" sounded like a joke. "There is no such thing, Hassa. Gschnas is not a word at all. It's impossible to pronounce."

"On the contrary, every Viennese pronounces it lovingly."

"But what is it, for heaven's sake?"

Smiling, Hassa shook his head. His wife was really a little savage. Fancy not knowing what Gschnas was.

"Gschnas is a fancy-dress ball. On that night, half of Vienna puts on fancy dress and goes wild in the halls of the Artisis' House. It is very gay, because wives are strictly forbidden to be jealous. You'll go as a bayadere, and I as a neanderthal man."

Asiadeh looked into his beaming face and laughed. "Strictly speaking, I don't need any fancy dress at all, Hassa. I'm in fancy dress every day, morning, noon, and night. I'm wearing dresses instead of wide Turkish trousers, and a hat instead of a veil. All right, I promise not to be jealous."

Hassa sat down beside her and caressed her face with his soft warm hand. "We do get on well together, Asiadeh," he said tenderly. "It was a good idea to get married. Is there anything you miss, being here with me?"

"Nothing, my lord and master. You are a good man. I don't think there can be a better man in the world."

Asiadeh stopped. Hassa was still a faithful machine whose mechanism was beyond her comprehension. "Are you never homesick for Sarajevo, Hassa?"

"For Sarajevo? No." Hassa laughed. "Only savages live there. I know: Whenever you are sitting there so quietly, staring at nothing, you are thinking of mosques, fountains, and Moorish collonades. But in the mosques you have to sit on the floor, the water in the fountains is undrinkable, and scorpions nest in the arabesques of the Moorish columns. I'd go mad if I had to live in the Orient. The world of the East is sick and decayed. I have often thought about it and know more than you think. It's like the underworld. Narrow damp alleys, houses impossible to live in decently, carpets full of germs. Trachoma and syphilis in the villages. Knifing as a pastime, and sluggish drowsing in horrible coffeehouses. Everything that makes life bearable in the Orient comes from Europe: trains, cars, hospitals. Since the beginning of time man has been threatened by nature and has battled against it. Only when he can tame the forces of nature can he become free and secure. Even smallpox germs are part of nature, and Western man has conquered them. We have conquered cold so our houses can be warm, we have conquered seas and rivers, space and time.

"But in the Orient, man is at the mercy of the elements. One breath of wind, and whole villages die of pestilence. A swarm of locusts, a sandstorm, and whole provinces starve.

"I know, I know! In Istanbul on the Bosphorus stand the palaces of the pashas. But whole quarters have regularly been destroyed by fires. In the Orient, man has not learned yet to rule nature, and so he prays to a god who only judges and punishes but does not love. No, the Orient is an inferno. A world of the Hereafter, full of misery, impotence, and pain. I am very glad indeed to live in a world that has conquered nature . . ."

He would have gone on, but the door opened and the fat baritone came in, stretching his hands out toward Hassa.

"Herr Doktor," he cried, "I've been waiting for an hour. I've got a dreadful sinusitis. I can't pronounce the 'M' anymore—and there you are, cuddling with your wife, you naughty man!"

"We'll conquer that sinusitis at once," cried Hassa, jumping up and rushing into the surgery.

Asiadeh was left alone. Hassa's words sounded in her ears like the muffled beats of a sledgehammer. He was right in everything he said. Man was a poor creature in the Orient, poor and naked at the mercy of the elements. And yet—everything in Asiadeh's soul longed for the quiet dignity of her life at home, for the world of miserable houses, wise dervishes, and calm devotion, for a world where nobody would dare to burst into a room where husband and wife were deep in conversation. When criminals in Istanbul, fleeing from justice, went to their women, the policemen stood outside in the streets, not daring to interrupt a man talking with his wife. Here a stranger burst into the room and her husband did not tell him to go away but went out with him to conquer nature.

This world was not a bad world; perhaps there was no such

thing as a good or bad world. Any world could make its people happy. But all differed from the others, divided from one another since the beginning of time, strong and immovably rooted in their own individuality.

Many hundreds of years ago the khaliph Moawija married a simple woman from the desert. He brought her to the khaliph town of Damascus, and she bore him an heir, the khaliph Jesid. But when the heir mounted his first war steed, the woman came to the khaliph, bowed before him, and asked him to send her back to her tribe in the desert, for she had done her duty in his town.

"We love each other," said the khaliph, "and we are happy. You have a son who is my heir, you have a husband who is a khaliph, you have palaces and servants. What more can you desire, why do you want to leave me?"

The woman knelt down before her husband and recited a poem:

A tent through which the wind is blowing
Is more to me than marble halls,
A piece of bread in my tent's corner
Tastes better than the choicest dish.
I'm longing for my desert homestead—
No king's palace can take its place.

The khaliph was astounded and let his wife go with honor.

Hundreds of years separated Asiadeh from the wife and mother of the old khaliphs. But the mystic dance that joins the living and the dead passes on through the centuries.

Yes, Hassa was right. The world of the West was a secure, good world. Hassa could never be happy in any other. But

Asiadeh lived in a different world, with different feelings and desires. And between these two worlds, on a narrow frail bridge, stood John Rolland, who was waiting for her, and Hassa, whom she could not leave, even though he was enclosed in this proud world that had conquered nature.

Hassa dismissed the happy singer from the next room. Outside other patients were waiting. They came in, sat in the examination chair, and told Hassa about their complaints. Hassa wrote prescriptions and gave advice. Suddenly he realized he was humming a soft gay tune in the middle of testing a patient's hearing. The hard-of-hearing patient did not notice anything, but the assistant nurse gave him a surprised look, and Hassa blushed with embarrassment. But life was fine, he was a good doctor and had a beautiful wife whom he loved very much. He was a considerate husband who never neglected his wife. Of course his wife was very young and had not quite found her equilibrium yet. But hadn't he just now had a serious conversation with her? He had convinced her that Europe as a beautiful continent, and she had listened attentively. Life was good and simple. One could explain anything to an intelligent woman, especially the simple fact that a world without smallpox is better than a world with smallpox. That was the way to conduct a marriage; that way there would never be any surprises.

Thus thought Hassa, and a few houses away, in the massive building on the Karlsplatz, workers were dragging heavy planks along, bent double under the strain.

The floors were washed and scrubbed, waiters, still with traces of private thoughts showing on their faces, put up tables, mechanics checked electric cables. A fat man manipulated a coffee machine, lean, long-haired youths covered immense sheets of paper with charcoal flourishes, and the whole big

Artists' House became smothered with posters, drawings, and slogans.

Counters were put up and batteries of wine bottles brought in. In the office the telephone was ringing nonstop. Gentlemen with crushed faces were talking in hoarse voices to the manager, demanding press tickets. Policemen paced across the halls with measured steps and checked posters, tables, bottles, and fire risks.

The great house was living a strange, confused life: The preparations for the Gschnas were going ahead full speed.

TWENTY-FIVE

Harlequins, gypsies, bayaderes, and knights crowded in on the wide brightly lit staircase and flooded in gaudy chaos through the house. Painted faces wore their gaiety like masks. Men who thought themselves too dignified to wear fance dress, but wore white ties and tails, were disrespectfully addressed by the colorful crowd as "Hey, waiter!" and looked like penguins stranded in this whirling multitude.

Noisy laughter and suppressed giggles came from the semi-darkness of the niches. Women in wide trousers or colorful skirts were dancing with medieval alchemists and Russian boyars. Lone recluses wandered through the halls, stiff disdain in their eyes and false noses on their faces. One man, wearing a three-cornered hat on his broad skull, stood unmoving in the middle of the great hall, his arms crossed over his chest, his face a victorious mask.

Tired dancers were sitting on long benches, wiping the sweat from their hot faces. A photographer stood at the door of his den and caught with his lens the harlequins, gypsies, bayaderes, and knights.

A strange magical play, a scene from an ancient bacchanal, seemed to be enacted in these great halls, men and women, as if touched by Circe's wand, changed into creatures of ghostly fantasies, a change denied to them during their drab everyday lives. On this night a solicitor could change into a gypsy, a chemist into a highwayman or a knight. Their souls, negligently shed, hung in the cloakroom together with their ordinary coats, and the halls were filled with hotly flushed people who had taken a holiday from fate for a few short hours and were throwing themselves with wild abandon into the ocean of their fulfilled dreams.

Asiadeh sat at a narrow table between a silently brooding harlequin and a French marquis with a powdered wig and a long, sniffly nose. She was wearing a gypsy costume, and golden coins tinkled on her brow.

Hassa had vanished. From time to time she could see his high pointed alchemist's hat above the crowd. Once his smiling face appeared near her. Two women were hanging on his arms; he looked at Asiadeh, and she had the certain feeling that he did not even recognize her. The surgeon Matthess was running after him, wearing the robe of a Chinese mandarin and carrying a bottle of champagne under his arm. He waved to Asiadeh and cried in a rather squeaky voice that his name was Li-Tai-Pe and he was having a wonderful time.

Asiadeh laughed. The harlequin put his arm around her shoulder. She pushed him away gently and landed in the embrace of the marquis, who offered her a slivovitz and sniffed at her back. She refused by rattling her coins and putting her tongue out to him—the rules of polite behavior had emphatically been lifted for this one night.

Dazed by the brilliant lights and colors, she rose and walked with undulating steps through the halls. When she came across a thin man in the flowing robes of a pasha from the olden times, she winked at him. He grabbed her hand and dragged her to the dance floor. While they were dancing, she adjusted his turban. "That's how you wear it," she explained severely. The pasha said he would take her into his harem and invited her to have a glass of champagne.

"I am already in a harem," Asiadeh said, laughing, and nibbled at a sweet.

"I'll buy you from your owner. We pashas are always buying women."

"I'm sold out," said Asiadeh, and walked away.

She went to the bar and asked for a mocha. She talked to strangers, and a lyrically beautiful youth caressed her hand. Men surrounded her, their eyes wooing, ordering, requesting. A white-faced Pierrot grabbed her and took her to an alcove. He had the pleading frightened eyes of a man who wakes from a bad dream and has not yet found reality.

"I have a wife, and I don't love her anymore," he said, and took Asiadeh's hand. Then he laughed, and Asiadeh caressed his powdered face and told him about Hassa, her father, and the flat on the Ring.

Suddenly the Pierrot disappeared—perhaps he had never existed—and in a blinding vision, Asiadeh understood the magical meaning of this night: Here the borders of the visible world were wavering and shifting, and nature, forever untamed, grinned at her victoriously, rejoicing in her triumph over the centuries, wretchedly spent in the vain attempt to tame her. For here the tamed souls arose from their everyday hiding places and, in a sudden attack, overran all barriers and baricades of the Western world . . .

The vision disappeared as suddenly as it had come, and Asiadeh saw Hassa, in his alchemist's costume, surrounded by women, grinning broadly. He came up to her, embraced her, and took her to the dance floor.

"Is it dull for you? Are you angry?" He spoke as if in a dream.

"No, it is very nice here. It should always be like this."

They danced, and the French marquis sniffed past them. Later Hassa was sitting on a bench, holding the hand of a slim woman, telling her fortune. Asiadeh went down the staircase. A giggle of young women surrounded the policeman at the entrance. His blue eyes looked at the pagan festivities with the calm, even temper of authority. Asiadeh touched his arm. He was a real policeman, not in fancy dress. Here was a glimpse of the world that began outside this house, the world that was called reality. With one quick gesture, one movement of his hand, he could make the nocturnal spook of the liberated souls change back into the tamed stagnation of everyday life.

Asiadeh shuddered at the thought. In the semidarkness of the ground floor, scantily dressed women were clinging to men in white ties and tails; the air was hot, oppressive, smelling of scent and wine. Asiadeh felt suddenly very tired and sat down on the corner of an empty bench. Men passed by and smiled at her, but she did not smile back, just sat there in her many-colored gypsy costume, the golden coins lying on her forehead like a wreath.

A bayadere sat down on the other end of the bench, turning her back to Asiadeh. The back was brown, young, and slim. Asiadeh saw slender arms, full silk trousers, gold-embroidered slippers, and a silk turban. Thoughtfully and silently, the woman sat there, obviously tired of the tumult around her.

Then she turned. From the turban an oval pearl hung down

on the woman's forehead—and there was the face with the nobly curved eyebrows, haughty brown eyes, and the narrow nose with the trembling nostrils.

"Good evening, Marion," said Asiadeh. Suddenly she was not tired anymore. She moved closer to the bayadere.

"Good evening, Asiadeh." Marion scrutinized her curiously, and Asiadeh looked back at her admiringly.

"You look like a real Indian girl. The turban suits you."

Marion laughed. "You should really be the one to wear a turban and trousers."

"Oh no, that would be too realistic. Don't you know that I'm a savage and should wear a veil?"

"A savage? You? Who was the last woman in your family to wear a veil?"

"The last one? I, myself, six years ago. No, it's really true, I really am a savage."

Asiadeh took Marion's hand, and the astonished Marion raised her eyebrows. "Why don't you run away, as you did that time on the Semmering?" She laughed.

Asiadeh's voice sounded sad. "I was a silly goose, Marion, that's why I ran away. Please don't be angry with me." As she looked at Marion, her serious eyes were putting out delicate feelers of curiosity.

Marion shook her head. She couldn't understand this sudden friendliness. "Is Alex behaving himself? You don't have to worry about him?"

"Our husband is very good, Marion. Just now he is an alchemist, telling a blonde her fortune. And Matthess is sitting next to him, and he's really Li-Tai-Pe. Kurz should be around somewhere, and the others too. No, he is a good man, and I have no worries at all."

Peter the Great walked across the hall, his arm around

Queen Nefertiti's shoulder. A youth with a big red nose and a raffish-looking Indian with horn-rimmed glasses were talking earnestly, if rather incoherently, about aesthetic problems.

Marion was deep in thought, her face still a bit haughty. "Let's go and have a mocha," she proposed abruptly. "I know from experience that our husband stays at the Gschnas till the break of day."

Asiadeh nodded, and there they sat, a bayadere and a gypsy, gray eyes looking into brown eyes. The intoxication of the nocturnal feast began to wane, and the packed hall slowly became less crowded.

Suddenly both women felt very embarrassed.

"How are you, Marion?"

"I? Oh, fine, thanks. I've been skiing in the Tyrol. Now I'm in town again."

"Isn't it strange, Marion? This is the first time I'm talking to you, and yet I already know so much about you."

Marion blushed faintly. "Yes, Alex must always have someone to unburden his soul to. Does he still talk about his patients, and does he still rave about the *apfelstrudl* his mother used to bake?"

"Oh yes, he does. And the waiting room is still full of patients, and the same journals are still on the table. And after surgery he still goes to the same café."

"And afterward he drives up to the Kobenzl or the Prater, doesn't he? I feel quite young again when I hear you talking."

She did not go on. The band was playing a gypsy song, lovers were cuddling in the corners, no one was dancing anymore. At the next table two men were talking about the stock exchange. Through mysterious hidden peepholes, reality had begun to seep into the hall again.

"It's not very often," said Marion, "that two wives of one man sit peacefully together at one table."

"Oh, but why not? My grandfather had four wives at the same time, and they got on very well together. Even better than with their husband."

Marion opened her bag, took out a small mirror, and gently touched the powder puff to her face.

"I'm so glad to hear that Alex is all right. He had taken this thing very badly at the time. But my God, it does happen that two people separate. I had to go, there was no other way. Alex is lucky. You do get on very well together, don't you?" Marion's voice was cool and impersonal. Asiadeh hid her nose and eyes in the mocha cup. Then she smiled shyly.

"Oh yes, we get on very well. You see, I'm a savage, and so very different from Hassa. But he is always very patient with me, and very pleasant. Anything I want him to do, he does. And I don't even believe he does it for my sake, he's just an ideal husband. Very busy, very tender, very obliging. He would be as nice to any other women, I'm sure. He is just made for marriage. It is very easy to be happy with Hassa—and so we are happy."

Marion laughed. She thought of the flat, of the bed, of Hassa in his white coat, and the journals in the waiting room.

"Do you always sit in the drawing room, at the bow window, and Alex shouts: 'Say twenty-two'?"

Asiadeh nodded enthusiastically.

"Yes, and the patient answers: 'Fourteen' or 'Beg your pardon?' and then the instruments rattle. At first I wanted to help Hassa in the surgery, but he wouldn't allow it."

"He allowed me." There was a tiny triumphant note in Marion's voice. "I could pass him the instruments, write out the bills, and give chocolate to the children. At first I loved it. But it is not a good thing for man and wife to be always together. As I knew all his patients, he talked of nothing but patients to me—all the time. And that just didn't do."

Marion's rigid face became soft. Her long, slender hands crumpled a handkerchief. It was strange to think that there had been a time when she was passing instruments to Alex and had been jealous of beautiful patients. But all that was long ago. Between then and now there had been Fritz. All the women had been after Fritz. There had been others too—but it was best not to think about that.

Asiadeh sighed.

"Sometimes I envy you, Marion. You know Hassa so much better than I do. I know so little about European men. Except for Hassa, all I knew were a few colleagues in Berlin. They had bald heads and deciphered hieroglyphs. We'll have to meet more often and talk about our husband."

"Stupid chick," thought Marion, "or is there something wrong in the marriage? Funny, this sudden friendship!"

With newly aroused interest, she looked at Asiadeh, and the strangely formed eyes looked back at her with naive unconcern. Her arms lying awkwardly on the table, the silly little girl was sitting there, probably jealous because her husband was dancing with other women.

Marion smiled graciously. "Very well, Asiadeh. Yes, I'd like to meet you sometime. I do know Alex quite well, or at least I think I do."

By now the great hall was nearly empty. Only Napoléon was left there, sitting in the middle of the floor, lonely and victorious. The floor was covered with paper streamers, the paper lanterns threw an unreal flickering light on the walls. Waiters were standing about in corners, their official faces slowly set-tling back into their private lines.

Loud laughter came from the staircase. Four gentlemen in very high spirits tumbled into the mocha bar. First the surgeon Matthess in the silk robe of a Chinese mandarin and with art-fully made-up slit eyes, followed by Sachs and Halm, and then Hassa, his alchemist's hat slightly askew.

"There you are, Asiadeh," he cried gaily, "and we've been looking for you everywhere." He came to the table.

"And while you were looking for me," Asiadeh said, laugh-ing, "your two wives have found each other and have been drinking mocha."

Hassa's laughing face stiffened. Only now he recognized Marion.

"Good evening Alex," said Marion blithely, "take a seat—or should I go?"

"Oh, but please, Marion. No . . . it's very nice . . . we could have a glass of wine . . . so you're here too?" He was terribly embarrassed.

"There's the pasha, surrounded by his harem!" shouted Matthess. "Must be celebrated! Waiter, wine!"

Noisily he pushed chairs together, Dr. Sachs poured the wine, and the gynecologist Halm raised his glass. "In vino veritas!" he cried. "Here's to a happy meeting!"

The glasses clinked. No one noticed that Asiadeh had emp-tied her glass in one quick gulp. Her heart beat like a hammer. How right the great scholar Sheik Ismail of Ardebil had been when he asserted that there were moments in life when alcohol was allowed.

Marion smiled dreamily.

"To think," said Dr. Sachs pensively, "to think that I was a witness at your divorce. And now here we are, all sitting together peacefully together around the table. Such is life."

He shook his head and filled his glass.

Hassa sat down next to Asiadeh and embraced her victoriously—but she felt he was asking for help. His slanting eyes stared at Marion, and his hand nestled in Asiadeh's hair.

Halm laughed. So far he had been divorced twice. "My first wife—she remarried a long time ago—well, even today she choses my ties. But on the day of the divorce, she threatened me with a bayonet."

Marion raised her head and, smiling, looked at Hassa. "Alex," she said, "what became of the toy pistol you threatened me with?"

It sounded like a triumphal fanfare. For years she had wanted to ask him that question. Hassa blushed. He really had threatened Marion with a pistol. And, except for Asiadeh, everyone at the table knew it.

It was embarrassing to be reminded of that incident.

"I've sold it. A bad bargain. Lost five schillings on it."

He blinked shyly, and Marion laughed.

"I'll refund you the five schillings sometime, Alex."

By now the hall had become quite peaceful. The band members were packing up their instruments, Peter the Great stumbled yawning toward the exit. A man passed by and smiled at Marion, but she turned away.

"How do you like my savage little wife?" asked Hassa. His hand was still buried in Asiadeh's hair.

"You are a lucky man, Alex. You have a charming wife, and she has just confessed to me that you are very happy together. I am very glad for you, really."

Her eyes were very humble; she put her hand out to him and

he took it. "Let's go!" cried Dr. Sachs. "This scene is becoming too sweet for words."

They all rose. Asiadeh grabbed fat Dr. Halm and, golden coins tinkling on her forehead, whirled him around in the hall till he became dizzy. Then she ran to the cloakroom.

"We'll meet sometime, won't we, Marion?" said Asiadeh, and Marion nodded.

Gray morning fog seeped in from the street. People slipped back into their normal clothes and souls. Narrow bits of paper streamers were still clinging to coats and cloaks—a shamefaced memory of a magic dream. And the moist fog drew mercifully protecting veils round them.

The overturned order of the universe slowly moved back to its natural course.

"A mad night," said Hassa.

"A very nice night," said Asiadeh, "a wonderful night. The Gschnas is lovely. I've had a wonderful time. Really, Hassa."

And she put her head on his shoulder and fell asleep at once.

TWENTY-SIX

In the afternoon Frau Dr. Asiadeh Hassa usually went to the café on the Stephansplatz and met Marion. She would sit next to her, hands folded like a little girl, and tell about her happy marriage, of Hassa's practice and the flat on the Ring.

"You know," she said on the first day, "I just can't imagine a life without Hassa anymore. He is so good." Her big naive eyes glowed with artless pride. "Isn't it strange," she went on, "you've been married to Hassa too, and so you know all about the wonderful life I have. And just because of that, you seem closer to me than anybody else in Vienna."

Marion listened patiently. Asiadeh was a childish creature who wanted to babble on about her happiness and who, for some strange reason, trusted her. Asiadeh never stopped talking about her marriage all through the afternoon, then she went, and when Marion finished her cigarette, she paid and walked across the snow-covered Stephansplatz. Her proud eyes glanced boredly at the window displays on the Graben and indifferently at the Pestsäule as she turned in to the Kohlmarkt.

Cars, hooting like trumpeting elephants in the twilight, splashed through the slush, and the semicircular facade of the Hofburg stared at her with resigned disdain. Kings and

emperors had driven through these enormous gates. Emperor
Franz Joseph and Napoléon had looked down on the round
square from these windows. Gold-embroidered uniforms had
been mirrored in these big panes. The Hofburg had seen so
much, had lived through so much. What did the fate of one
woman matter?

The Herrengasse was shaped like a long, curved worm. On
the left side were government departments and museums, but
Marion knew neither their names nor what was housed in
them. To the right the endless row of shopwindows blazed
through the dark, and the skyscraper loomed above the street,
cold steel and concrete.

Marion walked across the marble floor of the entrance
hall. The porter saluted her with familiar courtesy; softly,
silently, the lift moved up. Marion came into her flat, into the
cool, matter-of-fact modern room with the view to the paved
courtyard. It seemed a luxurious cell in a prison for million-
aires. Marion's face was not haughty anymore—far from it.
With a furious gesture, she closed the curtains. The gray
prison yard disappeared. She switched on the lights and stared
into the mirror. Yes—she was still very beautiful with her oval
face, brown eyes and hair, and smooth high forehead. The face
did not give anything away about the divorce from Alex, or the
affair with Fritz, or all the others who had come later, about
whom she did not want to think.

Marion sat down on the sofa. Her small white teeth bit
into the lower lip, and now she looked as unhappy as she felt.
The room with its soulless cool furniture seemed a sepulchre
to her—when and how had she moved into the flat and furnished it? Oh yes—it had been on one of those days she tried
to forget—and could not . . .

She shook her head. No, her life had become utterly confused, but it was certainly not her fault. Alex was a decent dull man with primitive ideas and the character of a child. He loved his wife, his flat, and his patients. She couldn't bear it . . .

Marion rose and walked up and down in the room. Suddenly she collapsed on the couch and stared at the window. She loved Fritz so much that she sometimes wanted to shoot him. Everything about Fritz was so colorful and alluring, so full of enigmatic mysteries and promises. He had more women than Alex had patients, and when he was talking, Marion would lie there with her eyes closed, just listening to the sound of his voice— and Alex disappeared forever in the pit of forgetfulness.

Marion lit a cigarette. The English tobacco tasted insipid and sweet. Well—and then it came to light that Fritz had a wife somewhere in the provinces, a regular wedded wife, and he was afraid of her. It had been a marvelous summer in the mountains. In this one summer Fritz had given her more than Alex had in three years of marriage.

And then . . . well, then came a robust wife with a croaking voice and a wicked nose, crooked like the beak of a parrot. And Fritz suddenly crumbled. All mystery and allure has abruptly and completely vanished, and before Marion stood a stupid, terrified, ashamed husband with lying eyes. Marion jumped up and threw the cigarette away.

Again she walked up and down, up and down, and did not know that Hassa had once walked up and down just like she did, before he put her photo into the drawer. She stopped in front of the mirror. She was all alone, and there was no sense in being haughty and superior.

Suddenly she did not like her face anymore. She looked at it closely for quite awhile, then she put her first finger on the tip of her nose and pushed it up. Now the face was haughty again, and stupid in the bargain.

"Serves you right," said Marion, and was glad she did not have a snub nose. That was a humble and quite harmless pleasure. Then she went to the sofa and sat down again. It was good that she was alone in the flat. No one could see her now and know that she was just a lonely girl, hurt, and frightened of life.

Again she remembered: Fritz disappeared with the parrot-nosed woman. He left her a pair of socks and the memory of a beautiful summer. "I will never forget you," he had said, and Marion had stood at the window, her face cool and proud, and she had been sorry that she was a civilized person and could not strangle him.

That was the end of Fritz, but not the end of summer. Gay in the endless rain, the town of Salzburg lay at the feet of its fortress. Stiff and proud, Marion sat in the café Basar, thinking of the bridge from which she would never find the courage to jump, much as she wanted to.

Englishmen in shorts passed by, and Americans in amazing clothes. The headwaiter of the café had the veiled eyes of a wise man who was master of all life's secrets, and Marion thought it would be nice at least to sniff cocaine. That does help one to forget, but then you get a head cold, the nose swells, and you look ugly. Not in vain had Marion been the wife of a laryngologist. So no cocaine.

She could hardly remember the names of all the men who had accompanied her to the Mirabell Garden and later came to see her in Vienna. Not that it mattered. The men left ugly memories, best forgotten.

Marion lit another cigarette only to throw it too away. She went into the kitchen and made coffee. She sipped it in the kitchen, standing by the stove, looking frightened. For she was afraid of the men who might still come and leave ugly memories.

The telephone rang in the corridor. Marion went and took the receiver. "Hello?"

"Hello Marion, Asiadeh here. We—Hassa and I—are going to the Tulbinger Kobl on Sunday. Dr. Sachs is coming too, and there is another seat in the car. I thought if you haven't got anything better to do . . ."

A very superior smile appeared on Marion's lips. "Thank you . . . well . . . I do have a sort of tentative appointment, but perhaps I can put that off to another day. Yes, fine. Sunday, eight o'clock in the morning. You'll come for me."

Really, this little Turk was a very stupid chit. It was not at all pleasant to be reminded again and again of those years she had spent with Alex. Actually they had been quite nice years, if a little boring. If the silly child's eyes were not so harmless and dreamy, one might think that this radiant Turkish happiness might well be a mockery. Marion shrugged. She was not interested in Alex. He was a leftover from the time before her soul was burned to ashes on the pyre that was called Fritz.

Hassa was not interested in Marion either. Dissatisfied, he stood in the drawing room and growled: "I don't understand you, Asiadeh. This friendship with Marion! I don't want to meet Marion. That haughty goose with her ruined life. It's simply not decent that I should go to the Tulbinger Kohl with my ex-wife."

"But I will be there too. And Dr. Sachs."

Asiadeh's voice sounded genuinely astonished. She rubbed her face on Hassa's collar, and her eyes looked up to her husband with childlike submission. Not in vain had she received the best Istanbul polish. Century-old harem experience spoke through her lips: "Look, Hassa—Marion is so nice to me. She is really pleased that we are so happy. And then, you know, I have such a bad conscience about her. I behaved so badly that time on the Semmering. And also: I've got you, and she's got nothing. Nothing at all. I want to be just a little bit nice to her. I think perhaps she'll marry Dr. Sachs. You know—we women are born marriage brokers. I want to marry Marion off. Then we'll really be rid of her."

"No sane man is going to marry Marion," said Hassa darkly. Then he looked into Asiadeh's big smiling eyes, sensed the faint fragrance of her blond hair, and calmed down. Actually, it did not really matter who would be sitting next to Dr. Sachs. Asiadeh would be sitting next to him, and that was all that mattered.

"All right," he said graciously, "let Marion come. Try to marry her off to Dr. Sachs, if you can, but I don't think it will come off. Sachs is no fool."

Asiadeh did not reply. Never mind what Hassa thought and who was a fool. A princess from Istanbul should be able to bring anything about, even build a house for a decrepit prince who wallowed in the dust before Allah and whose name was Rolland.

On Sunday at eight o'clock, Hassa's car stood in front of Marion's door. Marion was a bit late. She smiled haughtily, drew her collar close to her neck, and took her seat next to Dr. Sachs.

On Monday, Dr. Sachs was sitting in the café on the Ring. All Dr. Hassa's friends were there, and the heads wagged like trolls' heads. The coffee in the cups grew cold, and the water in the glasses became warm. The headwaiter listened, leaning against the nearest pillar. Dr. Sachs gave his report:

"I could have died laughing," he said, "Hassa with his two wives. We went to the Tulbinger Kobl. The little Turk kept jabbering away. I suppose it is a harem tradition that a man drives about with all his wives. Hassa was terribly embarrassed and did not dare to look at Marion. Only too understandable after all that happened between them that time. We had lunch in the hotel, and all the time Asiadeh was making amourous cats' eyes at Hassa, and once she even asked Marion: had Hassa been as nice to her too! Poor Marion nearly choked. You can say what you like, but Marion is a lady. She behaved wonderfully—unapproachable and yet very polite. It can't have been easy for her."

Dr. Kurz emptied his cup with the air of a connoisseur.

"Of course this Turk is a savage," he said. "All Asiatic men have several wives. As likely as not, Asiadeh in her Asiatic mind sees Marion as a sort of colleague who ought to share the load of a husband with her. I think Asiadeh is rather frigid herself. That's all there is to it." He smiled knowingly.

"Nonsense," laughed Halm. "The little Turk is quite simply head over heels in love with Hassa and feels the need to parade her happiness. Preferably before Marion. So that she bursts with envy. Rather a primitive way of boasting and vengeance. What she doesn't realize is that she's playing with fire. Marion is very good-looking, and one foolishness in her life should be enough for her. And Hassa did love her very much. I even suspect that he married Asiadeh, among other things, just to show Marion that he can get along without her. A sort of compensation for his inferiority complex."

The doctors' wagging heads came close together. The conversation became more and more scientific. The nomenclatures of different complexes were buzzing around in the air. Asiadeh—Hassa—Marion: Three naked souls lay there among the coffeee cups as if on an operating table. The doctors' faces became flushed. It was decided unanimously that Asiadeh was suffering from delayed puberty manifestations, while Hassa was inclined toward an Oedius complex.

In the end Matthess, the surgeon, raised his finger and said with the primitive directness of his profession: "It is simply the question of genetic stock. We know that Hassa is the descendant of Bosnian Mohamedans. We must never foget that Asiadeh awakens in him the suppressed Asiatic instincts. It will end in a triangle. Hassa will be as happy as a pasha in his harem. Asiadeh will fill the Asiatic sector in the range of his intellect, and Marion the European."

"Impossible," said Kurz. "Hassa hasn't got any Asiatic sector in him at all, and Asiadeh hasn't got a European one. It will end when the Turk pinches some sort of acid from Hassa's medicine cupboard and throws it into Marion's face. One should really warn Marion."

Dr. Kurz believed he knew Asiadeh very well.

The door of the café opened, and the doctors fell silent. Hassa came in and sat down tiredly.

"What's the matter, Hassa?" Kurz's voice was full of genuine sympathy.

"I've only got two hands," groaned Hassa. "I can't hold the scalpel, the mirror, and the probe at the same time."

When he saw his colleagues' astonished faces, he emptied his cup and said in despair: "Fridl has left me."

"Who?"

A picture of unspeakable vices arose before the colleagues' eyes.

"Fridl," repeated Hassa darkly, "don't you know Fridl? My theater nurse?"

"Oh," said the doctors, secretly rather satisfied, and Kurz patted Hassa's knee.

"Was Asiadeh jealous? These things happen."

"Nonsense, Fridl is lame and over forty. But fantastically efficient. Just one nod and she gives me the right instrument. Yes, even without a nod. She always knows in advance what I'll need."

The doctors laughed.

"So why have you frozen her out?"

"I haven't frozen her out at all. She's inherited a house in Graz, and now she's gone. Asiadeh, child that she is, told her that now she needn't work anymore. She wouldn't have thought of that herself. And I really feel I have lost my hands. After all, I'm no nerve specialist. I need a nurse who knows my ways."

The gynecologist Halm nodded understandingly.

"A good theater nurse is irreplaceable. Especially for the slight narcotic intoxication. A new nurse is like a new wife. You have to take a very good look indeed before taking her on."

"I won't find another one," said Hassa gloomily. "I know myself. I'm a creature of habit. You have to train a nurse to your ways, and then she runs away like Marion or inherits a house like Fridl."

He fell silent, brooding sadly.

"The best way is to marry your nurse, or make your wife into a nurse," said Kurz. "Then you're safe."

Hassa looked at him angrily. "Nerve specialists don't need nurses, only a couple of straitjackets. With us it's different. Today Asiadeh helped me, but that's no good in the long run."

"Why not?" The doctors waited with bated breath.

"Well—I ask you!" Hassa's voice was rather angry. "What do you think? Asiadeh is a sensitive girl. She can't chisel a paranasal sinus. She really did try today, but I've had to put all operations off. Just imagine what would happen if, in the middle of an operation, the nurse suddenly fainted dead away. She hasn't done so badly. But at the end of the surgery there was an old man with a rhinophlegma. Well—I know that isn't a very attractive illness. But poor Asiadeh felt sick, really sick." He shook his head. He did feel sorry for poor Asiadeh.

And while he was sorry for her, Asiadeh rushed into the café on the Stephansplatz.

"Marion," she said, with deep disgust in her gray eyes, "is that a part of a wife's duty too?"

Astonished, Marion looked up. Asiadeh was taking a seat next to her, the picture of deep despair.

"I can't even stand the smell," she said, "and then all these sick people. I nearly fainted dead away. And tomorrow Hassa has to operate on a throat excrescence. What can I do, Marion? Surely there are enough nurses around?"

The words came out, one tumbling over the other. She told about Fridl who had inherited a house in Graz, and without whom Hassa was helpless. She told of the old man with the repulsive rhinophlegma, and how she had felt sick, and how Hassa had stared at her and not understood her at all.

"And tomorrow he will operate, Marion. That's just too much for me." She sat in her chair, a broken reed, and her tongue was gliding over her dry lips.

Marion laughed. "You are just a little lady of leisure, Asiadeh. A blossom from the harem. When I married, I took a course and became Alex's theater nurse. I was probably a better nurse than a wife. After the divorce Alex complained that he couldn't find a nurse. Well . . . about the pharnyx excrescence: It's quite easy, really. After each stroke you move the patient's head forward. And you get Beckmann's ring-shaped knife with the Gottstein bend ready before the operation. And afterward you give Alex the Pollitzer for blowing out. Do you understand?"

"No," said Asiadeh. "I don't understand a thing." She sat there, awkward and cross. "I admire you, Marion, all these things you can do. You're quite right, I'm just a lady of leisure."

Asiadeh went home. Hassa was sitting in the waiting room, leafing through the old journals.

"Don't worry about tomorrow," said Asiadeh meekly, "I know now exactly what I've got to do. First I give you a Pollitzer, and then a Gottstein knife with a Beckmann bend."

"Quite wrong," Hassa said, laughing. "Just the other way around. But I'll be all right. Kurz is sending me an experienced nurse. He really is a good friend. Let's go to the cinema, shall we? It's not your fault that you can't stand the work. Even though that time with the dervish, you managed quite well."

Hassa spoke timidly and looked sideways at Asiadeh. He was terribly sorry that she could not stand any rhinophyma and got the instruments in the wrong order.

"Oh, the dervish"—for a second Asiadeh's eyes shone. Once more Hassa was the great magician, master of life and death, he who had saved the holy man's life.

"Yes, the dervish," she repeated, and her voice was cold. "That was quite another thing, Hassa. The dervish was a holy man, and it was my duty to help him. But here it's just an old man with disgusting tumors. I'll go and change now."

Hassa nodded sadly. Asiadeh went into the dressing room, sat down on a low stool, and stared at her reflection. Tiredly, she brushed her hand over her forehead. It was so difficult to be a lady of leisure, incapable of helping her husband. So difficult to make oneself sick instead of handing him the correct instruments and see an answering smile in his eyes. She sighed. Marion must think her mad. But it did not matter. She had to reach the goal that had been set for her.

Asiadeh threw her head back and smiled. No, Hassa must not be sad because of her. She would arrange all.

She closed her eyes and folded her hands. If Hassa had come into the room, he would have seen her praying.

The next day came. Dreamily Asiadeh walked about the flat. At half past nine the new nurse arrived, a fat woman wearing a white cap. Hassa took her into the surgery, and Asiadeh tiptoed after them to listen tensely.

"It's just a small thing," said Hassa. "First a young girl—hypertropy of adenoids. We need a slight narcosis intoxication. Then an actress—a slight septum resection, on the left side. With injections. All right with you, nurse?"

"Of course, Herr Doktor," said the nurse in a deep voice.

Ten o'clock. Asiadeh went back into the waiting room. The first patient arrived—a slender blond girl accompanied by an elder woman, probably her mother.

Asiadeh heard Hassa's voice. "It won't hurt at all. You'll just be asleep."

The girl answered something in a soft voice.

Asiadeh stole into the drawing room. She heard steps in the surgery.

"Sit down, please . . . that's it . . . the mask, nurse! Count, please: one . . . two . . . three . . . four . . ." Hassa's voice became very soft. Then the instruments rattled. "She sleeps," said the nurse. Asiadeh listened. Seconds passed. Then—a strangled cry. Then loud sobbing.

Asiadeh flinched. Hassa drew his chair away. The sobbing

continued. The door opened, and Hassa came into the drawing room. His eyes were slanting slits.

"Quick—send for some ice, Asiadeh. The little girl must swallow some ice. She woke up too soon. The nurse gave too little narcosis. It's not a disaster, but it shouldn't have happened."

Asiadeh nodded. She ran for the ice herself and comforted the sobbing patient. The girl swallowed the ice. She could not be more than eighteen years old and had not expected any pain. With frightened eyes she looked at Asiadeh and did not know that mysteriously she had been drawn into fate's enigmatic round dance.

The robust nurse tidied the room. The instruments were boiling in a metal bowl.

"You understand, Nurse. A septum resection. On the left. You'll have to use the hammer. You're sure you understand?"

"Of course, Herr Doktor."

The bell rang. Asiadeh answered it. The actress had dark hair and wore a mink coat. Asiadeh showed her into the waiting room. Suppressed whispering came from the surgery. Obviously they were not quite ready there yet.

"You are Frau Doktor Hassa?" breathed the actress. Her hands tore bits off an old journal. "Your husband is going to operate on my nose. No, unfortunately not a polypus. That would be child's play. A friend of mine had her polypus taken out by your husband. Didn't feel a thing. Very satisfied. But with me—there's something wrong with the bones. I can't talk properly—there's something."

She stopped and looked at her watch. It was a quarter to one. The suppressed whispering was still going on behind the closed door.

"I am sure my husband will do it very well," said Asiadeh.

"I hope so." The actress looked down anxiously. "Why does it take so long? Your husband said twelve sharp. I haven't asked anyone to come along. Your husband said it would not be necessary. I can go home immediately afterward."

"Yes, of course," said Asiadeh. She felt sorry for the actress.

The surgery door opened, and Hassa appeared, the nurse behind him. Asiadeh suddenly felt a pang of a very bad conscience, as if she were responsible for the fate of the actress. Softly she tugged at Hassa's sleeve.

"Hassa," she whispered, "the nurse does not seem to be very good. May I come too? Perhaps I can help. I promise not to faint."

Hassa nodded. Asiadeh put a white coat on. The actress sat in the operating chair, her head slightly back. Her narrow nostrils trembled. Hassa sat down in front of her. The light of the reflector was full on her face.

"It won't be too bad, will it?" she asked.

"No, of course not. You won't feel a thing," said Hassa.

He put his hand on her forehead. With his thumb he turned the tip of her nose upward. The eyes of the actress looked terrified. Asiadeh stood next to her. She saw the nurse handing Hassa the injection needle and thought of the dervish who had once sat like that, and whose life Hassa had seved.

Hassa worked silently. The actress sat unmoving, her lips trembling.

"That's it," said Hassa. "Chisel, please."

The nurse handed him the chisel. Asiadeh's mouth stood open. A little hammer glittered in the nurse's hand.

"Now," said Hassa. The hammer came down. "Ouch," said the patient, and moved her head to the side. There was pain in her eyes.

Hassa looked up, his face flushed angrily. "Nurse, what are you doing—you haven't hit correctly!"

The hammer came down again.

"Oh—oh—oh!" The actress's head was turned far back, her eyes full of tears. She gripped Hassa's hand.

"Stop, Doctor, stop," she whispered, "I can't stand any more."

Hassa gritted his teeth. Sweat was running from his brow. "Nurse, you still haven't hit correctly," he hissed.

Asiadeh put her hands around the girl's head. "It will be all over in a second," she whispered, "just a little patience. Sit still." Quickly she kissed the woman's forehead. Then she was standing behind the chair, her hands firmly gripping the strange head.

At last—on the third try—the hammer hit the chisel correctly. Tears flooded the sick woman's face.

"Finished. Gauze, Nurse." Hassa rose. His face was dark red, "Like a village quack," he thought bitterly. The actress was crying. Asiadeh was sitting next to her, drying her tears.

"Better stay here a bit to recover. Perhaps in the drawing room." Hassa's voice sounded embarrassed. He gave her a pill, and Asiadeh took her to the divan.

"It was dreadful, Doctor," the woman whispered, "is it all right now?"

"Perfectly all right," said Hassa, furious that anyone could imagine it would not be.

Then he went back to the surgery.

"You should be nurse to a veterinary," he said, "but then we'd get complaints from the Animals' Protection Society."

Offended, the fat woman packed her things.

"Your patients are too high-class, Doctor. You'd think anyone could stand a bit of pain without going on so."

She went, her head high.

In the drawing room the actress was sleeping, her eyes swollen from crying. Asiadeh dragged Hassa into the bedroom.

"My lord and master," she said, "it can't go on like this." Her face was very serious. "You'll lose all your patients if you can't get a decent nurse."

"I'll get one all right," growled Hassa. "Vienna is a big place. It's just a question of time. All the good assistants are booked. I'll just have to operate in the clinic."

"Hassa," said Asiadeh, and her face became ecstatic, "you must not wait, and I won't be responsible for your patients' suffering. No, Hassa. I love you too much, and I will make any sacrifice for your sake. You must think of all those poor sick people who depend on your help. Our personal feelings must not come into this at all."

She stood before him, her head held high, looking at him passionately.

"What do you mean, my child?" Hassa did not understand at all.

"Hassa," said Asiadeh, "I am going to ring Marion. You are used to working with her. And poor Marion will be glad to help us. It is my duty to do this. Our marriage is too secure, we needn't be afraid of Marion."

She did not wait for his answer but ran to the telephone and dialed Marion's number. A few minutes later she came back, her face flushed. She felt a bit dizzy.

"She is coming at four o'clock for the afternoon surgery. She says she is happy to take on a part of her former duties again."

Then she stood there, her head slightly bent to the side, looking humbly up at Hassa. All ancient Asia was in her eyes.

Hassa did not see it. He went to her, put his arm around her shoulder, and said, completely at a loss: "Asiadeh, you are almost a saint."

Asiadeh did not answer. She was very ashamed of herself.

Marion came at four o'clock. There was a puzzled look on her face when she put the white coat on.

"Alex," she said, "I'm only too pleased to help you. For the time being only, of course. Until you've found the right nurse. You'll see, I haven't forgotten anything."

She walked through the flat and stopped at the door of the surgery, surprised that her heart was beating so strongly.

Dusk was falling when Asiadeh tripped gaily into the café all by herself. Her lips were pursed, she hummed a Turkish song. Dr. Kurz came to meet her.

"I hope your husband was satisfied with the nurse I recommended."

"He's already fired her. I've found something better for him." She was silent for a little while, then gave Kurz a mocking smile: "Marion is helping him until he finds the right nurse."

Smiling, she walked on and took a seat at a table near the window. Kurz returned to the doctors' table. She watched the doctors' heads bending close together like ears of wheat in the wind. She could guess their astonished whispers.

The surgeon Mathess rose, came to her table, and bowed. His hair was gray, his features clean-cut. He sat down and looked attentively at Asiadeh.

"Please forgive me," he said, "it's got nothing to do with me. But I feel I must warn you. Asiadeh—you are playing with fire. I don't understand you. One really shouldn't make sinning too easy for others, and in this case it would be best to stop it altogether. You trust Marion too much, or else you are too optimistic. One mustn't play with one's own happiness. You're nourishing a viper in your bosom."

Asiadeh leaned backward against the wall, raised her head, and half closed her eyes. Her face was soft and relaxed. She laughed a little and only her throat was trembling.

"You are a good man, Dr. Matthess. That is because you collect Chinese books and go to the Gschnas as Li-Tai-Pet. I do thank you. Marion is a poor thing, and I want to help her. And she's my friend. Friendship is holy, isn't it, Dr. Matthess?"

Her face had become very solemn. She looked at the big windowpane. White snowflakes were falling from the black sky. Bent under the weight of the snow, the trees lowered their branches, saluting the window. She rubbed the glass with her glove. Imperceptibly, the street became wider and wider—the snow turned into sand. The smell of burning arose from the earth, and camels came from afar, their heads bending like ears of wheat in the wind.

She looked at her watch. Hassa's surgery had taken a long time today.

TWENTY-SEVEN

E arly that morning the telephone rang.

"*Merhabar,* Hanum Effendi"—Good morning, Madam.

Asiadeh was fully awake at once. "*Merhabar,* Hasretinis"— Good morning, Excellency.

She sat up in bed. Hassa turned to her and listened with astonishment to the twittering sounds.

"Has my house been built yet, Hanum?"

"Nearly. Just a few stones are still missing. Did you go to the grave of the holy Abdessalam?"

"Of course. I have brought you a blessed rosary. And I have said farewell to the desert. It was a happy farewell. When can I see you, Hanum?"

Asiadeh put her hand on the receiver.

"Hassa," she said, "it's the two countrymen I crashed into in the summer. You know one of them. They are here again and they want to see me."

"Ask them to dinner," said Hassa indifferently, "or meet them tonight at the ball at the Hofburg."

Asiadeh nodded and took her hand from the receiver.

"Excellency," she said, "there will be a meeting of sages

tonight at the palace of this country's monarch. Come there. I will meet you in the halls of the palace."

She put the receiver down. Hassa jumped out of bed and dressed quickly. "I'm going to sleep again, Hassa," said Asia-deh, "I . . . I'm so tired."

She closed her eyes. Hassa kissed her quickly and was gone.

She lay in her bed without moving, her hands folded on the covers. The weak rays of the winter sun fell on her face. Her eyelashes trembled. So this was it. John had come back from the desert, and she did not even know whether his house was ready.

She opened her eyes. The room was so empty. A strange feeling overcame her, as if her mind and body were stretching, as if the things in the room were slowly dissolving and disap-pearing into her. She looked down. The rays of the sun broke in the mirror, the air had suddenly become visible, multi-colored, almost tangible.

Asiadeh rose and put her feet into slippers. Then she sat on the bed, trembling. She was suddenly afraid to move her head and look around. The room—wardrobe, tables, chairs—it all pressed heavily on her shoulders. The polished wood blinked at her, strange and distrustful, and filled her with a fear she could not understand.

Quickly she opened the wardrobe. A dark cool cavern stared at her. Clothes were hanging there, one by one, like soldiers on parade. Asiadeh's hand touched the colored rags. Each garment had once enclosed her body, a piece of her life was clinging to each dress. Mute guards, they framed the road of her life.

Here, under this old silk, her heart had beaten when she was driving with Hassa to Stolpchensee and he bought her a bathing suit. She had not worn it since her marriage but could not bring herself to throw it away. The summer dress next to it was a souvenir of the five o'clock tea on the Semmering, of a collision and a strange man into whose face she had thrown a torn-up hundred-dollar bill.

The blue suit she had worn in Sarajevo, and it had kept the smell of the Orient in its folds. Next to it, creased and gaily colored, the gypsy costume of the Gschnas. And in front—untouched and virginal, backless and sleeveless—a shimmering white ball dress, to be worn for the first time tonight, in the splendor of the Hofburg halls.

Asiadeh pushed the dress aside. It was a battle uniform, but the horn had not yet sounded the attack. Her eye fell on a simple dark suit at the back.

Lovingly she touched the plain material. This she had worn during the long hours in the library, when she was discovering the secrets of strange sounds, and Hassa had sat in the car on the corner, waiting for her. Why had she kept it?

Asiadeh put her hand into a pocket and found a creased bit of paper. Where and why had she put it there? She blushed violently when she read: "Everything which is offered to you comes and goes. Only the Blessed Knowledge remains. Everything which this world holds must end and vanish. Only the written word remains, everything else flows away."

How well she remembered the library and the excited girl who had opened the *Book of Blessed Knowledge* to try and find the secret of life in the flourishes of the ancient script. Carefully she put the paper back. It was unbelievable that she herself had been that excited girl. As she closed the wardrobe, an old Persian saying came into her mind. She went into the bathroom, but the saying came with her. She took it into the soft scented water, and it accompanied her to the dressing room, the dressing table, and to breakfast. Sadly, thoughtfully, she repeated it: "Only the snakes shed their skins so the soul can blossom and age. We humans are not like snakes. We shed our souls and retain the skin."

Hours passed, like pearls on a rosary. At half past one Hassa came and brought her orchids. They looked like brightly colored crawling snakes.

"For tonight," he said.

At lunch he ate his soup and talked about a dish of game with cream sauce, and of Italy, where he wanted to take Asiadeh in the spring.

"It will be wonderful," he said, and Asiadeh nodded.

"Yes, it will be wonderful."

Suddenly he put his spoon away. "Are you looking forward to seeing your countrymen at the ball?"

Asiadeh looked up. His face was suspiciously harmless.

"Of course, Hassa, very much so."

"I can just imagine it," laughed Hassa, "you'll talk Turkish all night, and I won't understand a word and will feel very lonely. While he was talking, his eyes were looking piously at the ceiling. "I'm just thinking . . . such a ball is always so formal. If you want to be with your Turks, what can I do? By the way, Kurz will be there too. Would you mind if he—er—I mean to say, if he took Marion to the ball? Of course only if you don't mind."

He talked very fast, still looking at the ceiling, and did not realize that he was blushing.

"But of course, Hassa. Poor Marion! She has so little fun. Yes, do let her come with Kurz."

Asiadeh looked at the window. There! She had heard the bugle blowing for the attack.

Evening came. The big facade of the Hofburg shimmered in the floodlight that bathed the muscles of the stone titans in its glare. Festive and proud, the Burg looked down on the brightly lit square. Tonight, once again, was Gala Night. How many had there been in the past! The fate of realms, peoples, and tribes had been decided in its halls. There had been feasts, dignified receptions, and secret cabinet sessions, and at balls as grand as this one, jewels, decorations, and gold embroideries had glittered. Shining coaches, drawn by high-spirited horses, had driven up to its portals, and ladies in sweeping long skirts, holding their trains, had stepped out, helped by gentlemen in splendid gold-braided uniforms. Tonight, shiny laquered boxes were drawing up, and slinky-skirted ladies extended silk-clad legs to step out, helped by gentlemen in white ties and tails. Tonight, as in the past, crowds were standing at the entrance, trying to catch a glimpse of the splendor.

The guests came flooding over the wide staircase. Lackeys in old court uniforms were standing on the steps, their faces stiff and sad. Men-about-town in white ties and tails walked in through the marble foyer, together with dignitaries wearing all their decorations, highborn and not so highborn ladies in shimmering low-cut dresses, and old officers who still wore their prewar uniforms.

The great ballroom was filled with couples dancing to shrill foreign rhythms. The sounds rose up to the ceiling and recoiled from the marble walls, filling the hall with the latest hits.

Then the music changed. Now it was Vienna's very own dance: the waltz. The silver tinkling of spurs that had sounded so wrong with fox-trots and quicksteps was just right now, as the colored uniforms looked right among the black and white of the men and the clinging skirts of the women. In the corridors the court, lackeys served at small tables where Hassa and

Asiadeh were sitting. Her eyes were small slits, and greedily she breathed in the atmosphere of the old palace. Shades of the past seemed an arch, covering the white and gold ceiling.

"The Holy Roman Empire," said Asiadeh softly, and thought of the world that had broken into two parts: the world of the Viennese Caesar and the world of the Istanbul khaliph.

"We have come too soon," said Hassa. "Your Turks aren't here yet, and Kurz not either. Perhaps they are looking for us and cannot find us."

Timidly he looked into Asiadeh's eyes and gripped the champagne glass. "They'll find us," said Asiadeh calmly. She was still hearing the call of the bugle, sounding the attack . . .

She raised her head. John Rolland and Sam Dooth stood in the doorway. She waved to them, and they threaded their way across the red marble hall, among the dancers. As John shook Hassa's hand, there was something feline and lurking in his movements.

They took their seats and Hassa filled the glasses. John sat motionless, looking at Hassa's forehead, his eyes cold and expressionless.

"My wife has told me about you," said Hassa. "I'm very glad to see you. Your occupation and your name show that you too have shed the dusty robes of Asia and become part of Western culture. But my wife would even today rather sit on the floor, and even eat from it."

Hassa laughed. John looked at him for a long time. Then, abruptly, he nodded.

"I know what you mean. You mean that a people who sit on the floor, and eat from it, cannot possibly have a culture of their own. But the floor—it is man's earthly home, from which he should not divide himself. Man comes from the earth and

should not deny it. On the contrary: The lump of earth from
which he descends should be part of his spiritual life. The man
of Asia feels his unity with earth and is happy to humble himself before the floor that has created him. It is like an eternal
mysterious stream that comes from the earth to fertilize
mankind. Therefore we pray, sitting on the floor, and touch
with our foreheads the earth, to which we will return."

John fell silent. Far away the English band was playing. Sam
looked at Asiadeh over the rim of his champagne glass. She was
sitting there quietly, and her eyes went from John to Hassa.

The attack had begun in deadly earnest.

"Yes," said Hassa. "I know about prayers beneath the mosques'
domed cupolas. But even born from the earth, mankind strives
upward, toward the sky. And because of this striving, man has
ceased to be an animal. And the visible form of this striving is
the Gothic dome. That is nobler than all earthbound mosques,
with their crude plain cupolas."

John nodded. His eyes were on Asiadeh, on her short,
slightly raised upper lip, and on her eyes, now as gray as ashes.

"The mosque," he said, "the soul of Asia in the shape of
stones. Untold foreign eyes have beheld our mosques, but
no unbeliever could ever understand their symbolism: that of
the cupola, the cubic basic plan, the many angular components,
and the minaret, symbol of the flame. All over the Orient the
houses of God are composed of these four parts, and everywhere their meaning is the same: that of the spirit of a man
from beyond who takes on his earthly form through the media-
tion of the two worlds, which are forever merging into each
other, and who thus makes this the foundation of God's will for
redemption.

"You are right—the unadulterated straight lines and vehe-
ment movements of the Gothic style are missing in our

mosque. Its weight reposes on the wide clear plane, formed in the same design as the building that covers and unifies it."

Hassa shook his head violently. "What is missing in the mosque," he said, "is the kind of design that uplifts the heart, in the same way as in your pictorial art the representation of living beings is missing. A sad world, a world without pictures."

John nodded politely and sipped champagne. "You are quite right. Asia is orientated toward the Hereafter, and Europe is orientated toward the visible world. Therefore Europe needs naturalistic representations of living beings. Asia is trying to express ultimate ideas by direct formal symbols, seeking to give shape to platonic thoughts without using the roundabout way of human or animal forms, thus renouncing the representation of living—and therefore transistory—beings."

Astonished, Hassa looked at John. "I disagree," he said, "that is why I live in Vienna. If I thought as you do, I would live in Sarajevo. One's outer life must be in harmony with one's inner consciousness. I live a European life, repudiating the East. But you—you are a film writer in New York, and yet you carry Asia in your soul. How do you bridge that gap?"

Hassa spoke slowly and a bit mockingly. It was very easy to wax enthusiastic about the dust of Asia when one was living in America. Sam moved restlessly in his chair. He knew only too well how John bridged this gap.

But John smiled guilelessly.

"The home," he said, "that is the bridge. As long as you have that, there is no contrast between the outer being and the inner consciousness. Once I thought differently. But I was lost in the world of visible forms. Home is not the bathroom you're using every day, nor the café you go to every day. Home—that is the structure of the soul, formed by the earth of the homeland. Home is always there, always in man's heart. As long as he lives, man is within the magic circle of his home, regardless of where he happens to be. An Englishman goes to the African bush, and his sleeping tent is England. A Turk goes to New York, and his room in Manhattan is Turkey. Only he who never had a home or a soul can ever lose it."

Hassa could not parry this stroke.

Marion and Kurz came to the table.

"There you are! And we've been looking for you for the last hour." Marion's voice, soft and melodious as always, suddenly stopped, her beautiful mouth was agape, and there was fear in her eyes. She had seen John Rolland.

"Oh—h," she said slowly and timidly, "I believe . . ."

But she did not go on. She was convinced he would jump up at once and command her to do a belly dance, there and then. Yet John did not say a word. He rose and bowed stiffly, for he too remembered the scene on the Semmering only too well. Kurz and Marion sat down, dumbfoundedly looking at Rolland.

Hassa made the introductions ". . . Asiadeh's countrymen. Mr. Rolland is a well-known film writer."

Dr. Kurz nodded. Yes, these things happened. Typical dual personality. Should be in a home. First imagines himself to be a prince, then a film writer. *Casus gravissimus.* Prognosis unfavorable.

Kurz squinted sideways at Hassa. It was really typical—an ignorant laryngologist could not see immediately that the man was a lunatic. Typical skull formation, thought Kurz, and made secret signs to Sam, whom he took to be the nurse. But the nurse did not seem to understand.

Abruptly John rose. Marion flinched, terrified. But nothing more terrifying happened than John bowing formally to Asiadeh, asking her to dance, and Asiadeh following him.

Obviously she was instinctless enough to dance with an

escaped inmate of a lunatic asylum. When the two had disappeared into the crowd, Kurz cleared his throat and bent across to Sam: "Is the gentleman better now?"

Sam looked angrily at him. "Much better, and soon he will be very well indeed."

It sounded like a prophesy. Marion looked for protection from the two doctors.

"A raving maniac," she whispered to Hassa. "I know him. He attacked me once. How can you let Asiadeh dance with him?"

Aghast, Hassa looked up. "A maniac?"

"No, no." Sam Dooth became very lively. "He's all right. Just don't irritate him, then he's quite all right. He's just a bit nervous."

Hassa rose. "I'll be back soon," he said worriedly.

He made his way across the hall. There was John Rolland, bending forward slightly, his face stiff and severe, his arm around Asiadeh's waist. Her eyes were half closed.

"Is my house ready, Hanum?"

"Nearly. Only one stone is still missing."

"Who will live in it?"

"We two."

"And the home?"

"It will always be with us."

She looked up at him. He was smiling—for the first time since she had known him.

But back at the table in the red hall, there were hasty whisperings.

"How dare you take a maniac to a ball?" hissed Kurz.

"I can't answer that," Sam hissed back, "you send a bill for every word."

His face did not give anything away, but he was very angry. John was a fool. Now he'd either be taken away or confess that he planned to kidnap another man's wife. Sam emptied his glass of champagne and managed to look conceited and unapproachable.

Kurz and Marion were still whispering together excitedly. Suddenly they stopped. John Rolland stood at the table.

"Dr. Hassa is dancing with his wife. May I . . ." He bowed to Marion.

Marion blanched. "I . . . thank you. I don't dance."

John sat down and laughed as Sam had never heard him laugh before. "I really must apologize," he said. "You think I'm a maniac. And I realize I did behave rather strangely that day on the Semmering."

"Typical," whispered Kurz to Marion, "but basically harmless."

Marion nodded and John ordered champagne. Hassa came back with Asiadeh on his arm. Her eyes were still half closed—perhaps this had been her last dance with Hassa in this life.

She looked at the orchids on her shoulder. Suddenly they were heavy, pressing down on her like stones. Slowly she took one orchid and gave it to Marion.

"For you," she said with sudden warmth, bent forward, and fastened it on Marion's breast.

Marion thanked her and whispered: "Asiadeh, take care with this Turk. He's not quite all there. A maniac. He attacks women."

Asiadeh looked at Hassa, who had once kissed her in his car, and at Kurz, who was no maniac and therefore had no excuse for attacking women. She laughed.

"I know—he is a maniac, but not because he attacks women.

On the contrary, I believe he would be very good at defending women."

Marion shrugged, and Kurz rose. He had quite enough to do with maniacs during the day. In the evening he could do without them.

"It's getting late," he said, "shall we go?"

Hassa nodded. They went through the halls, down the staircase, into the dark side alley where the cars were parked: Hassa's little two-seater, and John's rented limousine.

"We'll take you home, Kurz," said Hassa, "and Marion too, of course."

He took his hat off to say goodbye to Asiadeh's countrymen, and John too made his goodbyes with stiff politeness, standing in the snow, shaking Hassa's hand.

Suddenly Asiadeh cried in a foreign language, which the prince understood very well indeed:

"Your Highness! This man"—she pointed at Kurz—"enticed me to his house and tried to rape me while my husband was in the next room!"

The top hat fell from John's hand. His body was suddenly tense, his face a mask of fury. His eyes glittered like those of a wild animal; his lips trembled. With a sudden blow his fist struck into Kurz's face. And again. Short heavy blows rained on Kurz's face and body. In the cold moonlight John seemed a wild wolf from the steppes on a nocturnal chase.

"Help!" groaned Kurz. Hassa threw himself at John, Sam was waving his hands about. Two policemen came running. John tore away from Hassa and, with a wild leap, jumped into his car, followed by Sam. The car raced away even before the policemen arrived on the scene. Kurz was lying in the snow, his face distorted with pain and fury.

"A maniac," he panted, "a raving lunatic. Didn't I tell you? Into a straitjacket with him!"

Asiadeh stood at the side, her feet sinking into the snow. She was silent, smiling quietly and thoughtfully.

The last stone of her house had been laid.

TWENTY-EIGHT

"**I**n the name of God!

"Highly honored Excellency, dear father Achmed-Pasha!

"The world is big, and much land separates me from you. But space and time—what are they before Allah's throne? A piece of paper, a stamp, an envelope—and while space and time are bridged, you are reading the thoughts of your daughter, who is attached to you in deep veneration. Know then—oh Father!—that great events have occurred in the town of Vienna, and great are the miracles of the Lord. Behold—before my lord and master turned the eye of his favor on me, a beautiful slave by the name of Marion shared his nights with him. But in sinful lust she left her master and, going about in the country to the town of Salzburg, was leading an unchaste life in the arms of a stranger.

"Then the All-Merciful took pity on my husband—Herr Doktor Alexander Hassa, peace be with him—and sent me to be his slave and comfort in this vale of earthly misery. And I lived with him, and served him, oh Father, as you had taught me, and as it was my duty.

"And my duty was also pleasure and joy, for my husband's eyes smiled when they saw me, or my eyes, lips, or bosom.

"But inscrutable are the ways of Allah!

"He punishes and judges, and mortals are but tools in the hands of providence.

"There is a mountain near the town of Vienna called Semmering. On this mountain the hands of men—with God's gracious help—have built a house of recuperation. I was there once. But there was no recuperation for me in this house, for there I met Marion, my master's unchaste slave. Great fury filled me then. I left the house, for it is unseemly for the daughter of a pasha to share a roof with a fallen woman and breaker of marriages.

"Then God punished me for my pride and sent great trials onto me.

"For behold, Father, it was a sore trial for me to meet the man for whom I had been destined, for whom I had learned Arab prayers and Persian poetry. But twice as heavy was the trial to me, because John Rolland awoke my love and caused sinful thoughts to arise in my heart, even though my husband was lying in his bed at home, waiting for me.

"But God protected me from sin, and I did not step onto the road of unchastity and shame. God is just, and his wrath fell on Marion, for whom the doors of hell were waiting. I found out that the man with whom she had been united in sinful love had forsaken her, and that she was alone and lonely, even though she is a very beautiful slave, skilled in the arts of love and life.

"So I stayed with my lord and master, but my eyes opened, and my senses became alert.

"The life these unbelievers lead, oh Father, is very good indeed for them. But for a woman from Istanbul, it is not good at all. There are too many men in this life, and too few children, while in our country it has always been the other way around: too few men and too many children. But here the men are like children, yet what the children are like I do not know, for I have never met any.

"Be amazed, Father! A strange man dared to kiss me, and my own husband stood by and laughed, even though he is a good man and not a castrate. So strange are the customs of the people here!

"But inscrutable are the ways of Allah! In his wrath he punished the fallen woman Marion, and in his mercy he saved her again. And it was I who was destined to be his tool for this, yet great astonishment fills me—for at the same time it was Marion who was just a tool to bring me away from the world of unbelief to the tents of peace.

"We were, both of us, nothing but tools in the hands of the Almighty. Yet while I began my task with open eyes, Marion was struck with blindness, and even today knows nothing of the thoughts in my heart. And it is good that this be so, oh Pasha, for there must be a difference between a princess from Istanbul who keeps faith with her husband, and a sinner who runs away from him.

"Days passed, and I sat at one table with Marion, looked into her eyes, and examined her heart. Nights passed, and I lay with my husband, looked into his eyes, and examined his heart. But during these days and nights John Rolland was in the desert, wallowing in the dust before Allah, and I tried not to think of him, yet had to think of him.

"No, oh Father! Never would I have followed John had I not known that the fate of my lord and master Dr. Alexander Hassa—peace be with him—would be in safe hands.

"But Marion's hands are now very safe, and she will be a good wife to him, humble and thankful for the favor and mercy my master is showing her.

"But I am getting lost in the labyrinth of words, Father, and you still do not know what happened in Vienna, and how strangely life plays with us humans.

"It was in the monarch's old palace. The halls were lit festively, and people were dancing. There were many uniforms, the halls were made of marble, there were mirrors and pictures everywhere, and I realized that the monarchs of this country live in quite a different way from the sultan, our ruler, in the palaces of Ildis Kiosk or Eski Serai.

"We were all assembled around a table. But it was only I who was aware of the secrets surrounding us, and I seemed to hear the plaintive call of a bugle sounding the attack.

"Then we stood on the street in the snow, and I saw that John is really the right man to win forever the love of a princess from Istanbul. For he struck the face of Dr. Kurz, whom you do not know, oh Father, but who is a villain, believe me! So he struck the stranger in the face and was like a gray wolf chasing his prey in the night. Then he suddenly vanished, we took Kurz home, and they were all angry with me, my customs, and my friends. We went home, and my lord and master spoke very bitter words. He called me a savage who had shamed him and brought great troubles to him. I was lying in my bed and kept silent, for he too had brought great troubles to me, even though he did not know it, and he would now be very lonely and unhappy if I were not a savage. Therefore I lay there and was silent, for the wise one does not need appreciation.

"Then a very exciting day came, Pasha. For first Marion came and put on the white coat to help my husband drive away illnesses from strangers' bodies. Sick people came, and Hassa was driving their sicknesses away. But I was sitting in the next room, for I could still hear the plaintive call of the bugle sounding the attack.

"Then the sick people had gone, but Marion was still there, in the room of pain, and my husband was there with her.

"It was very quiet, and suddenly I heard my lord and master complaining about me, because I was a savage and could not understand the world of the West. And Marion spoke too, but very softly, so that I could not understand what she was saying, oh Father!

"And now it became quite quiet. My heart was beating violently, Pasha, for I am only twenty-one years old and not used to life's malevolence.

"But I have inheritated your clear head, Father and Excellency, and for that I will always be grateful to you. I went quietly to the door and listened. I could not hear much, but what I heard was enough.

"I opened the door. Marion was sitting in the chair in which the sick people usually sit, and her head was leaning back against the soft leather cushion. The light fell on her face, and I could see her quite plainly. She was very beautiful and her eyes were shining. And Hassa was standing beside her, her head in his hands. And he was kissing her lips, her eyes, her cheeks, and her nose.

"That, Father, was what I saw, and though I wanted to stay calm, my heart was beating violently. But one can have a clear head and yet a stupid heart.

"Then I came into the room and closed the door. They were both very frightened. My poor lord and master looked away, and Marion jumped up and tidied her hair. And I stood there and looked at them, for I did not know whether to laugh or to cry. Then I cried a little, for I am a woman who is not used to life yet.

"But when Hassa came to me and tried to comfort me, I wiped the tears away and raised my head. I said something but cannot remember clearly what I said. They looked at me with astonishment in their eyes. Then I laughed, and Marion laughed too; only Hassa did not laugh, for he is a man who has a conscience. But I stroked his hair and talked to him, and his conscience became smaller and smaller.

"These, oh Father, are the events which God in his wisdom let happen to us, and I do not know who of us was God's tool. I believe we all were.

"But then, when I was content about Hassa's fate, I went to John Rolland. He is sitting next to me, a smile on his lips, reciting to me the true words of our prophet: 'Man's most prized treasure is a virtuous wife.'

"Believe me, Father, I was virtuous, I am virtuous, and I always will be virtuous. Only stupid women step onto the path of sin, whereas a clever woman reflects and knows how to avoid sin so as not to bring harm upon herself and others. For many things lie in the hand of a woman: happiness and unhappiness, life and death. A woman must be wise to master the narrow path of virtue and thus be free to look calmly into the eyes of the world.

"And now, oh Father, I am traveling with John to the far-away country on the other side of the ocean. But our home is traveling with us, for we carry it in our hearts, in our arms, our eyes, our thoughts, and our children, who—God willing—will be born in New York. A fat man called Perikles is also coming with us. His family comes from the Phanar. He is very skilled in the matters of outward life. So we are all on our way, Father, Hassa is on his way with Marion, I with John, and Perikles is on his way with us, and so is our child, but it does not beat its feet on my stomach yet, for it is still too early.

"And you too, Father, should now be on your way to the town of Bremen, where we will all meet to go together to the end of the world. For John thinks that the house of an Osman prince is not complete if there is no pasha living in it. And he is right. You must live with us, to teach our children the commandments of faith and virtue, so they will never forget that their ancestors once came from the yellow hills of Turan and conquered three continents.

"Now I will finish, Achmed-Pasha. I have said goodbye to Hassa and Marion and have seen happiness in their eyes. Now I must go once more to the coffeehouse on the Ring. There I will drink a cup of coffee and see the astonished faces of the doctors who are masters of life and death and yet as awkward as children in the world of feelings.

"I know it is not good to mock other people. But the people in the big coffeehouse have often mocked me, and I am only twenty-one years old and want a bit of joy before I go away. Therefore I go to the coffeehouse and shake their hands and look into their astonished and disappointed eyes. For they all hoped to see my tears, and now they must see my smile instead.

"Great are the miracles of the Lord, Pasha, and inscrutable are Allah's ways. We will await you in the town called Bremen, to walk together, smiling, the short road from birth to death, the road God has made for man to walk, on which a foolish one travels with fear, a strong one with pride, and a wise one with a smile.

"Your daughter
Asiadeh Rolland."